THAT ASIAN KID

SAVITA KALHAN

troika

Published by TROIKA

First published in 2019

Troika Books Ltd

Well House, Green Lane, Ardleigh CO7 7PD, UK

www.troikabooks.com

A CIP catalogue record for this book is available
from the British Library

ISBN 978-1- 909991-97-2

3 5 7 9 10 8 6 4 2

Printed in Poland

For Hish and Jad

Knowledge is power.

CHAPTER 1

I'm taking my shortcut through the woods, all innocent and minding my own business, when I hear the sound of laughter coming from somewhere behind me. I slow down. I'd know that laugh anywhere. It's like a boom: loud and deep, a guffawing that emanates from the ground beneath his boots, and rumbles through the belly before erupting out of his mouth, Father Christmas-style, but raised to the power of ten. It can only be Mr Green, my History teacher. I glance back. It *is* Green. He's with a woman, but I can't make out her face. I grind my half-smoked cigarette under my heel, silently cursing my one-every-other-day habit (yeah, I know, I'm such a rebel), and Mr Green and his companion for invading my space.

Did he see me smoking? Cos if he did he won't let me off with a simple lecture or a look of disdain. He'll be massively disappointed – and he'll make sure I know about it on a daily basis.

They're coming my way. Damn. The smell of smoke is sticking in the air like an accusatory finger pointing directly at me. They're still some way off, so I could easily make a break for it, but I hesitate, curious about who the woman is. It could be Mr Green's wife, but I've never seen his wife and there's something oddly familiar about this woman. I duck behind some bushes. As they approach, they slow down, and I get a good look at the woman walking beside him. What a shocker! It's Mrs Greaves, my English Lit teacher.

I use this shortcut every day – the bus drops me off on one side of the woods and I cut through the woods to get home, shaving fifteen minutes off my journey. I've never once seen any teachers from school down here, and as for these two particular teachers, well, I've never even seen them speak to each other at school. Any thoughts I might have had about surreptitiously creeping away are fast disappearing as I wonder what the hell my favourite teacher and my least favourite teacher are doing skulking round the woods on a freeze-your-nose-off January day.

Whatever they're here for, I have a sneaking suspicion that it's not for an innocent chat – you'd choose a warmer venue than these damp, cold woods for that. I hunker down further. There is a distinct possibility this could end in trouble – especially if they come any closer to the monster holly bush I'm currently being pricked to bits in.

I can hear them clearly now.

'This will make you laugh – I asked one of the boys

how his Christmas was and this is what he said,' Mr Green is saying. 'His cat climbed up the Christmas tree and toppled it over. The tree hit the dining table, and scattered pine needles all over the roast potatoes and veg. Then the cat landed on the platter of sliced turkey breast, his mum screamed, his grandmother grabbed the cat, and the cat clung on to the turkey for dear life and took half of it with him. So his family ended up eating all the trimmings minus the turkey for their lunch, which his grandmother was ecstatic about because she's a vegetarian and she said it served them right for forgetting to make her a special vegetarian dish.'

That's my story!

Mrs Greaves laughs. 'Shame he didn't record it – it would have gone viral if it really happened. Cat videos get the most hits, apparently.'

'I agree.' Mr Green chuckles. 'He's got a way of putting things, that Jeevan.'

What? *Mrs Greaves is laughing?* Apart from the fact that I've never in the eighteen months she's been my teacher seen her smile (it would put a serious crack in her face), much less laugh, the real surprise is that she's laughing about *my* story.

'I suspect he probably made the whole thing up.'

Mr Green shrugs. 'He had the whole class in stitches – me included.'

'There's a class clown in every form.'

That's when an idea explodes into my brain and my

phone's in my hand before I've given it another thought. You'd think I'd think before I acted – I mean, I get straight As in everything.

But I don't stop to think.

The idea has me on autopilot – I've accessed the camera, flicked to Video and pressed Record faster than most people can blink.

'Anyhow, good to see the smile back on your face,' Mr Green says. 'You sounded so upset earlier. Are you going to tell me what's happened?'

'It's horrible, Daniel. I don't really know where to start.'

Mr Green pats her arm. 'It can't be that bad.'

'I wish you were right. The Head called me in for a meeting. He wouldn't tell me much except that he's concerned.'

'Concerned about what?'

Greaves looks away. 'Someone's sent in an anonymous letter.'

'What do you mean?' says Mr Green.

'Never mind. It doesn't matter.'

'It obviously does matter. Isn't that why you asked me to meet you here? You said you needed to talk.'

'On reflection I think I would rather put all that out of my head – it's very distressing.'

'Hang on – distressing? What was in the letter?'

'Someone has made certain – *allegations*, in the note, which the Head says he feels bound to look into.'

'Allegations? Christ. That sounds serious.'

'Yes, it must be for Rawson to give it any credence.'

'So what are they alleging?' And then it's like the penny has dropped, because Mr Green's tone changes. 'You haven't told anyone about what happened, have you? Because it was only the once, so—'

'Of course I haven't. Give me some credit. My reputation would be at stake too, you know.'

'I'm sorry, I'm sorry. So what is the note alleging?'

'I'm pretty sure that one of the boys is playing the race card because he doesn't like his grades. It's utterly preposterous. What kind of person does that? Clearly one with very little going on up here,' she taps her head, 'or otherwise they wouldn't be resorting to devious, underhand and frankly ludicrous tactics.'

Mr Green's mouth opens so wide it almost hits the floor. 'No!' he says. 'Seriously? I've never heard such a thing. I'm surprised Rawson's bothering to look into it at all.'

'I know. Unbelievable, isn't it?'

'What else did he say? What's he going to do about it?'

'Rawson said it's a serious allegation and it doesn't matter if there's no truth to it, he has to look into it regardless. He said he wasn't overly concerned, but I'm not sure what to think.'

'Christ! I can see why you're so worried. Something like that can get blown out of all proportion. Remember that case in the papers last year? You have to be careful. Things like that can stick – even when there's absolutely no truth to them.'

'I know. It's so good to know you care, Daniel. It's a real worry. I don't even know exactly what the note said. Rawson wouldn't show it to me. I wish he had – I'm sure I would have recognized the handwriting.'

'Whoever wrote it would have disguised their writing, Nic.'

'Yes, you're right. Of course they would have. It's such a cowardly act. If they really felt unfairly treated, they should have gone straight to the Headmaster instead of sending a backstabbing, slanderous note. I've never been accused of – of anything like this.' She sobs. 'It's a total shock! I've been a teacher all my working life. I love the kids, and I love my job. It's all I ever wanted. It's all I know,' she says, sniffing and wiping the tears away with her hands.

Mr Green rummages for a hanky and hands it to her. Greaves has put her hand on his arm, drawing him in. She lets her head rest on his chest as she cries. Mr Green pats her on the back, saying soothing words.

'It'll be all right. Don't let it get to you. You have nothing to fear. Rawson won't believe an anonymous note.'

'I know, but still, as you said, lies can stick.' She's really sobbing now. 'What should I do?' Green puts his arms around her, hugging her.

I hear kissing noises, which would make me puke if I wasn't so shocked.

They're an item?

Greaves and Green couldn't have picked a more romantic spot for their assignation.

I squat down, resigned to being stuck here a bit longer. It's only half past four, so I've still got half an hour before I have to give Maji, my gran, her insulin shot. Besides, this conversation might get even more interesting.

Mr Green's *married*. He's always talking about how his wife prosecutes criminals for a living: 'So you'd better watch your step, sonny Jim,' he threatens us on a regular basis. No one pays his threats any attention, though, because Mr Green's one of those all-right teachers. Unlike Mrs Greaves, who just doesn't get us. Well, she doesn't get *me*, that's for sure.

What I cannot get my head round is how he can fancy her. Some of the boys at school think she's all right, pretty attractive even. I've told them there's a two-for-one offer on at Specsavers and they should get themselves down there sharpish. Greaves has long frizzy blonde hair and watery blue bug eyes that would win a staring competition hands down, and she wears dangerously low-cut, close-fitting tops to show off her ample cleavage. On no planet would that be considered professional when you're teaching a bunch of hormonal teenage boys, imho.

'Oh, Daniel!' Mrs Greaves exclaims breathlessly. 'It's been too long.'

'Too long? Hang on a minute, Nicola, please don't misunderstand—'

'I know I'm not misunderstanding this,' Greaves replies, her voice suddenly low and husky.

Uh oh! I don't want to know what's happening – but at the same time, it's *way* more interesting than *EastEnders*, which Maji insists on watching even though she can't understand half of what the cast are saying. That's why I have to watch it with her, so I can translate for her. It's surprising how much of it she gets, though, just from the actors' expressions and the way they say stuff. Not bad for a woman who's never been to school in her life. What's unfolding before my eyes is in a totally different league – it's car-crash reality TV, and I'm hooked.

'Look, Nicola. Stop, please.' Mr Green seems reluctant. 'We came here to talk.'

Mrs Greaves is leading him the few steps towards the large oak tree almost directly in front of the bushes I'm hiding in, and he's allowing her to lead him.

What's wrong with him?

My heart is thudding so loudly, I'm surprised they can't hear it.

Sticking around for the show was not my best idea, I think.

And the camera is still recording.

CHAPTER 2

OK, this is seriously gross!

Mr Green isn't that into it if you ask me. Almost as if he's doing her a big favour – maybe he is, maybe this is how his sympathy manifests itself – hell, I don't know, I'm no psychologist. But it's seriously messed up. In PSHE, teachers are always going on about how we need to learn to say 'no', usually where sex and drugs are involved. Man, some of them need to practise what they preach.

Greaves has unbuttoned her coat. She isn't giving up – and she isn't about to let Green get away. Pretty soon, after more buttons get unbuttoned, Green finally seems to realize that resistance is futile.

They're *at it* now. Shit, the huffing and puffing and panting are seriously messing with my gag reflex. I'm wishing I'd stuck my ear-buds in my ears to muffle the sound effects. Although it's obvious what they're up to, most of their clothes have, thanks to the freezing cold weather, stayed on. So that's one image that won't be searing itself into my memory to haunt me until the day I die.

I spoke too soon. Greaves is yanking her tights down. I look away, letting the camera do the watching for me, and wonder what kind of idiot I am. I should have legged it when I had the chance.

When it stops, I almost yell hallelujah, in sheer relief. Luckily for me, it hasn't lasted too long and both parties seem happy enough with their performance, so who am I to argue?

I'm kind of hoping there's more to the whole sex thing than that, though. Because if that's all there is then there's not much to look forward to. Here's a confession: I haven't got that far myself yet; but then again I'm only fifteen, I go to a boys' grammar, and, since my grandma got sick, I don't get out to parties as much as I'd like.

Mr Green lights up – another shocker. I'd never taken him for a smoker.

'Daniel! You told me you were giving up,' Greaves says. 'Another broken promise,' she mutters, buttoning up her coat.

Mr Green exhales a cloud of smoke. 'I didn't promise anything. I merely said that I was considering it. Besides, it's only the occasional one. No harm done.'

'My clothes will stink of smoke,' Greaves objects.

'Your cat is hardly going to complain.'

I muffle a laugh.

'What was that?' Greaves is peering round anxiously. Her eyes settle briefly on my holly bush. I'm trying not to shake the damn thing, but an attack of the giggles is threatening to give me away.

'Just the wildlife. Time we got going. I'm late.' Mr Green stamps out his cigarette and starts walking.

She catches hold of his arm. 'Wait! You promised me you'd talk to her.'

My ears prick up. I hunch forward, so I can hear better. He's not going to leave his wife for Greaves, is he? He must be mad!

'Talk to who?' Mr Green asks, baffled.

'Susan.'

Mr Green looks seriously troubled, so I'm guessing Susan is his wife.

'Look, we were both very drunk that night, and you've obviously misunderstood. I'm sorry, Nic. It was an easy mistake, considering what a state we were both in.'

'Speak for yourself, Daniel. I was driving that night. Remember?'

'Were you? Didn't we share a cab?'

Mr Green can't seem to remember anything about *that night*. He must have been well tanked. Either that, or whatever happened between them was so gross, he blanked it all out. So why would he do it again – here, in the freezing cold, stone-cold sober? He really has got one hell of a problem saying no. I'm kind of wishing that Mr Green had seen me smoking now – maybe none of this would have happened if they'd known that these woods were not as deserted as they appeared. I'd have happily taken all the detentions he demanded and promised never to smoke again; in fact, I don't think I'll ever smoke again after this. But it's too late – it's happened, and I've got the evidence on camera.

'Look, it doesn't matter. Susan wasn't well and things were difficult. It was a rough patch, but we're trying our best to get through it.'

Really? This is trying his best?

Greaves is thinking the same thing, judging from her arched eyebrow.

'Look, you were there for me then. You gave me a shoulder to lean on when I really needed it, and I'm grateful for that.'

'I think I gave you a bit more than that. I seem to recall you were more than happy to take things further.'

'I'm sorry.'

'So you were just using me.'

'No, it just happened, and I'm truly sorry.'

'And what about what happened just now?'

Mr Green is squirming. It's not a nice thing to see. When you so rarely see teachers out of school, you don't think they can be much different to what they're like in school. One thing's for sure: I don't know if I'll ever be able to see Mr Green in the same way again.

Plus I don't honestly know who to feel more sorry for – Green, who's acted like a complete idiot, or Greaves, and the less said about her the better.

Just last week, Greaves reported me to the Head for 'answering back in a belligerent manner'. One thing I don't do is *belligerent*. Sarcastic, yes, smart-alec, big yes, but generally I'm not a stroppy kind of guy. By the time Greaves had finished telling Mr Rawson, the Head, about my unacceptable behaviour, even I believed her.

Anyway, to cut a long and miserable story short, I ended up with my first detention ever, and had to get the school to call my mum – it was an after-school detention, which meant I was going to be late back for Maji. Mum blew her top at me. I could practically see the flames from where I stood in the school office thirty miles away. Needless to say, I got scorched.

'Don't tell me you were just doing me a favour because I was upset,' Greaves is saying.

'Of course not!' Green says.

But it does look that way, I'm thinking. It's not just Green, though – it takes two to tango, except that I'd call what they were doing a little bit more than tangoing! In fact, I don't even want to think about what they've just been doing.

'Oh, come on. Please don't be like that. You've got a lot on your plate at the moment, what with that ridiculous anonymous note hanging over you.'

'It *is* ridiculous, isn't it? Rawson should have put the

note exactly where rubbish like that belongs – straight in the bin!'

He takes her hand. 'You're frozen. Come on, let's go. I'll walk you to your car. And whatever happens over this note thing, try not to worry too much. The Head isn't going to give an anonymous note the time of day – he's just making you aware of the fact that someone's making a false accusation. And, of course, I'll back you up and support you all I can . . .'

I can't believe Green's saying he'll back her up! Now would be a good time to stroll out of my hiding place. I'm *so* tempted – just to see the look of complete horror on their faces.

I resist the temptation. As soon as they're out of sight, I have to get home. My gran is waiting for her insulin shot, and I have an X-rated video on my phone that's already started feeling like a ticking time bomb.

CHAPTER 3

'Maji, I'm home,' I call out, kicking the front door shut. I push my shoes off and zip up to the bathroom, wash my hands, and gargle with extra-strength mouthwash. It always peels off a layer of skin on the inside of my mouth, but nothing else nukes the lingering smell of smoke quite as effectively. That one-every-other-day cigarette was my sole act of rebellion. Lame, I know, and it's never going to happen again after today. There's no need to let my gran find out. The concept of rebellion is alien to her, and why her favourite grandson might feel the need to indulge in it would be incomprehensible.

'You have everything, *beta*,' she would say. 'You are not like one of those English boys who don't know any better. Your mother and father have brought you up well, educated you, fed you with the *most* healthiest food. They buy you what you want. You have your own room. So why do you do these bad things? When I was growing up in India . . .' I'll stop there as Maji's stories of

'When I was growing up in India' can run on and on and on. I love my gran, and I love her stories, but you can see why I can never let her find out, can't you?

Smoking is a seriously evil crime if you're a nice Indian boy from a nice Indian family. And if I was a nice Indian *girl* it would be a far, far worse crime – practically being akin to a slag right there. Luckily for Shanti, my older sis, the word 'rebellion' never entered her vocabulary. She's the virtuous one, the daughter that every single Indian parent dreams of, although some might prefer her accomplishments to be their son's. Shanti's at Oxford, studying medicine, following in Mum and Dad's illustrious footsteps. Good for her, is what I think – as long as Mum and Dad don't expect me to do the same. I can give Gran her insulin shot, but I can only just about dissect a frog or a pig's heart in biology, and that's because there's no getting out of it. The last time I had to do it I felt sick and the yellow and green shades I turned made everyone else feel sick. Do I want to spend my life turning varying shades of yellow and green? Definitely not! Being brown is challenging enough sometimes.

As soon as I've given Maji her insulin shot, made her a cup of tea served with two chocolate digestives, and promised to come down in ten minutes to hear about her day, I'm taking the stairs up to my room two at a time.

'But my day was so very interesting, Jeevan,' Maji calls.

Not as interesting as my day, I'm betting. 'I'll be down soon,' I reply.

The video is so hot it's practically burning a hole in my pocket. The sooner it's off my phone and stored somewhere inaccessible, the better. Maji would be scandalized – she's hot on adults setting a good example to children. She'd make sure I was out of that school in a heartbeat and into a *good school where teachers knew how to behave properly*. Mind you, if Mum or Dad got a whiff of this, they'd do the same.

I shut and lock the door, then double-check it's locked. I don't need any interruptions while in possession of this highly sensitive material. Then I boot up my laptop. Time to sync my phone to my laptop and work out what to do with the fizzing bomb in my very nervous hands.

It's like a gift from God – powerful, perfect, and the timing couldn't have been better. But in the wrong hands, it's an extremely dangerous gift.

Is it time to call for backup? I need advice and I need it now.

Backup are Jonathan and Sandi. Jonathan Fellowes, aka Dread, is half-Nigerian and half-English. His nickname is something of a misnomer; if he could, he'd have dreadlocks, but, apart from the fact that he's not allowed to and never will be, his hair is more like his dad's than his mum's – curly, but not Afro-curly, and it's not black but golden brown, like his skin. So to dread up his hair he'd have to dye it black and get a tight perm first, and – 'that ain't happ'nin', bro. Big mama she said no.' No one argues with Dread's mum, especially Dread.

'What would she do if you used your own money and went and had it done?' I asked him once.

Dread gave me a withering look; he was good at those. 'Stop putting dumb-ass ideas in my head – unless you want to see me homeless.'

'She wouldn't! Would she?'

'You know my mum. What do *you* think?'

Sandip, aka Sandi, is like me – his parents are Punjabi like mine, but he's Sikh. His dad owns the local Indian shop. Because it's walking distance, Maji often pops in for a gossip with his mum, or dad, or anyone else who might be unfortunate enough to have run out of onions and popped out to the shop. Sandi doesn't like trouble – and this video is exactly that. Trouble with a capital T. All of us have pretty strict parents – strict about school and getting homework done, and about doing well. It's always been that way, so it's not something we think about much.

But now I've got this video on my phone and I'm wondering what to do with it. I'm afraid my friends might tell me to delete it.

Or would they?

I can trust my friends, that much is for sure. But this is *so* totally way out there. The temptation to load it up on YouTube is *so* strong – and if it's that strong in me, it'll be crazy for them. There's no way they would be able to resist the call of the dark side. And that's exactly where uploading this vid would take us, to the dark side where trouble awaits.

Here's the thing – neither Dread nor Sandi have Greaves for English Lit, the lucky bastards. But I do. The trouble is Mr Green's all right, so uploading that X-rated video would be a bad thing to do to him – even though I know lots of kids have posted 'caught-you-out' videos about their teachers on the Internet.

I download the X-rated vid and store it in a password-protected file within a file within a file. It's buried so deep in the vaults of my laptop that only someone with an intimate knowledge of my filing system, and of my offbeat sense of humour, would be able to locate it and hack the password.

I feel better now that I know only I can access it. It's still on my phone, so I watch it with the sound low just to see how bad it actually is.

Jesus Christ. The picture quality is almost *too* good. During the few minutes of the *act*, Greaves is centre stage. Luckily, Mr Green's in a pair of jeans and a fleece rather than one of his usual slightly eccentric and easily identifiable suits, and his back's to the camera, which helps.

The temptation to upload the video on to Instagram and YouTube is even stronger now. But if I post that video, everyone will see it and they will know that it was me who put it online. *Me*. My phone would crash with the amount of calls I'd get. I'm not sure I could handle that. The idea of making the video public is losing its allure.

I'd like to say that I know it's wrong to do it to Green and Greaves, you know, morally and all that (and I do), but I think it's more that I'm just a chicken. To test it out I hover with my finger over Share for an agonizing moment.

Just do it, Jeev!

No! Don't be an idiot!

Do it!

No!

Without warning, my finger stabs Delete, and I breathe a sigh of relief as the video vanishes. Now, if my phone gets hacked or stolen, I won't be panicking about the vid getting into the wrong hands. Not that mine are the right ones. In fact, to be brutally honest, mine are probably the *worst* hands the video could have ended up in.

It's been far longer than ten minutes and I know Gran will have been counting them, getting more and more impatient that her debriefing's still on hold. She claims she doesn't see anyone or talk to anyone all day, but I know better. I head downstairs to humour her.

'So how was your day, Maji?'

She sets her knitting down. 'Very good. I went for my walk twice today, because your father tells me off if I don't walk for at least twenty minutes. He's become very bossy since he started reading that new research. He's drilled it into me: walking every day helps if you are diabetic. As if I don't know these things already. I watch that medical programme with that nice doctor every week.'

Gran's speaking in Punjabi, although if you were listening you'd probably understand at least half of what she's saying, there's that many English words here: *walk, minutes, bossy, reading, research, every, helps* and *diabetic, medical, programme, nice,* and, of course, *doctor.*

'He's been telling you that for years, Maji! And I know you're only doing it so you can have biscuits with your afternoon tea and not feel guilty about it.'

She winks at me. 'That's our secret, Jeevan. No need to trouble your father with these trivial details.'

Back in my room twenty minutes later, I put some Charlie Parker on and get my homework out. I'm seriously into jazz at the moment – bhangra isn't my style, unless I'm at a wedding. Dread's into juju music and Afrobeat, people like Fela Kuti and King Sunny Ade, and he's got me into it too. Sandi's into anything and everything to do with Rihanna, although recently she may have got knocked off the pedestal by Dua Lipa.

English Lit homework is due in tomorrow, so it can't be left for another night. Now I wish I'd done it yesterday. I picture the totally unnecessary red marks Greaves left on my last prep, and the one before that.

The video is kind of like an insurance policy. I

wouldn't even have to upload it – just the threat of it could be enough.

But blackmail? Seriously?

It's so not my style.

CHAPTER 4

'Remember: mocks are next week. If you haven't done any work over the Christmas break, you're so deep in it even I won't be able to drag you out!' Green emphasizes his point by slamming the textbook against his desk, which judders under the impact. A pen rolls on to the floor and settles near Sandi's foot and Sandi pounces on it at once. Mr Green snatches it out of his hand and stabs the air with it, punctuating his words: 'GET YOUR HEADS DOWN AND START CRAMMING!' He says, 'Thanks, mate,' to Sandi before addressing the class again. 'I am making myself available to you every lunch time this week. If you have any problems, I'll be there.'

He's wearing a dark blue suit, shot through with red pinstripes, with a deep burgundy lining. It's too cool for school, but that's his style. He has cauliflower ears and a nose that looks broken; the kind of bloke you'd think might eat babies for breakfast. He gets our respect. He still has mine – but barely, and I'm not sure how long it'll survive the massive dent it's suffered.

'Are you all listening?' Mr Green slams the book on the desk again, making us all sit up straighter.

Yesterday's dangerous liaison in the woods is making less and less sense to me. Was it really Mr Green? Did they really do it in the woods? If the evidence wasn't safely locked away on my laptop at home, I'd wonder if it wasn't just some kind of insane, horrific wet dream. Ugh!

Mr Green's lessons are legendary. A lot of discussion, a fair bit of politics background, and we all have a laugh. We know way more than the other History set, who have Mrs Pinner, droning through the dry bones of the curriculum and zombifying the class into a stupor. We've seen them troop out of their lesson looking stoned to oblivion. No surprise that hardly any of them put History down as one of their options for A level.

But today, we're told, there won't be a single word uttered during our entire lesson. Green is challenging us with a timed paper, '. . . as a kick up the backside, because I know you all need one,' he says. He looks round the room, steely glare pinning the slackers to their chairs as papers hit the desks. Fifty minutes later, we're stretching our backs and flexing the cramp out of our fingers. This is just a taste of what's coming next week.

'Jeeves, when you've finished your yoga exercises, collect up all the papers, please,' Mr Green says.

This is his little joke. He's given every one of us a nickname – some are funny, some are plain cruel. Mr

Green's sense of humour may incline towards derision, but because he's a brilliant teacher, no one minds. Mine is Jeeves. If you haven't read any P.G. Wodehouse, all you have to know is that Jeeves is a valet, who tends to his master's needs and gets him out of trouble. (He's also the clever one. Just sayin'.)

I gather up all the papers and shuffle them into a neat pile as I head towards Mr Green's desk. His back is to the desk. He's busy telling off Justin, aka Bieber (even though he looks nothing like Justin Bieber and stammers like hell when a girl even glances at him), for not handing in the last two pieces of homework. His phone is sitting in plain view. There are several text messages waiting to be read. I sneak a look and manage to catch a few words here and there.

Feeling terrible . . . Rawson . . . meeting . . .

Please . . . need your big shoulders

I dump all the papers on his desk, feeling strangely sordid and conflicted. And more disappointed in Mr Green than I've ever felt. This is getting kind of intense. Mr Green's in deep shit. I should ignore it. Greaves is not my problem. Well, she is, but not in that way. This is way too complicated. He might call me Jeeves as a joke, but there's no way I can get him out of the trouble he's landed himself in. But as I'm hurrying out, Mr Green catches hold of my arm.

'Everything OK, Jeevan? You're not your usual cheery self today.' His blue eyes search my face for a clue.

'Yeah, sure. All good. Thanks, sir.'

He holds my eyes for a moment and my face reddens with a sudden flush. I almost blurt out, 'How could you?' Instead, I look down at my shoes. They're flecked with spatters of mud from the woods. I meant to wipe them clean last night, but totally forgot.

'Are you sure?'

'It's all good, sir.'

'Well, if there's anything you want to talk about you know where to find me,' he says, finally letting me go.

'Thanks, sir.' I beat a hasty retreat, quick as I can without actually breaking into a giveaway run. It's not written on my face, is it? Does he know? No, that's impossible.

I look around for Dread or Sandi, but they've gone to their next lesson. I groan out loud when I realize what mine is.

English Lit!

It had to be, didn't it? How am I going to get through it?

Because Mr Green kept me, I'm three minutes late for English – a punishable offence, unless you're one of the Favoured Ones. Which I'm certainly not. Just to prove my point, Harry Pearce barges in right after me from his Geography class, takes his seat and Mrs Greaves doesn't bat an eyelid. He doesn't even have to give a reason. I'm about to do the same, but Greaves is already right up in my face.

'Why are you late? No! I don't want to hear your feeble excuses. Sit down. You've caused enough disruption.'

She's in a filthy mood. Her text to Green said something about another meeting with the Head.

'I'm sorry—' I begin.

'Sit down! Now!' she barks.

I should, but I don't. I do nothing. I'm taking a stand. It's a point of principle. She should hear me out, shouldn't she? She should at least be polite. Instead, she talks to me like I'm the mangy dead mouse the cat dragged in and it really pisses me off. Golden boy Harry didn't get the same treatment.

Her voice drops several decibels. 'You do understand plain English, don't you? English Lit is *not* optional. If you can't manage in this set, then perhaps it's time you dropped *down* to a less demanding set.' Her mouth is working away like she's chewing gum, but I know she's grinding her teeth – a sign of how livid she is. She takes no prisoners when she's like this. It should serve as a warning to me. The last time it happened, only last week, I ended up in the Headmaster's office.

I ignore the warning. I'm clever, sure, but not so smart I can't be stupid sometimes. But I *am* a human being, and I like to be treated like one. Not a big ask. Besides, with the accusation in the anonymous note hanging over her head, there's no way she's going to send me to the Headmaster.

I open my mouth to speak, concentrating on

maintaining an even, level, non-confrontational tone. 'Sorry for being one of the *two* people three minutes late for your lesson, Mrs Greaves. But I was talking to Mr Green.' She gives a sharp little intake of breath – and that's when I screw it all up, smiling as if I know something I shouldn't. (Which I do.)

She takes another step back, her eyes narrowing. I'm desperately trying to suppress the wink that's twitching at the corner of my eye, but it's hopeless. My cheeky wink sends her over the edge. Before I know it, I'm standing outside the Headmaster's office for the second time in a week.

'Headmaster will call you through in a minute,' Mrs Dere says. She gives me a sympathetic look before getting on with her work.

At least I don't have to use the school phone to call my mum about the inevitable detention on the horizon. Mum is seriously going to kill me when I get home. And I'm missing my sis more than I thought I would. Shanti would pop home from sixth-form college for Maji if I was going to be late, but she's at Oxford now, so it's a bit far for her to nip back.

Mrs Dere's intercom buzzes and I hear the Headmaster telling her to send me through.

'I hope you're not intending to make a habit of this, Jeevan?' Rawson says.

I'm standing in front of his desk praying for a miracle. 'No, sir.'

'Take a pew. So Mrs Greaves sent you here, did she?'

'Yes, sir.'

'More belligerency on your part?'

'Definitely not, sir.'

'No? Well, don't keep me in suspense. What did you do?'

'A couple of us were three minutes late for her class. Mr Green kept me back a few minutes, which made me late for Mrs Greaves.'

'But there's only one of you here.'

'Yes, sir.'

'Who else was late?'

I hated to do what I was about to do.

'Speak up, Jeevan.'

'Pearce, sir,' I say reluctantly. I'm not a grass. Saying Harry's name makes me wince. On the other hand, he's never in trouble, so he has nothing to worry about. He may be slightly challenged personality-wise, but otherwise, he's safe.

'I see.' Rawson taps his chin with his pen. His desk is cluttered with files and papers. I catch a glimpse of the corner of a sheet of bright yellow paper, and I recognize it. My hands suddenly get clammy. The room is stifling hot and I feel a bead of sweat trickle down my back. 'Mocks next week, Jeevan. Are you ready for them?'

I drag my eyes up to meet his. 'Well, sir, I'm doing my best.'

Rawson looks thoughtful for a moment. 'I'm sure

you're feeling the stress – you and the rest of Year Eleven. Tell you what – I'm giving you a library pass. See you stay there until your next lesson.'

I almost jump for joy. I was expecting a bollocking and a detention as the minimum. But a reward? There is a god! 'Thank you, sir.'

'I do NOT want to see your face in here again this term, however. Got it?'

'Yes, sir. Oh, should I go and tell Mrs Greaves?' I'd like to see her face when she hears. It may be petty, but the small victories count.

'No need. I'll be seeing her shortly.'

I'm betting I know what that's about. And why I've just been given a library pass, too.

CHAPTER 5

'You're kidding me! For real?'

'No way, man!'

There is a fusillade of swearing going on in my bedroom – from Sandi, anyway; Dread rarely swears.

I've just told them about the lethal weapon on my laptop. At first, they refuse to believe me, but that's no surprise – I wouldn't have either. Then they realize I'm serious. And then, of course, they want to watch it, which makes me realize I've just made a blunder of epic proportions.

'No can do, guys. It's seriously bad. It'll mash up your heads and flip your stomachs inside out. I ain't having anyone puking up in my room.'

'Come on, Jeev, you've got to play it for us,' Sandi says, ignoring me.

He's sprawled on my bedroom floor; Dread's lounging on the swivel chair at my desk. We're drowning in past papers: Chemistry, Biology and Physics, which both

Dread and Sandi can A-star blindfolded and with one arm tied behind their backs. Wish I could say the same for me! But that's what all these group revision sessions are in aid of. Tomorrow night we're hitting History and English – that's where I come into my own. In Maths, we're pretty even, and Latin is all learning by rote, so you just have to put the hours in. Dread has a photographic memory, the jammy bastard; my hours of slogging are mere minutes for him.

I shake my head. 'Can't do it. Sorry, guys. I'm only looking out for you here. Once you've watched it, you can't unwatch it, and, believe me, you'll wish you could.'

Dread gives me a scathing look. 'It's not for real, is it?' he says. 'Man, you're a time-waster. What's going on inside that little head of yours these days? You got a bad case of exam-fever or what?'

'Yeah, you're sick, man! And it's not even funny,' Sandi says, but he's grinning his head off. 'And did you *have* to use Green for your sleazy little fantasy?'

'Fantasy?' Dread says. 'More like a B-movie horror.'

'You could have picked someone else, *anyone* else. Like Holder – now *that* I might've believed. He needs a bloody magnifying glass to see anything, and he'd definitely go for Greaves. Although he might need a couple of Viagra pills to get things going!' Sandi adds.

I shake my head. 'Gross!'

Mr Holder teaches Chemistry. He probably should have retired at some point in the last century, but he knows his stuff and he's not a bad teacher. Luckily for him, and us, he has a lab assistant who sets up all his experiments. Otherwise, I'm pretty sure the school would not still be standing.

'Man, she'd eat him alive!' Dread says. 'Whiskers, wrinkles and warts – and magnifying glass an' all!' Something about the image cracks us all up and we laugh until tears pour down our faces.

They've switched back to thinking I've made it all up, which is fine by me. I was a dumb-ass to tell them in the first place.

I tell them about what happened in English Lit instead.

'Fool!' Sandi says. 'What happened to keeping your head below the radar? You know she's never liked you much.'

I still can't get used to Sandi's new look. After much thought and deliberation, and a lot of agonizing – trust me, I got it all – he decided to drop the turban last week and get himself his *first* ever haircut. He had to persuade his parents that he hadn't lost his religion to stop them freaking out. So now he goes to the *gurdwara*, the Sikh temple, on Sundays to keep them happy and has to wear a hanky on his head when he's there. He's not used to his new look either. Every now and then, he pats his head and looks startled. He finally realized how much it made him stand out, he told me, that and all the funny looks, and the abuse he got for it.

'More to the point – how the hell did you get away with a library pass from Rawson?' Dread throws a perfectly designed paper plane in my direction. It sails right at my head. I swat it away. 'What are you not telling us?'

Trust him to guess.

'Come on, Jeev, spill.'

'OK, OK! You know she marks me down – and before you say anything, no, it's not just me that thinks so. Tom does, too. We've compared our essays. Tom's are good, but mine are way better.'

'All right, Shakespeare, calm down,' Dread says.

'Come on, guys, you know me – I'm not into bigging myself up, but facts are facts.'

Dread rolls his eyes.

Sandi pointedly yawns. 'Get to the point, will you?' he says. 'You're losing us. And, yeah, your head's definitely way too big for that little brain it's hiding!'

I ignore him. 'So, we finished our Lit controlled assessment last week. Greaves had already checked our plans the week before, and she said mine was fine. Well, *adequate* – that's the word she used.'

'Don't tell me she said Tom's was better?' Sandi says, yawning again.

'Quit that, Sandi. What do you know about what happens in my lessons?' I say, getting angry.

'Cool it, Jeev. Just tell us what happened,' Dread says.

'She told Tom that his was *superb*, and I overheard

her telling him how to make it even better. But when I asked her how I could improve mine, she said she couldn't offer any guidance.'

'Uh oh, I think I know where this is going,' Dread says. 'You didn't go all *belligerent* again, did you?'

I pull a face at him. 'No, cos I've learnt from my mistake. One detention a week is more than I can handle.'

'So, the controlled assessment's done now. What did she give you for it?' Sandi asks. He shakes his head. 'Damn shame we're not in the year below. We wouldn't have to worry about controlled assessments.'

This is the last year we have to suffer controlled assessments – they've been phased out. 'Give me exams any time. At least no one can fiddle those results,' I say with feeling.

'True,' Dread says. 'Some private schools are doing the IGCSE – so they'll still get to do controlled assessments and coursework. They'll still be able to fiddle the hell out of their results. Can't have the kids of the rich and famous getting anything less than A stars, can we? Who would run the country?'

'Yeah, we all know that game. If Dad could afford to put me in one of those schools, he would have. I heard the teachers wrote out all the notes for the essays. And get this, some of them let the kids bring in the whole essay prewritten to submit. Imagine!' Sandi says, clearly unable to imagine how they got away with it. 'Always wondered why your parents never put you in a private school, Jeev.'

'You know what they're like: a level playing field, doesn't matter what school you go to, it's all down to you what you make of your life, and all that crap.'

'So what did you get for your controlled?' Dread asks.

'I find out in the next lesson.'

Greaves has already predicted me a B for the controlled assessment. In fact, I'm betting that even though I haven't even sat the mock exam yet, she's already put me down for a B, or even a C after today's incident. I know the GCSE is marked externally – but the thing is, people should be fair, shouldn't they? Or what's the point in bothering? My gran just says get over it, of course. Nothing's fair in this world. That's the way it is and that's the way it'll always be. Then she'll launch into another one of her stories about 'when I was young.'

'Well, you can appeal anything. They pick a random sample of controlled assessments to go off to get marked externally, so just make sure yours is one of them,' Dread says. 'It'll be a hassle, though. Parents will have to get involved. There'll be no escaping that.' His tone is doom-laden, and with just cause.

Dread avoids his mum going in to school at all cost. Even though he's the golden boy, parents' evenings are akin to the rack for him. Mrs Fellowes, his mum, is a perfect copy of Ripley in *Aliens*. *No one* messes with her kid – not her kid, or her sister's kid, or her brother's kid, or even her friend's kid. You get the picture. If she found out what Greaves has been up to, she'd tie her hair back, roll up her sleeves, get out her AK-47 and drive her Mini straight into Greaves's classroom, guns blazing. The fallout would be mind-blowing.

Sandi prods me. 'What did you do, Jeev?'

I lower my voice. 'OK, so I wrote a little note and posted it to Rawson. Anonymously.'

Their ears are practically flapping.

Sandi shoves me, and I fall backwards on the carpet. 'Get out! What did you say in it?'

'I presented Rawson with my sneaking suspicion. He bloody well better take it seriously. Can't be every day that a member of his staff is accused of marking certain kids down.'

'No-o! You actually said that in the note?' Sandi says, shocked. 'You actually said she does that? For real?'

'Yeah, kind of. I want him to look into why she always marks me down.'

'Dude, we could have told you why,' Dread says.

'Because you've got a big mouth, or she doesn't like the fact that you know more than her – or *think* you do! That would piss anyone off,' Sandi says as though he understands where she's coming from.

'Exactly. That doesn't necessarily make her a racist, Jeev,' Dread adds. 'Unless she's been doing that with *all* the non-white kids at school, and then a claim like that has to be backed up with proof. It's a pretty massive thing to allege about someone.'

Trust Dread to approach this with logic. 'Well, I don't have proof. When Rawson looks into it, he'll find out what she's been doing. You'll see I'm right about this.'

'And he's going to look into it, is he?' Dread says. 'Because he doesn't have to, Jeev. He could chuck your anonymous note in the bin and forget all about it.'

Sandi echoes Dread, but much more emphatically. 'Especially as your name wasn't even on it. It's a helluva thing to accuse a teacher of something like that and then leave it unsigned. Jeev, you need your head examining!' Sandi says.

'I know, I know. It was a risk, but you seriously think I should have signed it?'

'No!' Dread and Sandi say together.

'Make up your minds! First you say I should've signed the note, and now you're saying no! Bloody hell!'

'*Obviously* you shouldn't have signed it. It's slander, for a start,' Dread says. 'Or defamation of character at the very least.'

'And when he calls Greaves in and says look what your pupil, Jeevan Kapoor, is saying about you, you would have been in for it!' Sandi adds. 'You think she doesn't like you now? Imagine what she'd be like if she hated your guts.'

'So here's the thing – Rawson hasn't binned it. I saw it on his desk.' What I can't tell them, without giving away the fact that I really *did* record a video of Greaves and Green doing it in the woods, is that I know that Rawson is definitely looking into the note.

'You're gonna be in so much trouble if he finds out it's you,' Sandi says. Did I mention that Sandi *always* stays under the radar? 'And seeing as Greaves has sent you to his office twice now, it's pretty obvious.'

'I sent the note after the first time. Anyway, she's always sending someone to his office. There's no way he'll find out it's me. It could have been anyone.'

Dread looks over his round black-rimmed glasses, which are perched precariously on the end of his nose. And I know he's got a list of exactly how many different ways I'm going to be found out. I brace myself.

He counts them off on his fingers. 'Prints on the note and the envelope, DNA from your saliva, handwriting analysis,' Dread begins. If you haven't already guessed, he's addicted to *CSI*, *True Crimes* and *Silent Witness*; basically anything that has anything to do with forensics. He's the only one of us who knows exactly what he wants to be: Grissom Number Two, Chief Forensic Analyst of CSI Las Vegas.

'No one's dead, Dread,' Sandi reminds him with a roll of his eyes. 'Rawson is not going to be that bothered by a silly note, no matter what it alleges.'

Dread ignores him and continues. 'He'll make a list of all the black and Asian kids who have Greaves – because it won't be any of the white kids warning him about a racist teacher, will it? So how many are there, Jeev?'

Oh God.

Sandi says, 'She only takes Years Ten and Eleven for English Lit.'

I don't know how many she has in her Year Ten class, but there are only three of us in my lesson with her, and one is mixed race. That leaves two of us, and maybe a few more from Year Ten.

'Wait. She takes some of the other years for English Language,' Sandi says. 'I know my brother has her.'

Yes! The shortlist has become a longlist again. I'm safe! But I'm beginning to wonder about that library pass today and whether Rawson has guessed it was me. No, he can't have. I was standing right in front of him – perfectly positioned for an interrogation – yet he let me go after asking me barely anything.

'Just don't do anything like that again, Jeev. You could totally screw up the year for yourself,' Sandi says, prophetically as it turns out.

'He's not out of the woods yet,' says Dread, and then he turns to me. 'Did you specifically say English Lit in the note?' he asks.

I nod slowly, feeling myself turning that sickly shade of green I dislike so much.

CHAPTER 6

I'll deny it. That's what I have to do. 'It wasn't me, sir,' I'll say with just the right amount of shock, conviction and wide-eyed innocence. Besides, no matter what Dread says when he's in full-on channelling Grissom mode, no one can prove anything.

Anyway, there's no way the school are going to bother with any forensic analysis because I didn't commit a crime, though I have to keep reminding Dread of this. Rawson hasn't passed the note on to the police. The time and expense involved, not to mention the bad publicity for the school, would put him off, anyhow.

In fact, all I've really done is make an observation. But if the anonymous note were to come to light, or, somehow, end up in the wrong hands, well, that *would* be serious – especially if the allegations made in the note proved to be true, and I think they are. I've been checking into it.

Well, I've messaged a couple of Greaves's ex-pupils

on Facebook Messenger. So that makes three of us who think she marked us down.

OK, maybe the note was a bad move.

This is turning into a game of chess, and chess is not my forte. Dad beats me every single time we play. 'Jeevan, what have I taught you?' he asks me at the end of every game.

'Yeah, I know, Dad. Think it *all* the way through in my head *before* making a move.' But the carrots he's dangling, my potential reward for the first time I do beat him, are slightly distracting. He lays them on the table before we start a game: two crisp fifty-pound notes.

I do try to think the move through. I just can't visualize all the moves my opponent might make, and then all the moves I might make after that . . . Chess is not a game about a single move. It's far more complicated than that. I wish I'd never asked Dad to teach me now.

Lessons can be learnt from thinking like a chess grandmaster – even from a lesser grandmaster like my dad.

The anonymous note was one thing. The ticking bomb embedded in my laptop is quite another. It's on a whole different level.

I need to talk to Dread.

'You've got to use it or lose it,' Dread says. He's sharp. He knew the video was for real straight off – and he realized it was only because Sandi was there that I'd clammed up about it. One whiff of trouble and Sandi runs the other way. Not surprising, really. Sandi's the first one in his family to go to a grammar school and his parents, and uncles and aunties and cousins, have high hopes for him. Sandi's smarts are in the sciences – you know where I'm going with this, right? Yes, they, too, want Sandi to be a doctor. Realistically, no parent wouldn't, right? The thing is, Sandi wants it too. And that's why he ducks under the radar, which is easier for him than me as he doesn't have the liability of a smart-alec mouth like mine to contend with. And he also doesn't have Greaves for English.

'Lose it?'

'Yeah, get rid of it. Delete it. Wipe it. Erase it. That kind of ammo is gonna mess with your head if you hang on to it. Every time Greaves does something that gets your back up, you're gonna be thinking about it, thinking about what you saw, what you recorded, and how you're gonna have to use it against her and how it'll be all her own fault because you gave her all these chances and she blew them. You'll hold out for a while, but soon she'll just have to *breathe* wrong, and WHAM, you'll hit the button.'

'I wouldn't do that!' I say, but realize it's Dread I'm trying to kid. 'OK, I was tempted to use it, who wouldn't be? Not any more, though.' I think I might still be trying to lie through my teeth.

Dread waves away my denials. 'You're tempted all

right!' he says. 'But you'll end up doing it on the spur of the moment cos that's how you roll, Jeev.' Dread's been helping me raise my chess game so if anyone knows how my brain works, it's him. 'And then there's Mr Green. Man,' Dread shakes his imaginary dreadlocks, 'why did it have to be him? I had some respect for that dude. Ain't nothing big about him now. You gonna land him in it too?'

'He can be edited out,' I say, wincing at how unconvincing I sound.

Dread raises an eyebrow. 'You sure about that?'

'Maybe not.' I take a deep breath. 'So, you still want to watch it?' I think about asking him to swear an oath of secrecy, but Dread's the safest guy I know.

There are two clips: Act One and Act Two. Act One is the conversation that starts with Greaves telling Mr Green about being called in to see the Headmaster. This is the interesting bit as she basically convinces Mr Green that some scumbag – that would be me – is unfairly using the race card to get at her. Yeah, right, she's a poor innocent lamb. So, of course Green is gonna be there for her, the damsel in distress. See? I'm not the only one playing cards.

In Act Two Greaves's co-star could almost have been anyone, until she murmurs, 'Oh, Daniel!' towards the end. That's Mr Green well and truly incriminated, unless Dread can edit it out. I suggest a voice-over, but Dread gives me a look. 'Maybe not,' I mutter.

Now that I've watched the two clips again, I see their

potential, the possibilities. I might never need to use more than a few minutes' worth. The clips could also be turned into three or four acts – maybe even a mini-series. Dread's good at this kind of stuff, but if we got a techie to take a look maybe they could blur Mr Green to protect his identity. His voice might have to be altered too. Is that possible? I don't know. Dread might know, but he's staring at the screen.

I wait awhile, and eventually he speaks.

'Holy shit!' Dread's voice is barely above a whisper. He rarely swears, so I know the video has made an impression. He whispers it again.

'Or not so holy!' I glance over my shoulder to make sure my bedroom door is shut. My mum hates hearing me swear, so I never swear at home. But Dread's mum would literally have his guts for garters and make him wear them if she heard him cussing.

And his mum is currently downstairs chatting with my mum about an upcoming PTA meeting, where school dinners will be topping the agenda – again. Just as an example: last Tuesday the vegetarian option was a sprinkling of plastic cheese served on fashionably wilted lettuce, garnished with a sliver of wrinkly cucumber and wedges of tomato. The vaguely acceptable veggie pasta dish had run out – all the non-veggies had it. The non-veggie dish was liver, grey and curling up at the edges in embarrassment, and doing its best to swim out of the highly toxic brackish-brown puddle it was drowning in.

From our year, only Toby Ross was dumb enough to eat some, and that was because someone had dared him to for a fiver. Inevitably, the consequences were dire and the toilets had to be declared a no-go zone.

If one of us had reported the offending lunch, it would have been disregarded. 'Everyone complains about school dinners, so you simply cannot take a pupil's complaints seriously,' the Deputy Head had said at one PTA.

But someone had taken a photograph of all the school dinner options that day, and one thing you cannot argue against is visual evidence, timed and tagged and captured for posterity. A bit like my ticking bomb.

'Dread!' I give his shoulder a shake to bring him back to life.

'That's some serious shit,' he breathes.

'Can't say it's a show I ever want to see again.' I'm being flippant about it now – it's not as shocking the third time round. But Dread is still in that totally-shocked-by-it moment.

'How stupid could they be?'

'Very, it turns out.'

'And they didn't see you? Or know anyone was watching?'

'No. Soon as I saw them heading my way, I hid. Although Greaves thought she heard something for a second. But no. They haven't got a clue that they were caught on candid camera.'

'When you winked at her in class the other day,

didn't she clock it then?'

'No, I don't think so. There's no way she would have put two and two together.'

'OK, first thing – no more winking at her, otherwise she's going to start getting suspicious.'

'And then?' I ask.

'Got to think this through.'

Dread falls silent again.

'I was thinking we could divide it all up into smaller segments and post them as snippets, a mini-series.' I'm getting into my stride, thinking this thing can be done, should be done. It's only a matter of how and when. 'We could try out various edits, but save the original version. Maybe blur out Green—'

'Jeev! This is so out there – there's no way we can touch it!'

'Why not?'

'It's just not right, man.'

'Don't go all Sandi on me, Dread.'

'Have you given him a private showing too?'

'No way! He'd have insisted on handing it in to the Headmaster. Look, I know it's not right and it's not fair, but that's how life rolls sometimes. Take Greaves – she's never been fair with me, so why should I be fair back? And I've done nothing wrong – she has.'

'I take your point. But this video – it could destroy people's lives. And for what? Because you *think* she's being unfair to you.'

Dread's definitely got his I'm-too-sensible hat on today, which is probably why I went to him for advice. 'Come on, Dread, you know that's not my aim. The threat of using it might be more than enough. I could write a note and allude to its existence – and include a few choice details to verify its authenticity.'

Dread finally cracks a smile before saying, 'Another note?'

I ignore his barb. 'That might be enough to prod Greaves into being fair. That's all I want. To be treated the same as everyone else.'

Dread groans. 'You and me both.'

'The difference being you haven't got Greaves.'

'Let me think it through. Don't post it anywhere for now. OK?'

I feel offended that he doesn't trust me with it. I know he's right about keeping it under wraps, which I'd been doing until I got to the point of bursting. It *needed* to be shared. 'I wasn't about to. You could take a copy though, see what you can do with it in your editing suite. Saving Mr Green any embarrassment being the top priority.'

'Yeah, no need to land him in it.' Dread takes his memory stick off his key ring and inserts it into my laptop to copy the files.

So now, there are two time bombs ticking in unison.

CHAPTER 7

Friday lunchtime, I head over for Mr Green's lesson.

I did a timed essay yesterday and emailed it to him. He's marked it already and said he'd go through it at lunchtime, give me some pointers on where I went wrong: '. . . which wasn't in too many places, so no need to get your knickers in a twist, Jeevan. I'll see you later.'

Christ sake! Unwelcome images of Mrs Greaves's twisted knickers spring to mind immediately. Dread is sitting next to me in the lesson, and neither of us dare look at each other. One small turn of the head towards him and I know exactly what'll happen. Forget an exchange of a small smile, or a smirk, or even a suppressed snigger. Hysterics of epic proportions would erupt, ugly snorting would be involved, inevitably resulting in us both being sent out of the room, or worse still, to Rawson. I'd have to feign an asthma attack regardless of the fact that I don't have asthma. So, no, we daren't trade a look.

'It's the *mocks* next week, not the real thing. There's

plenty of time to hone your skills,' Mr Green continued. 'That goes for you, too, Goldilocks.'

'Yes, sir,' Dread replies. His voice sounds strained.

I almost make the fatal mistake of looking at him to see if he's all right, and it's a superhuman effort that makes me hold myself back at the last second. Dread proceeds to have a major coughing fit and gets sent to the water fountain in the corridor. By the time he gets back, Mr Green has moved on, as has the moment, and it's safe to look at each other.

'Man, that was close,' Dread murmurs. 'How're we gonna get through the rest of the year when we can barely make it through one lesson? He uses that expression all the time! But it's got this whole new meaning now.'

'I warned you the video would mess with your head! As long as he doesn't say it again today, we'll be all right,' I say. But Dread's right – it's one of Mr Green's catchphrases.

'What are the chances?' Dread mutters.

And he doesn't say it again – today, that is. I've no idea if he literally gets anyone's knickers in a twist again, but then I've been taking the long way home. The woods have been spoilt for me, adulterated . . .

The one-to-one with him at lunchtime is going fine too, until he asks me a question that makes me sit bolt upright in my chair.

'Time to get it all off your chest, Jeevan. What's

going on with you? Problem shared and all that.'

'Nothing's going on, sir.' This would have been the right time to practise my innocent look, but instead I shuffle my papers together, getting ready to make a quick exit. A quick smile and, 'Thanks for your help, sir,' and I'm halfway to the door when he says, 'Sit!'

I come back and sit. In pensive silence.

'Not a single quip in class all week, no hand shooting up with all the answers. Barely even a glance up from your books.'

It's been hard to maintain any kind of eye contact with him, since, you know, the scene in the woods. But obviously, there's no way on earth I can tell him that. Or can I? It would be a relief to get it off my chest. But NO! What am I thinking?

'Jeevan?'

'Yes, sir. Sorry, sir.' I need to get my brain in gear. Offer him something, anything except the truth. 'Well, it's the mocks, I guess. You know, the pressure. Family,' I mutter, eyes downcast, brow a crochet of frowns.

'Yes, I know they have very high expectations of you. You have a sister at Oxford, don't you?'

I'm almost grateful to my parents for mentioning my genius older sister at every parents' evening. I nod, oh so bleakly. 'She's studying medicine.' Just the right amount of awe mixed with fear of failure in my tone brings Green's sympathetic shoulder out.

He nods with understanding, and looks concerned for

me, which makes me feel bad. 'I see, Jeevan. That's quite some pressure. And is that what's expected of you too?'

'I guess so, sir.' I'm warming up to it now. He doesn't know that my parents have given me a special dispensation to follow my heart – even if my heart doesn't follow the science route. 'I have to ace every single one of my exams if I want to carry on with History, English and Latin at A level, otherwise . . .' I allow my doom-laden voice to trail off.

'Jeevan, you are predicted an A star in History and I know from Mr Hartley that you're on for an A star in Latin too. In fact, from what I remember of your report, you're predicted A stars for most of your subjects.'

Yeah, in everything except English Lit. Don't you have anything to say about that? I wait. He clears his throat. I prompt him.

'English Lit.'

He's nodding his head. 'I've seen your predicted grades. Some work to do there, Jeevan, but I know you're up to it,' he says. 'You're not a million miles off an A.'

Oh yeah? The controlled assessments are going to bring me down big time. I've got Lit this afternoon, so I'll know what grade she's given me soon enough. And it's not an A I'm after. It's the A with the bright twinkly star that I want. It's a matter of pride for me – I have to match my brilliant sister's grades.

My leg has started jigging up and down under the table. It happens when I'm nervous, or extremely angry, or a bit of both, or a lot of both, like now. He knows Greaves is being 'investigated' because of the anonymous note, but she has him thinking it's all a crock of shit. How do I tell him it's not? If he knew it was me who'd sent that note, he would definitely sit up and pay attention. Green has no hang-ups – not about colour or anything.

How do I let on?

It all comes back to the ticking bomb on my laptop, which is now on Dread's memory stick too. No. Aside from that and the anonymous note, I have one more card up my sleeve that I can play. I might not be much of a chess player, but I've played a few hands of cards in my time. OK, it was only with my granddad from the age of about seven until Granddad passed away three years ago. We'd play cards most days when I got home from school. He taught me tons of different games, but we had a favourite, Getaway, and the aim of that game was to have no cards left in your hand. The origins of *Bhabhi*, its Indian name, are so un-PC it's no surprise Mum and Dad were deeply shocked when they found out what Granddad and I had been playing. Maji just laughed and told them it was only a name, but they were still livid, and I get why. *Bhabhi* means brother's wife, and it's the person who loses who gets called that – they get the honour of serving all the drinks and snacks, and, Granddad told me, if it's a boy they get the ultimate diss of having to dress up in girl's clothes . . .

Mum and Dad are so PC that they checked Dread's heritage with me in case they inadvertently offended him when he was over at ours. Like Dread would mind! He's so laid-back, that boy, besides, it's only intentional slurs that get to us. The rest we're really not that bothered about. We're not ducks, but not much water gets under our skin either.

Thinking about it, Getaway is the wrong card game for the game I'm playing. I need to hold my cards closer to my chest.

'Sir,' I begin.

'Have you been to see Mrs Greaves? Talked to her about some extra help?' Mr Green interrupts. 'I'm sure she'll be very amenable. She only wants the best for you.'

That's where Mr Green's thinking parts ways from mine. He knows nothing about my sneaking suspicion. I don't care that Dread and Sandi think I'm wrong about it – or not completely right, at any rate. And Green told her he had her back – I've got it on film.

Seems like no one's got my back. Time to play that card up my sleeve.

'No, sir. But my parents have an old friend who lectures in English and I've been to see him.'

Mr Green seems taken aback. 'Oh, I see. And this friend of theirs, how does he think you're progressing?'

'Fine. He's happy. He asked me to write a few essays and then I sat a couple of timed papers with him.'

'And?'

'It was fine.'

'How fine?' Mr Green is looking intently at me now. I stare right back at him. 'Solid A stars so far.'

'Ah. I see. Well, some teachers can bring out the best in kids, and this friend of your parents has clearly tapped into that brain of yours and made it work in a subject that you weren't exactly flunking, Jeevan, but you also weren't exactly excelling in.' He laughs. But it's not his usual deep-from-the-belly guffaw.

He must be wondering about Mrs Greaves and the validity of the accusations in the note. Or does he simply think that not everyone can be brilliant in every subject and English Lit is clearly the chink in my otherwise undented armour?

'Don't put too much store in the predicted grades. They are only meant to be a simple guideline, an indication of where you need to work harder.'

'I thought that's what mocks were for.'

'The mocks will help you hone your exam technique, get you revising early, and see where you're going wrong so you can get it right for the real thing.'

'I wouldn't care about the predictions if they weren't on my school record, sir.'

But because they are recorded, I do care – a lot. I don't care what anyone else says about how they don't matter. Anything written about you in black and white, or stored in a computer, matters. If you allow people to write lies about you and get away with it, those lies can come back and bite you.

And no one is going to bite *me*.

Besides, if she's been unfair to me, it's likely other kids have been treated unfairly too. She's been a teacher for a long time. Someone's got to stop her. I have the means to do something about it. The anonymous note was the plan, and it was my only plan. OK, it wasn't much of one and I don't expect much from it.

But if that doesn't do the trick...

Like Mr Green said, some teachers bring out the best in you.

And some teachers don't.

CHAPTER 8

'Come up and get your marks for your controlled assessment when I call your name,' Mrs Greaves says at the start of the lesson.

This is literally the last time Greaves will ever say that. How will she manage her thwarted sense of fairness in September when the new curriculum and grading system roll in? They're getting rid of As and Bs and Cs and putting in numbers instead. I'm guessing it won't be long before she finds a new way to keep kids like me in our place. Or am I being unfair to her because I can't stand her? Dread and Sandi would say yes, no doubts, Jeevs, and they'd pin me with red-hot glares until I shut up about it.

Next to me, Tom groans. 'I don't want to know mine. I did a crap job.'

'Tom, don't stress it, you did fine, mate. It only counts for about twenty per cent of the overall grade.'

'Twenty per cent? Shit, that much?'

I nod. Yes, that much. It could make the difference

between getting a B and getting an A. 'She practically told you that you had it in the bag and she didn't tell me that!'

'Yeah, I know. But this time you'll get what you deserve, Jeev. This isn't homework or class work. The controlled assessments get marked externally.'

See, Tom knows all about her tricks with me. 'Um, actually I think the school only sends a random sample off for external marking.'

'Oh,' Tom says, the light dawning in his eyes.

'Yeah, big OH.'

My heart's banging against my ribcage and I'm feeling a bit sick. If it's an A, then I was totally wrong about her. If it's a B, there are two possibilities: either I was right about her, or I messed up the paper. I *have* messed up a paper before – one year, I turned two pages at the same time during my History exam, but that was way back in Year Eight. I've never been that stupid again. Now I compulsively check and recheck that I've answered every single question on every single sodding page.

It would be impossible for me to have done that this time because we know the essay question ahead of time and we're allowed to take our plan into the exam. And we've got two or three lessons to do it in. And I thought I'd done a decent job of it.

Which means . . .

'Jeevan,' Greaves calls impatiently. She must have

called me once already and I missed it.

Great way to start, Jeev, get the woman's back up before you even get to her desk.

Here it is – the moment of truth.

'You got a B, Jeevan. There were a few points you missed in your answer and some that you could have explained better. But, on the whole, a reasonable result.'

So there it is. My jaw tightens and clenches. A B? She's seriously got to be kidding me! What's the betting my controlled assessment doesn't get *randomly* selected for external marking?

'You can go back to your seat. There's a lot to get through before the mocks next week. Justin, will you come up, please?'

I walk away, jaw still clenched, anger churning and somersaulting inside me like a washing machine on steroids. Tom knows as soon as he sees my face.

'Bugger,' he says when I confirm it. 'What are you going to do?'

Good question. What *am* I going to do?

Sitting at the back of the top of the double-decker bus after school, I put the question to the Dream Team. 'So, what am I going to do?'

Dread whistles through his teeth. 'That could drop you down a grade.'

I glare at Dread. 'Tell me something I don't know.'

'But did you mess it up?' Sandi asks. 'Because unless you see your paper, you won't know, will you? So you could have messed it up.'

Sandi gets a glare too.

'OK, I get it,' Sandi, says, holding his hands up. 'Just checking. It's possible, though, isn't it?'

'Did you lose part of your brain when you got rid of the turban, Sandi, cos for someone's who's supposed to be so bloody smart, you can be a total bloody idiot!'

'I guess that means no, Sandi. Jeevan absolutely did *not* mess up his controlled assessment,' Dread tells Sandi. He drops his voice a notch, and adds, 'By the way, best not to ask him again whether it was his own fault he messed it up.'

'Sorry,' I mutter. 'Didn't mean that, Sand.'

Sandi shrugs. 'No worries. I don't mind being your punchbag. That's what mates are for.'

I've really offended him with my turban remark, so I go in with a mock-punch, to show him I'm sorry. 'Look, I need to do something about her, guys.'

'Well, if you're *so* sure you didn't mess up the paper, then you're going to have to tell your mum and dad,' Sandi says. 'That's what *I'd* do, anyhow. Get them to make sure it gets marked externally.'

'Sandi's right,' Dread says. 'Hate to be a parrot, but you're going to have to involve them. What about the note? Have you heard anything?'

I shake my head. 'Not a thing.'

'Don't stress, Jeev. Let your parents deal with it for you,' Sandi says.

'I hate dragging them into this. You know what they're like. First they'll say it's all my fault for having such a big mouth and being snarky all the time, and aggravating a situation that could've been avoided. Then they'll say that my sister, Shanti, never had these kinds of problems.'

Last term, at parents' evening, when my parents told Greaves that I was considering studying Classics and English at Oxford, she choked on her water. Mum had to thump her on the back a few times. There were tears rolling down her face when she told my parents that university choices were still very far away and that it was important for me to focus on the GCSEs first. 'A little less sarcasm in the classroom wouldn't go amiss either,' Greaves had added. 'Perhaps you can have a little chat with Jeevan about it when you get home, Mrs Kapoor.'

Mum had smiled sweetly as she corrected her. 'It's Dr Kapoor, Mrs Greaves, and yes we will most certainly be chatting with Jeevan.'

And when we got home Mum and Dad told me to stop being so sarcastic in her class because she was obviously very strict. 'There is no need to get her back up, Jeevan, so don't aggravate her,' Mum had added.

'Don't punch me, but it sounds like you think that they might think that you messed up the paper,' Dread says.

I scowl at him. Tom's come up the stairs and he's

looking around for a seat, but the bus is heaving. 'Over here,' I call, waving him over. We squeeze up to let him sit.

'Worked out what you're going to do yet?' Tom asks.

'No. Yes. Maybe. No,' I answer, despondently.

'It's simple – he's got to tell his mum and dad,' Sandi says.

'And like I said, it's not that simple,' I snap, losing my patience again.

'Really? No way I'd do that – it wouldn't be worth all the aggro,' Tom says.

'But won't they ask you what you got?' Sandi asks him.

'No. I mean, they know the mocks are next week, but they don't really know much about the controlled assessments.'

'You've got nothing to worry about – you got an A,' I remind him.

'Even so. I didn't tell them about *any* of the controlled assessments – I got a C for the last Chemistry one.'

That's got me thinking. Both Dread and Sandi read my mind.

'It's a risky strategy,' Dread says. 'If they find out that you haven't told them, they're going to be pissed at you. But with the mocks coming up, you could claim it went right out of your head.'

'They'll find out. They always do,' is Sandi's verdict, characteristically delivered in a mournful tone.

'Look, work out the percentages. If you get a B in the

controlled, you can still get an A star overall. Especially if you're as good as you say you are!' Dread adds.

'Your mum and dad are like mine,' Sandi warns. 'Mine want the lowdown on everything that's happened at school as soon as I walk through the door!'

'For real?' Tom says. 'Mine just ask how my day was, tell me what time tea is, and then I go up to my room. As long as I'm getting the right grades and parents' evening goes all right, they're not too bothered.'

'God, you're lucky! Even my grandma gives me the third degree when I walk in,' I say. 'Well, not quite the third degree – but almost. If my uncle's over, he'll do the same, and my aunts. Basically everyone. They like to make sure you're keeping to the straight and narrow. Failure is not an option!'

Sandi's right about our families sharing a similar ethos. You might think our parents are pushy, but that's normal behaviour for them. *They* don't see it as being pushy. Feeding your kids good home-cooked food, instilling a set of religion-based morals into them (all you need to know about 'religion-based' morality is that everything enjoyable is wrong!) and making sure they get a good education is their life's work. That's it. Simple. And if their kid turns out to be a doctor then job done, *and* they get to lord it over all their Indian friends. All that stuff is virtually sewn into the very fabric of their DNA. It's impossible for them to understand that other parents don't obsess about their children in the same way.

Tom's eyes get wider and wider as I lay it out for him. Sandi's laughing at his shocked expression.

'God, if my parents were like that, I'd die!' Tom says.

'And I'm talking about the way *my* parents are – they're second generation. It would have been tons worse for them when they were growing up,' I add. 'I know because my gran lives with us, and she's way pushier than my mum or dad.'

'Oh, but I love your gran,' Sandi says.

'That's cos she thinks you're such a good boy, such a good example to me! Like I'm a layabout, or something!' I mutter.

'She knows what she's talking about, that lady,' Sandi says, preening.

I groan at Sandi. But it's true about how hard it was for the first generation – I've heard the stories from my gran at least a hundred times. I kid you not!

'We came with nothing but a small suitcase, Jeevan, and the coupon with the job that was promised for your grandfather.'

That's something that never gets taught in History. The British government handed out coupons in India for jobs in the UK. They invited people to emigrate here.

We get taught about European History, the Roman Empire, the Hapsburgs, both the World Wars, the American Civil War, I could go on, but do we ever take an in-depth look at the British Empire? Never. It's like it was a dirty secret or something.

Granddad spoke English 'like a native,' he used to say with a chuckle. He was super-clever – he had a degree in engineering. 'Not so clever that he remembered to tell me how cold it would be in this country. I came here only wearing sandals – in November!' Maji said. She'll never forgive him for that!

You see, my granddad had very little access to information, and that's what it's all about. Access to information.

The first generation had very little.

The second generation thought they had tons of it, but it was an uphill battle and a lot of them fell at the first hurdle.

The third generation have it at their fingertips, 24/7, and they aren't seeing the same hurdles.

I'm third generation. That makes me very different from previous generations because, by now, my DNA has mutated – and our mutated DNA can cause us third-generationers major problems.

We're not quite like our parents, nothing like our grandparents, and we're not quite like the indigenous population (the colour thing can get in the way). So what are we? Well, we have a rough idea of what we are: it's everyone else that has the problem. Which makes it our problem, I guess. Vicious circle.

So, the upshot is – I'm thinking about *not* telling Mum and Dad about my result.

I'll see if Rawson acts on the note, although I'm not

sure how I'd find out if he has. The video is still on my laptop – and on my mind. I'm trying not to think about it because it's still so tempting to bring Greaves down and hang the consequences.

And the mocks are next week and I haven't even started revising!

CHAPTER 9

I'm a crammer, so all the major distractions – the ticking time bomb, the anonymous note, the detention last week, the near detention this week – during the two weeks before the mocks, have been far from optimal. There's still time to cram but no time for anything else, sleep included. Dad, a mine of useless information, once told me that Maggie Thatcher only needed three to four hours' sleep a day, which probably accounts for a lot so I would in no way use her as a role model. If she'd got a bit more sleep, she might have done things differently. Or then again, maybe not. I put it to Dad and he declared that even twelve hours' sleep a day would not have made her more human. Maji adored the Iron Lady, but then Maji's got some funny ideas about politics and figures of authority. She won't have a word said against Boris Johnson and she firmly informed my mum and dad that nothing they said would stop her from voting Leave in June – you should have seen the expression on my mum's face when she came up with that one!

Obama gets about six hours' kip. I tried that for a while – well, for three nights. The first day was fine, the second not too bad – I was just a little ragged around the ages, but by the third day I'd totally unravelled. Forget about focussing – by evening my jaw ached from all the extra work I'd forced it to do yawning. But that was in a non-exam period.

'Lights out soon, Jeevan. If you haven't learnt it by now, it's too late,' Dad says. 'You need to sleep.'

He's right, but that ain't about to happen because the Master Crammer is pulling a long night shift and is about to roll up his sleeves and go to work. Adrenaline, desperation and a Red Bull (don't panic, it's not a habit and I'm not an addict), and the need to stay ahead of the pack, keep me wide-eyed and focussed into the early hours. I get three or four hours' sleep, then get up and cram another couple of hours of revision in before getting ready for school. Maji knows what I'm like during exams and no way on earth is she letting me leave the house without something in my stomach. She soaked a bowlful of almonds for me last night, like most nights, and slips their skins off before handing me the bowl.

'You know you can buy them already blanched,' I tell her.

'Why should I pay for somebody else to remove the skin when it takes me one second to do it myself? You children have no sense. What do you learn in school these days?' Good question, I ask myself. 'Don't be wasting a single one,' she says sternly. Nothing goes to waste in our house, ever. Maji's like the Waste Police – she's always on patrol, and God help anyone who dares to leave a single morsel of food on their plate or a sip of tea in their cup.

I shovel the almonds into my mouth, give her a quick hug and then I'm out of the door. Mum and Dad are on night duty at the hospital this week. Our paths will only cross briefly, which is a relief as Mum's a bit of an insomniac and she would have shot me if she even got an inkling of how much midnight oil I burnt last night.

Two papers a day are manageable, but the days I have three or four papers threaten to be murderously evil. Luckily, all is not lost. I may not have Dread's photographic memory, or live by Sandi's motto of learn it as you go along, but I do allow a generous portion of time to my homework and, shockingly, a surprising amount has stuck.

The GCSEs are spread across May and June. Everyone knows that. Everyone except our school, that is. Mocks are meant to emulate the real thing, but my school has crammed the mock exams together one after the other with no breathing space, because who needs to breathe? They shouldn't be called mocks. A mockery is a more fitting description.

The only upside is that I don't have Greaves for a *whole week*. The rain doles it out though by chucking it down in skipfuls. A soaking on the way to school and a soaking on the way back, red-eyed, sleep-deprived, head buzzing with facts, figures, quotes, useful information, possibly useful information, more quotes, equations, pages upon pages of bullet points, and with fingers that are still clawed around an imaginary pen but dare not be straightened out until the end of the week in case I can't get them to curl round a pen again. What's not to like?

It's a week when you wished you'd listened to everyone, and I mean everyone, and got your head in the right gear and started revising earlier.

'How did you do?' Sandi asks. 'What did you write for question 3?'

Sandi always likes to do a post-mortem after an exam. He likes to dissect the whole paper, analyse each section, collate our responses and compare them with his. Anally retentive? Yes. And he's the kind of guy who remembers everything he wrote for every single question. How can anyone do that? Apart from it being a total waste of brain space, it really, really does my head in.

'I dunno. 57%, I think.'

He nods. 'Me too. What about question 10? It was a three-parter.'

'Was it?' Damn. Did I realize that in there? Did I answer all three parts? Mind blank. That's why I don't like post-mortems. In my head, I've already moved on to what we've got coming our way after lunch, and today it's the one I need to ace.

'Lit this afternoon,' Dread says, after we've finished analysing the Maths paper to Sandi's satisfaction.

'Yeah, and don't forget most of the quotes are at the back of the book, Sandi,' I remind him.

'You're sure they're giving us the book, right, Jeev? Because I'm stuffed if they don't.'

'I'm not 100% because Greaves didn't tell us jack, but Dread told me.'

'Chill. We're definitely getting the book,' Dread says. 'Mr Marks told us so in class last week, Sandi. Don't you remember?'

Sandi's chewing his lip ferociously. 'No.'

'Don't panic. You'll be fine,' I say, trying to reassure him. It's his worst subject. By worst I mean he's more of a scrape-an-A than ace an A star.

Toby, on the other hand, has an issue with the particular brand of thought-provoking literariness of the kind promoted by the curriculum. He writes rap lyrics in his spare time, and he's damn good, or, as he puts it, 'badass'. Seriously, though, he is good; we've all heard him rap. But when faced with an exam question asking why an author happened to choose the colour blue for the blinds, or brown for the sofa, or grey for the sky, words desert him.

To make things worse for him, he's in my set with Greaves. 'We're getting the book? We're getting the bloody book?' His eyes flash wildly. 'No one bloody told me! I stayed up half the night learning those sodding quotes.'

Ears are wagging all around us and pretty soon he's drawn a crowd of Year Elevens.

'All the quotes are at the back of the book!' I announce to a chorus of muttered curses and groans, but mainly curses, and some daringly not even muttered but practically shouted out – a risk as we're standing mere metres away from the dining hall and therefore dicing with death, or detention at the very least.

Sounds as though a lot of them spent half the night learning useless quotes. That's hours of their lives that Greaves has snatched away from them. Unbelievably, she gets paid for it too.

Maths, English Language, English Lit, Physics, Chemistry, Biology, History, Geography, Spanish and Latin – they're my options and it's way too late to change them now, or drop any of them. I wish I'd gone for Combined Science, but there was no way the pair of science gurus, my parents, would ever have allowed such an anomaly to occur in *their* family.

The week of mockery drags on to a not so dismal ending. No one cares about catching up on sleep – who needs it? We've all done without it, more or less, for an entire week, and survived. We've planned a weekend of debauchery. No, just kidding. We're going to the bowling alley on Friday night – we're that edgy. We're not even risking *not* getting a lane as Sandi's booked one. Then we're going to stand in a queue that'll snake around the block, with everyone else in the town aged between 12 and 20, trying to get into Nando's. And then we're going to a party, and that's when it might get interesting, or not, depending on who's there and who isn't.

Dread fancies a girl at the girls' grammar and, according to reliable info on Facebook, she's going to be there. No one actually knows the person whose party it is. All we know is that it got announced on Facebook by a guy at the private school up the road. Oh, and his parents are away.

Yeah, he's got to be a bit of an idiot. I mean, why would you do that? It's wrong on so many levels. You wouldn't catch us succumbing to that level of brain fail. And it's not because we wouldn't love to have a party, because we would, but we value our lives more than we value making new friends or making an impression on our existing friends.

It's close to ten by the time we get to the party. The house is lit up like a birthday cake with lights blazing in every window. The iron gate stands wide open, welcoming us to cross the forecourt, which is big enough for at least six cars, and enter the house through the unguarded front door. There are no bouncers and no guest list. What was this kid thinking? What were his parents thinking leaving him on his own?

'Probably not a good idea to stay too late at this one,' Dread remarks.

He's right. Sandi can smell trouble already. 'I'm out of here by midnight latest,' he says. 'Are you with me?'

We nod, agreeing to meet out the front later, and then we plunge into the melee.

'Amelia's here,' Dread says out of the corner of his mouth.

'What?' I shout. The music is call-the-feds-out loud. Luckily for the guy, the neighbours are a good twenty metres away on either side, or their Ming vases would have been jumping to the groove and bouncing off the walls in time with the bass.

'Amelia,' he mouths. I'm pretty sure that the reason Dread's purposely not shaved for a week is to create an impression on her. I hope for his sake she goes for the patchy yet vaguely bristly look.

'Where?' I ask, trying to follow his gaze, but the room is heaving with bodies. Everyone's drinking, mainly beers, but I've seen plenty of WKDs, Bacardi Breezers, Smirnoff Ices and bottles of spirits floating round the room. The guy whose party it is is *seriously* loaded. I live in a decent-sized semi, but this house has got to be ten times the size of my house, and apparently there's a pool out back too. Luckily for him, and no I don't know the guy's name, it's winter, so that's one thing that's guaranteed not to get trashed. There's no guarantee it won't get used as the outside loo though.

Mega-loaded or not, his parents ain't gonna be happy when they get back. He'll wish he had an army of cleaners coming when he wakes up in the morning, his house swimming in bottles, cans, butts and takeaway boxes. Then again, maybe he does.

Pretty soon I've lost Dread to Amelia, who seems taken by him; well, she hasn't told him to go away yet at any rate. I have to give it to Dread – Amelia is probably the most attractive girl in the room. They look good together.

I'm looking for Sandi, who's done a disappearing act, when Dread waves me over. I squeeze through the makeshift mosh pit and emerge relatively unscathed at the far side of the room.

'What's up?'

'Thought you looked lonesome,' Dread says.

'Where's Amelia?'

'Bringing her friend over.' Dread nods towards the hallway.

'You're not trying to set me up, are you?'

'Me? Never.'

Amelia's hugging a girl, and then they're laughing about something and I've got a horrible feeling it's about me. They link arms and start heading towards us. 'Think I'm gonna go find Sandi.'

'Be cool, Jeev.'

Judging by my clammy palms, I'm not sure I'm any good at cool. Amelia's friend looks kind of scary – her hair is dark and streaked with pink, and a short skirt and cropped top, DMs and a leather jacket complete her look. She's seriously fine, and she knows it. 'She's got pink hair,' is all I say out loud.

'Hey, Dread,' Amelia's friend says, giving him a hug.

Dread knows her? No time to ask him how as Amelia's friend is holding her hand out to me. 'You've got to be Jeevan?' My tongue's tied itself into knots, which is so alien to someone who's got a problem with talking too much rather than too little that it stumps me. So all I do is nod. 'Call me Ree.' She shakes my hand formally and then smiles, revealing a perfect set of dimples. 'Dread said you were the silent type, but I thought he was exaggerating.' Now they're all laughing, and if the laughter wasn't directed at me I would be laughing at the silent idiot too.

I shrug like I really don't care. My brain is struggling to unleash a witty retort, but it's coming up blank.

'I like the pink.' *Did I say that out loud? What kind of idiot am I?*

She takes my idiocy in her stride. 'Thanks. It was blue last week.'

'Why? I mean, why dye it mad colours?'

'It keeps my parents on their toes,' she says with a wink.

'So it's your act of rebellion? I get that.'

'Yeah, I know, it's lame, but it annoys the hell out of them.' She laughs. 'Imagine if I drank and did drugs? They'd die!'

'So this is not your scene then?' I gesture at the room, heaving with people in various stages of intoxication, the smell of weed from the garden wafting in through the open windows.

'Why does everyone think that if you don't drink you don't like a party?' she says fiercely. 'It's so boring.'

I'm suddenly relieved I don't have a drink in my hands. 'No, I didn't mean it like that,' I say hastily. Somehow I don't think peer pressure, or parental pressure come to that, ever gets in her way. I like that. I like her. I just wish I could make words that made more sense come out of my mouth. 'Sorry, my brain's fried – we've just finished mocks so it's been a crap week.'

'We had ours before Christmas.'

'Seriously? I needed the Christmas holidays to revise!'

'So while you were revising, I was in Casablanca having fun, and then in Paris for a few days.'

'Casablanca? In Morocco?'

'Is there another Casablanca?' she asks, twirling a strand of hair in her fingers. 'We travel around a lot. Everyone thinks that's great, but sometimes it's nice to chill out at home, binge watch Netflix for a week.'

'We don't travel much. My parents are always working.' It's getting harder to have a conversation as someone ramps up the volume on the speakers. The room fills up with more bodies and we get shoved together. I catch her arm as someone barges through between us and she slips backwards.

'Hey!' she shouts at the retreating back. 'Thanks.' She smiles at me and I'm disarmed by the full force of her dimples. My hand is still on her arm and I reluctantly remove it.

Someone's put on Stormzy's 'Shut Up', and everyone heads into the mosh pit.

'I love this one!' Ree shouts, grabbing my hand and leading me into the fray. Dread and Amelia are already there. Dread's left eyebrow rises a fraction and he nods at me. I ignore him and focus on Ree, which is not hard to do at all.

To top it all, she can dance too. Mosh-pit rules mean I don't have to do much apart from jump up and down, and that much I can manage. Ree's an odd name. I'm guessing it's short for something. Renee? Rebecca? Reba? Rihanna? No idea. She looks Spanish, or maybe Brazilian, or a mix. I should have asked her. Next time I will, and I'm taken aback by how much I'm hoping there will be a next time.

The next half-hour is a blur of bodies and noise. Eventually we get split up and I can't see her any more. It's time to get some air.

I head out to the garden and find Sandi sitting on his own on a sunlounger near the pool.

'Hey. What's up?' I ask him.

'Not much. You?'

'I think Dread and Amelia just tried to set me up with this Spanish girl.'

'Right.'

'That's all you have to say? Man, it was bad. She's way out of my league.'

There's definitely something up. Sandi's never this quiet – he doesn't do sitting in corners on his own.

'Come on, spill, Sandi.'

'It's no biggy. Dad's thinking of buying another shop – a bigger one. We might have to move,' he says with quiet resignation.

'Move where? You won't go far. Will you?'

He shrugs. 'Not sure yet. Maybe closer into the centre of town. Or further out somewhere.'

'Why?'

'It's part of his dream. You know my dad: "From a small corner shop, to a bigger corner shop, to a supermarket – with no corners! Not bad for someone who came here with all his possessions in one plastic bag. Lucky the bags were free then!"'

I remembered the first corner shop. It was on an ex-council estate, a few miles from where we live now. Sandi was ecstatic when they finally moved. 'You try running the gauntlet on a daily basis. It ain't no fun,' he'd said at the time, trying to make light of how tough it was living there.

'Suppose there's only a couple of years left at home before uni, anyhow, but it's been good here. I don't want to start again somewhere else. And what if the area turns out to be like the first place we lived?'

'Yeah, but your dad won't want that either, Sand.'

'I know he won't, but you don't know what it'll be like until you live there.'

'Then we'll make sure to scope out the locations your dad is considering before he sells up. It might not happen,' I say eventually. 'We'll worry about it when it does. How much have you had?' I ask, pointing at the bottle of beer in his hand.

He holds it up to the light. It's barely been touched. 'Can't seem to get into the party mood. Here, have it if you want.'

'No, I'm all right.' None of us are big drinkers, but I guess we're all knackered tonight. 'Shall we get out of here?'

'Yeah. Oh, forgot to tell you, Sukh said that there was another teacher, Mr Roberts, sitting at the back of the class during his lesson with Greaves.'

'What?'

Sandi sighs and begins to repeat what he's just told me. 'Sukh said that there—'

'I heard you the first time!' I mull over what that might mean. 'They're watching her.'

'Why?'

'Because of that note I sent. It's got to mean that Rawson's looking into it!'

'Sukh said Mr Roberts only stayed for about ten minutes, though. Greaves was extra nice to everyone while he was there, but she turned the temperature right back down to frost setting as soon as he left. He didn't ask to see anyone's work, or their grades.'

I mull it over some more. 'Looks as though it might just be to let her know to watch her step.'

'Or just so they can later *say* that they've looked into it and there's no basis to the allegations in the note, which they didn't have to look into anyway as it was written on a scrappy piece of yellow notepaper and it wasn't even signed.'

'Whoa! Have you morphed into Dread?' I ask him.

And then I make the decision to tell him the whole story. Sandi thumps my arm hard and yells, '*I knew it!* I just knew it! Why didn't you tell me before?'

'I didn't want to put you on the spot. You know what you're like.'

'What am I like?' Sandi asks indignantly.

'You know,' I say.

'No, I don't know.'

'It might have put you in an awkward position. My bad, Sands. I thought it was better just to tell you that I'd made it all up.'

Sandi looks upset for a minute, but the thing about Sandi is that he's never pissed off for long.

'You couldn't have made up that kind of freaky shit! Who'd have guessed? Greaves and Green.' He whistles.

'I can't use any of it, though – well, not unless it gets edited. Some of it doesn't need to see the light of day, you know what I mean!'

And that led to Sandi's light-bulb moment. 'Hey,

you know that student who lives above Dad's shop? No, you don't, but his name's Davy, and you'll never guess what he's doing at uni.'

'English?'

'No, stupid! Guess again.'

'I dunno – what do I care? Media studies?'

'Nope.'

'Sandi,' I growl, 'the suspense isn't exactly killing me. Just tell me already, will you?'

'OK, OK. He's doing film and photography.'

'So?'

'And he's also a bit of a computer techie . . .'

I crack a smile. 'Cool!'

Pretty soon there'll be three copies of the video in existence.

CHAPTER 10

It is the Day of Reckoning. In other words, results day.

Is anyone looking forward to it? The answer can only be no. Most lessons start with a long lecture from the teacher. Some start with solemn warnings. Others with a silence so deep and deadly we instinctively know that some of us have underachieved so spectacularly that it's impossible to put our dire performance into words, or at least the kind of words that are appropriate for the classroom.

Physics starts like that.

I'm shrinking further and further into my seat as each minute passes.

Mrs Saunders is unique in that she has never ever had to raise her voice even a micro-fraction of a decibel to command our attention. She's a good head taller than Dread, which means she's practically a giant, and she's approaching fifty. We know this because she's told us, and we also know she has more muscle mass in her biceps than the PE teacher has in his entire body. She keeps her dark hair very short. We've taken bets on whether it's the banned grade one or the skirting-danger grade two on the barber's clippers. We are all convinced that she was a deadly SAS operative in her previous life.

No one *dares* to breathe, and coming after a week of not breathing, there are a few sickly-blue faces in the room.

'Alexander,' she calls.

Alex looks stricken that his name has been called first, despite the fact that after at least eleven years at school it is not an uncommon occurrence as he's first in the register. He makes no move.

Mrs Saunders removes her glasses and rubs the bridge of her nose before picking up the exam paper and holding it out. 'Come and take your paper, please.'

Alex moves so fast he knocks his chair over, but doesn't bother to pick it up in his haste to take the paper out of her hand.

'Anthony,' Mrs Saunders calls out.

One by one, we go to the front and collect our papers. Circled at the top of each paper in bright red ink is our mark. Mine's an A, close to border-lining a B, but no need to tell the parents that bit. Dad will be happy with the A, but Mum will say, 'So a bit of work to do there to raise it up.' We spend the rest of the lesson going through the paper. The majority of the class get Bs and Cs, but Alex was right to be stricken

– he got a U, which will lose him a few lunchtimes in revision sessions with Mrs Saunders. Poor sod.

Then it's Chemistry followed by PE. Double Maths is after break. Then two lessons after lunch. No English today, so a reprieve there. I end the day with As. Not a single A star among them, but a couple were close. So far, the parents will be reasonably happy.

I know I said that my parents were super-pushy Indian Parents. But maybe if I hadn't always been an A grade kind of guy, then they might have been satisfied with results that reflected my ability – even if they were only Bs or Cs. So I guess I've made a cross for myself and I'll have to carry on staggering around under the weight of it. But that's OK, because now I kind of demand it of myself too, if you know what I mean.

It's all about expectations, and one of my expectations is never to be forced to be a slave to anyone. My grandma cleaned offices at night when she first arrived in the UK, because she and Granddad were saving like mad to buy their own house. Granddad, who was brilliant at his job but for a long time never got a pay rise, and was never quite the right shade to join the management team, eventually got recognized for the genius he was and got promoted. So my grandparents got their house, and Grandma finally got to give up her cleaning job.

That's how I see education – as a means to an end.

That's also how I see the video that's embedded deep inside my laptop – as a means to an end.

'Davy said he's almost done if you want to have a look,' Sandi says at lunchtime the next day.

Davy the techie has been working on cutting the video up into bite-sized chunks. Don't panic – I'm not planning a general release; there will be no red carpet premiere with A-list stars in sequins, paparazzi and flash photography.

There might be a few red faces though. That's if I don't chicken out and drop it back down into the black hole it's been festering in. Who am I kidding? I know damn well that's where it's going when I get it back from Davy. There's no way I'm going to post it anywhere. Even using it to blackmail Mrs Greaves makes me feel physically ill. Why? Because of that nagging feeling that there might be the outside chance, the faintest possibility, that I could be wrong about her.

Did I just say that?

Cold feet, that's what I've got.

I'm all talk and no action, a fence-sitter who means well, fully in possession of the highest principles, someone who knows right from wrong and how things should be. Somebody's got to put this right. But does that somebody have to be me?

Toby would pay me good money to rap those lines.

And then we have English Lit.

The English Lit mock paper was like a stroll down the beach on a summer's day: the sky an intense blue, the sea a calm turquoise perfection softly rolling on to warm golden sands. Pure magic, in other words, because all my favourite questions had come up and I knew that I'd nailed them bang on the head. So I'm feeling pretty good when I take my seat in class. This time, there can be no doubt, no ambiguity.

Greaves has marked all the papers, she says, and she is going to read out our grades. There are a few muffled groans. No one likes their marks being read out loud to the class because it's a public shaming and it stinks. Most of our other teachers are tactful, allowing us to decide if we want to tell other people how well or badly we did.

But not Mrs Greaves – ritual humiliation is an art form that she's perfected.

Judging from the marks I've heard so far, she's been a bit harsh, like a few of our other teachers. We may be able to claw back a few marks when we go through our papers with her; well, some of us might be able to. I'm not one of the Favoured Ones, so I'm not holding out any hope there. She carries on reading out our marks, making snide little remarks on practically every other paper, while the class shrink further and further into their seats.

By the end of it, I've adopted Alex's stricken expression when he found out he'd got a U in Physics, but I've discovered whole new unexplored depths with it. I've heard my result, and I ain't happy, not one bit. I'm shell-shocked to be honest.

'I'll call you over one by one during the lessons this week,' Greaves tells us, 'so I can go through them in detail with you individually. There's still a lot of the curriculum to get through so no need to waste everyone's time.'

I barely hear what she's saying. Everyone's opening their books and writing things down and I'm sat here doing nothing, numbed.

Tom's nudging me. I look blankly at him.

Maybe I misheard her. Maybe she called a C for the person before me or the person after me, or for both of them. But I know I didn't mishear her; it's the reason I'm feeling so numb.

It takes an age for the feeling to come back. Greaves has been talking for a while and I haven't heard a word she's said. She's written a few words on the blackboard.

COLLECTIVE RESPONSIBILITY
VERSUS
PERSONAL RESPONSIBILITY

CHRISTIAN DUTY

Tom's opened my copy of *An Inspector Calls* to the right scene for me. Looks like we have to write notes on it. My blank page stays blank. The feeling is coming back to me, but it's not the kind of feeling conducive to writing or thinking about what J.B. Priestley thought of the world he lived in.

'What did you get?' I ask Tom, when I've managed to make my mouth work.

From the way he looks so guilty, I've already guessed.

'A star,' he confirms quietly.

'That's great, really great, Tom.' And I really am happy for the guy.

'I don't understand your grade,' Tom says. So I *did* get a big fat C. 'What happened? Did you miss a question out?' he asks.

He's trying to work out what could have gone wrong for me. He's seen my essays – we don't mind other people looking at our work if it helps them, especially with revision, because we all know that we're not competing against each other but against the system. Some of us are good at working the system, some of us aren't. So anyone who wants to look at my work gets a look. Tom knows my essays are worth a look. Everyone does.

'Must be something wrong with the way your paper got marked,' Tom says.

Ain't that the truth!

But hang on. Did *I* do something wrong in the paper? Did I misread a question? Did I miss a question out completely? Am I sure it wasn't me?

Sandi made a point of pointing out that it was possible *I* had messed up the controlled assessment, but I didn't want to hear it.

What if he's right?

What if Greaves is right about me not being a shit-hot A-star candidate?

She's called Tom up. I watch as she pats the seat beside her and smiles at him. She really likes Tom, so she marks him too generously. He wants to do English Lit for A level too, so I've made sure he doesn't get a shock in the real exams in the summer by going through essay questions with him. He knows what he has to work on now. But hang on – again – what if it's *me* who's been wrong all this time? I've had a few tutorials with Mum and Dad's friend and he thinks I'm good, but then he doesn't teach Lit in a school. I'm doubting myself all of a sudden and it's not a great feeling.

Tom's come back with his paper and he hands it to me straight away. He's always been a bit of a mind reader.

'I've got to hand it back in at the end of the lesson,' he says.

I flick through it quickly, scanning the questions, remembering them and recalling my answers, and knowing, just knowing, that no way did I miss a question big enough to bring me down to that C.

As the lesson progresses and we're called up one by one, the numbness wears off, leaving something more dangerous in its place: a simmering anger that's got a life of its own. Pretty soon it's bubbling and churning and then it's morphing into a rage that's redder than any red

I've ever seen, and that scares me, because I don't know what to do with it.

I'm ready to face her down on this.

But then the lesson comes to an end without Greaves calling me for a one-to-one.

'The rest of you will have to wait until the next lesson,' she says, slamming her folder shut.

And now I don't know what to do with all that anger. I'm having real trouble understanding what could have gone wrong. I feel like a pressure cooker that someone's forgotten to turn the gas down under. Red-hot heat is channelling out of the top of my head. I've seen Maji with her pressure cooker, seen her wait for it to whistle and turn it down, seen her release the pressure slowly by letting the cold tap run over the edge of it to bring the temperature down slowly.

I need someone to pour cold water on me.

I need to keep my mouth shut and make it out of the classroom without blowing up. Because I know for a fact that if I blow, it'll be a matter of seconds before I'm sent out of the classroom and back before the Headmaster.

I need to cool down, lose the emotions, and approach things logically and rationally. And I need to talk to Dread and Sandi.

CHAPTER 11

I'm on autopilot as we leave the classroom. I don't even look her way, until she speaks to me.

'Disappointing result, Jeevan,' she says. I almost choke. 'But not entirely unexpected,' she adds, smirking. 'Justin, we'll go through your paper tomorrow, but you did very well. It bodes well for the exams in the summer.'

Now I'm seriously choking, but Tom's got my back and he shoves me out of the door before I erupt. I glare at him once we're outside her door. He puts his hands up in a gesture of surrender. 'That was for your own good,' he says quickly. 'You don't need another detention.'

I'm still so pumped up with rage I can almost feel my skin turning a Hulk-like shade of green, with my muscles ready to pop out of my skin and shred my nasty navy blue uniform to bits.

Luckily, I'm not a violent kind of guy. I've never even knowingly harmed a spider, and of course I'm not thinking of causing Greaves actual bodily harm. I just want to say my piece.

'Can't let it go, Tom. Gotta say something. You heard her – 'disappointing' and 'not entirely unexpected' – I mean, WTF!'

'Leave it, Jeev. Take a look at your paper first. Maybe you really did eff it up, had a blind spot, misread the question big time, I don't know. I mean, no one's perfect.'

He's made a little pinprick in my bubble of self-righteous hot air, and the logical, rational part of my brain knows that he is right. There *is* an outside chance that I had a major brain fail and missed a question. I vent some of the pressure that's built up inside me as we walk back to our lockers, and Tom pours cold water on the rest.

'I flunked my Physics. I told my dad I was rubbish at it. But would he listen? Combined Science I could have handled, but not all three separate sciences,' Tom says. 'It won't stop Mum and Dad being narked with me when they find out my result.'

Tom's been struggling with Physics, and because of that he has to start revising practically before we've even covered each new topic in class, because it takes him much longer to learn the stuff. No way could he rely on last-minute cramming like me, and he doesn't have a photographic memory like Dread. Sandi starts revising early too, but that's partly because he's a class-A swot. Mostly it's because revision gets him out of having to help in his dad's shop.

'We'll do some revision sessions together if you like,' I offer. 'I'm not brilliant at Physics – Dread and Sandi are the guys you need.'

'Can they work miracles?'

'Hope so – for your sake!'

We laugh and the last bit of the pressure in my head is released.

By the next day, it's back to being fully pressurized when I'm called up by Greaves. I take a deep breath because I know I'm going to need it.

'Keep cool,' Tom hisses at me as I get out of my seat.

'Paper 1 wasn't too bad. It's a middle B, so plenty of room for improvement as you'll see from all my comments,' she says after allowing me to glance through it briefly.

Middle B? That means I must have flunked Paper 2 to drag my overall grade down to a C!

Paper 1 is covered in an ominous scrawl of red scribbles. Others would cower in fear at the sheer quantity of them, but not me. I'm used to her ways. The point is, and always has been, that none of her comments are particularly relevant or significant. Even at a glance, I know I've covered each question fully. The red marks are placed at regular intervals throughout my paper to justify her low opinion of me, and consequently the low grade. I know I'm going to have to show the paper to Dad's friend for a second opinion.

We go through it question by question. I point out where she should have given me full marks, and she responds by pointing out that in her opinion it wasn't answered fully enough, or that I had wandered off the main point, or that my answer was too waffly, not succinct enough.

'But that's just saying the same thing in three different ways,' I tell her. 'If you read my answers properly you'll see that I've answered them all completely and succinctly and without repetition.'

'Do you *want* my help, Jeevan? Because I have to say that I don't care for your attitude,' she responds icily.

And so it goes on until I can practically feel the blood pouring down my face from banging my head against the brick wall so damn hard. We're through with Paper 1 quickly because there is virtually nothing she can add to what I have already said on the paper. She takes the paper and sticks it back in the file.

'I'd like to take the paper home, please, Mrs Greaves.'

'I'm afraid that's not possible. Off you go back to your seat. Justin?' she calls. 'You're next.'

I don't move. 'Why?'

'Why what?'

'Why can't I take the paper home?'

'Because we'll be going through them all in class later this week,' she snaps.

I see Tom glance worriedly in our direction. Sorry, Tom, this time I'm not backing down. 'I don't see the problem, miss. I'll bring it back tomorrow.'

Her lips are drawn in a thin hard line. 'No. It stays in my file. Now take your seat.'

'But we haven't finished. We haven't gone through Paper 2 yet.' The second paper is the one that's brought my grade down to a C. It's the one I must have got a D on. A *D*! I'm desperate to see it, to try and make some sense out of it. To know with absolute one hundred per cent certainty if it was my fault – or hers.

'We'll go through it next time. You got a D so there's a lot to go through, and I'm running out of time today.'

'Everyone else has got to see both their papers. I really need to see Paper 2, see where exactly I went wrong, miss. It's important to me.'

'Now you think it's important? Surely you should have considered how important it was when you were revising, or was it all last-minute revision? Well, you'll just have to wait.'

My heart is drumming hard now. Something's going on. She doesn't want me to see the paper – and I know the reason why.

'Everyone's seen both their papers,' I repeat. 'So I'd like to see mine.' And I cross my arms and wait.

'Fine. You'll see it tomorrow. It seems to have gone missing. I'm sure it will turn up.'

I knew it!

'Have you *lost* my paper?' I'm speaking too loud. The whole class is listening. They all know me. They know

I'm pretty chilled, that it takes a lot for me to react. Tom's shaking his head at me, but I can't put the brake on. 'You've lost it on *purpose*,' I say. 'So no one can see how you marked me down unfairly – again!'

'Don't be so ridiculous! I said I mislaid it. And as for the grade I've given you – it is an entirely fair reflection of your lack of preparation for the exam!'

Lack of preparation? She has no idea how much work I've been putting in over the year.

'I'm sorry if I've put a dent in your rather over-inflated opinion of yourself, Jeevan, but there it is. I did warn you. Now, get back to your desk!'

I'm so angry, I don't know what to do.

I stand up too fast, too abruptly, and accidentally send my chair flying over. One of its legs snaps off. Damn! Now I'll get accused of destroying school property to add to my long list of alleged crimes. It's hardly my fault they haven't replaced the rickety old chairs in this classroom. I pick up the wooden chair leg and hold it aimlessly, wondering what to do with the stupid thing.

Greaves has jumped to her feet and is backing away from me.

'Put it down, Jeevan, and go and sit down right this minute . . .'

'What, or you'll send me to the Headmaster? Fine by me. Let's go.' I drop the chair leg on the floor. Rawson will side with me, I'm sure of it. He'll still have the anonymous note in the back of his mind, not to mention that Greaves has definitely marked me down – and contrived to *lose* my paper.

'You know the way,' she says, her voice so tight I'm amazed she's managed to squeeze the words out at all.

I'm not going to let her wriggle out of this one. I want to see her squirm. I want to see her head on a platter. 'You're going to have to take me.'

'You're going to regret this,' she says through clenched teeth. 'Get on with your work – in silence!' she shouts at the rest of the class. She stalks out of the classroom, down the corridor, to the Headmaster's office, her heels going clickety-clack on the wooden floor, leaving indentations like she wished it was my face beneath her shoes.

All of a sudden, this Walk of Shame has become part of my weekly school routine. It's shocking because I barely even knew where the Headmaster's office was before a few weeks ago. Rawson is *not* going to be happy. The last time I saw him, he told me not to make this a habit. I'm even thinking that maybe I should have signed the anonymous note, or just sent it directly to Ofsted where it might have had more chance of being logged and properly investigated. After what Sandi told me at the party, I'm pretty sure the whole thing has been swept under the carpet.

The closer we get to his office, the edgier I get. Rawson is either going to bawl me out of the room, put me on report and ring my parents, or he's going to listen to my side of the story. I'm relying on the latter. He's a reasonable man – and he's had the heads-up from the anonymous note. He's got to side with me, hasn't he?

'Not necessarily' is the answer to that question.

He sees Greaves on her own first to get the lowdown before calling me in. Judging by his glowering expression, he's clearly not a happy man, and he doesn't ask me to sit. I'm wondering if I should have brought in witnesses.

'Belligerency,' he begins, 'and a threatening demeanour are not acceptable modes of behaviour in this school. But to physically threaten a teacher? You've gone way too far, Jeevan.'

What? Physically threatening? What's he talking about? 'Sir?' I say, genuinely puzzled.

'Throwing chairs around. Talking back, disrupting the class, non-cooperative behaviour, and then to use a chair leg to threaten your teacher – that is what I am talking about!' he thunders.

Mrs Greaves is standing quietly at his side, her expression neutral. Jesus Christ, I never imagined she would take it this far. There's no way out of this. I am well and truly effed.

'Mr Rawson, that's not what happened. I knocked the chair over accidentally and the leg snapped off. I picked it up and I was just holding it. I wasn't threatening anyone. I promise. I was upset about—'

'Yes, he was absolutely beside himself about his

exam result. But to go as far as brandishing a chair leg and shouting at me? I think the stress has been too much for him. I'll leave you to deal with him now, Mr Rawson. I should get back – the rest of the class are waiting for me.'

He nods. 'Yes, of course, Mrs Greaves.'

'I suppose you'll have no choice but to call his parents regarding the suspension, Mr Rawson,' she adds.

'Wait! Please! I haven't done any of those things. I knocked the chair down accidentally, and I wasn't—'

'It was no accident, Jeevan,' Greaves says, her voice so cold she could freeze hell over. 'We both know that, don't we?'

'But it was! Ask—'

'Jeevan! That's enough,' Rawson says. 'I will *not* tolerate any shouting.'

Shit! Shit! Shit! 'Sorry, sir,' I say, and take a deep breath. I've got to keep cool. 'Everyone in the class was watching – they all saw what happened and why I was upset.'

'A low grade – no matter how unexpected – is not an excuse for you or for anyone to behave in such a manner. Or do you think it is?'

Greaves butts in before I can open my mouth. She was supposed to be leaving a few minutes ago, but I knew she wouldn't be able to resist staying to watch me squirm.

'I tried to help him, I really did,' Greaves is saying, her

voice oh so reasonable and understanding. 'But instead of listening to me he threw the most shocking tantrum. It was – it was just so intimidating, so frightening. I'm so sorry.'

'No, no, wait! That's not what happened,' I say again, but Rawson isn't listening to me.

'As we both know, Mr Rawson, Jeevan does seem to have a problem with female teachers.'

What? 'Wait, that's not—' I begin.

'Did I ask you to speak, Jeevan? Then shut up,' Rawson says curtly.

I stare at them open-mouthed while Greaves carries out her softly spoken but deadly character assassination. I'm not allowed to respond. I've been told to shut up by Rawson, that I had my chance and now it's Mrs Greaves's turn to say her piece.

Her piece is an indictment. And her indictment of me is so thorough that she is barely out of the door when Rawson picks up the phone and calls my parents.

I'm in a state of shock as I'm sentenced.

I'll be on report following a two-day suspension. Each day I will report to Rawson himself, in the morning and the afternoon. Each week my teachers will be asked for a report of my behaviour and general demeanour in class.

She has screwed me big time.

CHAPTER 12

'Did we not teach you anything, Jeevan?' Mum asks. Her disappointment in me is all too evident.

We're sitting at the dining table because this conversation is *that* serious. Maji has gone out for a walk, which is a relief because I know she would never understand why I did what I did, which wasn't anything really, but she'd certainly think it was. As far as Maji's concerned, teachers are *always* right – it's that black or white for her. She doesn't see the grey areas in between.

'Make the system work for you. You are at school for one thing – to learn, and to achieve your potential.' I almost point out to Mum that that makes two things, but sometimes even *I* know when to keep my mouth shut. 'Your father and I have both had teachers like Mrs Greaves when we were at school. We have all had to deal with such people, so as much as you may believe it, you are not unique, Jeevan.'

'Your mum is right,' Dad chips in. 'The sooner

you learn how to deal with them, the better. Now this particular teacher won't tolerate any talking back. So what did you do? You shouted back at her.'

'She's had it in for me since last year,' I remind them.

'And you managed to get through the whole of that year without any of this nonsense happening,' Dad says.

'Until last month,' says Mum.

Then it's Dad's turn. They're tag-teaming me WWE-style, pinning me to the ropes. 'Twice she sent you to the Headmaster, and on each occasion you could have backed down and denied her the satisfaction.'

'But you didn't. You played right into her hands,' says Mum, 'and did you learn your lesson?' I shake my head because the answer's obvious and it'll only be worse for me if I open my mouth at this stage. 'So what did you go and do – for the third time? Where is your sense? You are not a child, Jeevan.'

'Technically I still am, Mum,' I mumble. Sometimes I just don't know when to keep my mouth shut.

Water would instantly turn to ice with the frosty glare she's giving me. 'That is why we are grounding you for a month.'

A month! 'Mum, that's so unfair!'

'Yes, maybe it is, but it will help you to remember to think about the consequences of what comes out of your mouth *before* you speak – not afterwards, when it's too late.'

I turn to Dad, hoping for some clemency. 'Please,

Dad, a month is harsh considering I'm being punished for something that wasn't my fault,' I plead. 'You know what Greaves is like. You know my English Lit paper got *lost* for a reason. I had to stand up to her. And then she told this whole pack of lies to Rawson. No way was I threatening her with a chair leg!'

'This, we will talk to the Headmaster about,' Dad says. 'We'll ask him to talk to the other pupils who were there.'

'There are other ways of standing up for yourself, Jeevan. You chose the wrong way. And, no, we do not know for sure that the paper got lost for a reason as you seem to believe. It is possible she was telling the truth about mislaying it.'

'She's marking me down because I'm not white! She's racist!'

'Jeevan! That's enough! You can't go around accusing people of being racist just because you're in conflict with them. It's a serious thing!' Dad says.

'Not without some kind of proof,' Mum adds.

'The rest of my class know what she's like. They know why she marks me down,' I say.

'What the rest of the class believes is hardly proof of anything, Jeevan,' Dad says. 'You clash with her – that much is obvious to everyone.'

'I'm sorry, but you'll have to apologize to her, grovel if needs be, but you must make amends. Another couple of months – that's all you need to get through.'

Mum's words have an ominous ring of finality to them. The thing is, I know she's right. I was an idiot. I let my anger and frustration get in the way. But considering the circumstances . . .

There's only one thing for it – I have to do my best grovelling act. It's my only chance to get some leniency. 'I know, and I'm sorry. Really sorry. You don't know what she's like. I'll try harder, OK? I really will. I'll find a way to get through to her.' The grovelling seems to be working because my parents' expressions have softened – a bit, and they don't look quite so disappointed in me. And I *will* find a way through to her – just maybe not the way my parents are expecting. 'I promise.'

'Sonia, perhaps we're being a little heavy-handed,' Dad says in my defence. 'I think two weeks is more than enough, no?'

Mum shrugs in agreement before giving me another look, you know the look – somehow it conveys a thousand messages, namely: *if you dare do anything like that again your life will not be worth living; you think being grounded for a month is harsh? Then try six months, try a year! Or how about the rest of your life?*

You get the gist.

Yes, I may be grounded, but at least I'm allowed the occasional visitor. We're in my room, brainstorming, just me and Dread. When I rang Sandi to come over, he said he had to help out in the shop – in that mournful tone of voice he always uses when he has to work in the shop, as though he's unreasonably put-upon when he has far more important stuff to be doing. Personally I don't understand why he thinks it's so bad. His dad is a real joker, a laugh-a-minute guy, and I know all the locals go in just for a bit of banter with him. His dad winked at me and said, 'It's good for business' when I pointed it out to him.

'Listen, why don't you guys come to me?' Sandi asked. I could hear the hope in his voice. It would have got him out of having to work in the shop if his parents thought he had to do homework with us.

'I'm grounded,' I told him.

'Count yourself lucky it wasn't worse than that,' Sandi says. 'I would have been six feet under by now, without a phone, no *FIFA* until the summer holidays, no pocket money. Nothing!'

He's not joking. His dad might be a joker, but he takes anything to do with school very seriously, which is why Sandi runs at the first sign of trouble. Lucky for him none of his teachers are anything like Greaves.

But unlike Rawson's bulldozing tactics, every time I tried to open my mouth to explain what happened, my parents heard me out, even if it was in unnerving silence and with their arms folded and a set of firmly fixed frowns. But still, at least they heard me out. And they believe me, well, of course they would because I'm their son, but let me just add that if they thought for

108

one second that I was guilty as charged, they would have marched me up to the school and forced me to apologize to Greaves in the most humiliatingly soul-destroying way.

'So what did Rawson say then?' Dread asks.

'Greaves knows how to work Rawson,' I tell Dread. 'He went on and on about how disappointed he was in me, how he had thought of me as an excellent student, a good example, how I was on his shortlist for senior prefect next year, and how I had been head boy material, blah, blah, blah. The usual crap, you know, making me feel bad for letting him down. What he doesn't get is how he's let *me* down. I count too. Just because I'm not an adult doesn't make me any less in the right. No one listens to us. It's like all adults think they're right about everything. Bloody telling *us* to listen, when they've forgotten how to do it themselves. And he's definitely thrown that note I sent straight in the bin. I should have sent it to the local paper or something. I bet you they would have come sniffing round – anything for some local scandal, and then the national papers might have picked it up.'

'Jeevan!'

'What?'

'Take a breath, man,' he orders me. 'It ain't that bad. You never wanted to be head boy anyhow, and who wants to be senior prefect? You get all the bum jobs. The anonymous note wasn't the worst idea, and we can still do something with that. Tell me what's happening about your missing exam paper.' Dread does air quotes round the word 'missing'.

'OK, so Mum and Dad are going to write a letter *and* go and see Rawson.' My parents may have grounded me, but they have the bit between their teeth and they're not going to let it go. Unlike me though, they're going to be cool, calm and rational when they bring the full weight of their might down upon the school. OK, a slight exaggeration. The only situation where they'd do that is if I was expelled, and I'm not expelled, just suspended. No, what Mum and Dad will do is make Rawson feel a bit of heat for not looking into my missing paper. She will be held accountable, Dad said.

'And if Paper 2 is never found, my parents are going to ask for me to resit it – it'll have to be a different paper though – and get Mr Holly or one of the others to mark it.'

'Bummer.'

'Yeah,' I say glumly. 'Don't see why I should resit it. *She* lost it and I know it was on purpose so I couldn't challenge her about the grade she gave me. And she wouldn't let me keep my other paper, so that's probably gone *missing* by now.'

'You've got the means to sort this out, you know, Jeev.'

I think about the ticking time bomb, and it makes me shudder. 'Yeah, I do,' I say slowly. 'Would you do it?'

Dread chews his lip, pondering. In the end, he shrugs. 'Yes. No. Just don't know.'

'You're a big help.'

'We need a think tank,' Dread says. 'Just an idea, but how about we ask Amelia and Ree to meet up at the weekend? Between us, we'd work something out.'

'What? No way. I barely know them.'

Someone knocks on my bedroom door and says, 'Jeevan?'

Dread and I look at each other.

'Sounds like Tom,' I say getting up to answer the door. It is Tom. 'Hey.'

'I should have texted to say I was coming,' he says apologetically.

'S'OK. Come in. Dread's doing a post-mortem.'

Tom looks worried. 'A what? Who's died?'

I laugh. If that was Sandi, he'd know exactly what I was talking about. 'No one yet,' I answer, deadpan. 'But it's only a matter of time.'

'Just don't use a chair leg!' Tom says, pretending to cower away from me.

'Ha-bloody-ha!'

'All right,' Dread says, nodding at Tom.

'Hi, Jonathan,' Tom says. I always forget he doesn't know Dread that well. 'Sorry about what happened to you, Jeev. It sucks.'

'Tell me about it! If I'd listened to you I wouldn't be stuck in this heap of steaming dung. I'm going to need witnesses, Tom, cos no surprise whose side Rawson took!'

'No worries. The whole class is going to back you up.'

'Seriously?' That should put me in the clear.

'We all pissed ourselves laughing after she marched you out. I mean, we all knew you weren't threatening her. And when the chair broke and you picked up the chair leg and didn't know what to do with it, the expression on your face was priceless!'

'The story's so much better when Tom tells it, Jeev,' Dread says, laughing.

I glare at the pair of them.

'Yeah, sorry. None of us thought she'd stitch you up like that. OK, look, I've, um, I've got something you might be interested in,' Tom says.

He opens his school bag and takes out a paper, holding it gingerly between two fingers like it might bite him. 'Thought you might want it.'

It turns out that when someone's offering you gold dust, they don't need to worry about their sales technique. Tom's got me gold dust – no, better than gold dust; it's a bar of pure solid twenty-four-carat gold!

He's only gone and pilfered the paper that Greaves refused to let me bring home out of her file and just handed it to me. 'You never!'

'I did,' he says proudly. 'As soon as she left the classroom with you, I went and had a look in her folder.

Thought things might go down badly for you. No one saw me – they were all too busy taking bets on how long you'd get suspended for.'

I'm not really hearing him now because I've just looked properly at what's in my hands.

Forget the gold dust or the twenty-four-carat gold bar. Forget the one ring that will rule them all, forget the Arkenstone held by Smaug, sought by Thorin, yeah, I'm a total mega-Tolkien fan, and no, that doesn't make me a saddo or a nerd.

This is not like any other precious stone.

Tom's handed me the biggest diamond in the shop. It's not the paper I went through with Greaves in class.

IT'S THE MISSING PAPER 2.

The one Greaves said she had *mislaid*.

It's been sitting in her folder all along.

CHAPTER 13

I could hug Tom. I don't because it would embarrass him too much and he looks embarrassed enough already, so I just say, 'You're a bloody star, Tom!'

And then I can't help myself and hug him anyway, which makes him go red, and then I hug Dread because I'm getting carried away, and then I hug them both again because if you can't hug someone when you're this happy, when can you hug them?

I am unbelievably ecstatic. No, that word's too tame. Overjoyed? Nah. Enraptured? Not quite. Euphoric? Yeah, that pretty much covers it! I'm unbelievably euphoric!

They're grinning at me and shaking their heads like I've totally lost the plot, and I have, because one minute my life felt like it couldn't get any worse, and then the next it can't get any better. Well, it could, but you know what I mean. Man, I love diamonds!

Until Dread pisses on my parade.

He's taken the missing paper from me and is flicking

through it. 'Good answers, Jeev,' he starts. That's high praise coming from him. 'But there's just one thing – she didn't bother marking it.'

'What do you mean? She said I'd got a D for this paper and a mid B for Paper 1 – the one I went through in class with her. It brings my overall grade down to that sucky C.'

'For a D, you'd expect her to have put few red marks on the paper, Jeev.'

'So she didn't bother marking it because she was always going to lose it,' I say. '"Why waste time?" she thought. She probably meant to take it out of the folder and leave it at home. My bloody good luck she didn't – otherwise Tom couldn't have lifted it!'

'You do know what that means?' Dread says.

I'm not liking his tone and I'm wracking my brain trying to work out where he's going with it. I come up blank. 'What does that mean?'

'Think about it, Jeev.'

'I don't want to think about it!'

'Um, I think Dread's trying to say that because she hasn't marked it then, you know, she could say . . .'

The penny drops, except it's not a penny but a great big boulder dropping from several thousand feet directly on to my head, cartoon-style – and I'm definitely not the Road Runner but Wile E. Coyote, who, as we all know, is not so wily.

'No, no, no,' I say. 'No way!'

'Yes way,' Dread responds.

I slump on the bed, deflated to the point that I feel thinner than a 3D stickman who had his last supper a month ago.

'But all is not lost,' Dread says, mulling over the problem. He tugs at his short light-brown mini-dreads, which no amount of tugging is going to help turn into real dreadlocks but it's turned into a habit. When he hits sixth form he's going to colour his hair jet black and grow his locks as long as he can get away with. Thing about Dread is that if anyone could pull it off he could. His mum might want to kill him initially, and she'll literally chew his ears off, but he's on for eleven A stars at GCSE and that counts for a lot. At A level, he'll be predicted four A stars, possibly even five if he decides to push himself a little.

For guys like me, that would mean signing away every single second of every minute of every hour in a twenty-four-hour day, three hundred and sixty-five days a year. Except this year it's 2016, so that's three hundred and sixty-six days for the leap year, But even then, we wouldn't get anywhere near Dread's illustrious heights, and definitely not with the same aplomb.

So what I'm trying to say, in my typical roundabout way, is that I've worked for this; I've worked damn hard. I'm not going to hide this diamond away where no one can see it. Diamonds are meant to shine and sparkle in the light, not get stuffed away in a dark place. This diamond has to be seen, so it can get marked, so I can get what I deserve. It's only right. It's only fair.

Both Dread and Tom disagree, of course, and they don't hold back about telling me exactly why, tag-team-style, just like my mum and dad.

'She'll call you a cheat,' Dread says.

'She'll say you took the paper home at the end of the exam,' says Tom.

'Instead of handing it in like everyone else,' says Dread.

'So you could finish it at home properly,' Tom adds.

'And get an unfair advantage.'

'She'll say that's why she couldn't find it,' Tom says. 'She never mislaid it.'

'Because you had it all along.'

We sit there in silence, until Dread says, 'Unless you want to drop Tom in it.'

That last statement kind of hangs in the air. I hadn't considered that.

'You won't be dropping me in it. I can make something up – like say I was looking for my paper and saw Jeevan's. The whole class heard her say she'd mislaid it,' Tom says. 'She might be pissed off with me for looking in her folder, but Rawson won't care.'

'That could work,' I say, looking at Dread.

'Yeah. That would work.' He doesn't seem convinced, though. 'How are you going to play it then?'

'I'll have to tell Mum and Dad. Let them do the talking this time.'

Dread winces – no doubt imagining the scenario if it were his mum involved rather than mine. 'Not ideal, but knowing you and your big mouth and where it lands you, probably for the best.'

Tom heads off home, and once he's gone, Dread says, 'No need to worry yourself with the video now, right?'

'Yeah, for now,' I tell him.

Although Sandi did tell me that the video had been turned into bite-sized chunks. One little bite-size clip is all I need. I'll keep it in reserve as my backup plan if all else fails.

'So this is the paper that your teacher supposedly lost?' Dad asks for the tenth time.

'Yes, Dad.'

'And Tom found it in her folder and gave it to you?'

'Yes, Mum.'

'I'll ring the school in the morning and set up a meeting with Mr Rawson,' Dad says. 'I'll take a copy of the paper now, and ask Peter to have a look at it tonight if he can.'

Dad's on my wavelength, or I'm on his. I've already emailed Dad's friend Peter, the English lecturer, to mark it for me.

'Good,' Dad says when I tell him. 'I'll give him a call too. Let him know it's urgent.'

'She will claim that it got muddled up with other papers in her folder. An innocent honest mistake,' Mum says. 'And

118

the fact that she accused you of aggressive behaviour will still stand, Jeevan. The suspension will remain in place – even if the whole class stands up for you.'

'But the D she gave me won't because it's obvious she didn't even mark the paper,' I point out.

'True. I wonder if she even looked at it before giving you that D,' Mum says.

We all know the answer to that question.

Mum sighs wearily. 'I think we may have to ask to move you out of her class. There are other English teachers in the year.'

Yes!

'But will it go on my report, on my school record?'

'Even if we argue mitigating circumstances, it may do. We will see what we can do, Jeevan.'

'No, they can't do that, Dad! It's not right. It wasn't me!'

'But you dealt with it badly,' Dad points out.

'And the grounding stays in place, Jeevan. You still need to learn how to deal with people like her,' Mum adds.

I groan at the injustice of it all. That euphoria I felt only a few hours ago, severely dented by Dread, has now shrunk to the size of a pea. It looks like I might get a fair mark for my Lit exam if another teacher marks the paper, but I know the rest of the matter will be hushed up because, well, that's what happens. We all know it.

Rawson is away for the next two days, it turns out – the two days I'm suspended, which takes us to the weekend.

The secretary, Mrs Dere, tells my dad that we can see the Deputy Head that afternoon, but we won't be able to see Rawson until Monday morning. Dad makes an appointment for Monday at 9 a.m.

'Use the next couple of days to catch up on your homework, get ahead with your preparation for the GCSEs,' Dad tells me. 'Don't waste the time you have. And absolutely no *FIFA*.'

Yeah, I might be fifteen years old, but when my dad uses that tone, I feel like I'm about ten.

Now I know how it feels to be given a red card and get sent off the pitch for a legitimate tackle on a seasoned diver – it sucks. What Dad doesn't get is that the mocks have only just finished, so there's zero space left in my brain. I crammed it to full capacity. I need a break, but with the grounding still in place and the *FIFA* ban, the days are going to drag.

And if I so much as open my mouth and moan about how unfair it all is, the grounding will be straight back up to a month, and the special dispensation I've managed to wrangle to go out for Dread's birthday on Saturday night will be withdrawn so fast it'll leave me spinning.

CHAPTER 14

Thursday isn't so bad. Maji loves having someone at home during the day, but she's also cross with me for getting into trouble with a teacher *and* the Headmaster. Like I said, in her book, authority figures must be obeyed and teachers are never wrong. I try to explain the situation to her but she's not having any of it. 'Instead of answering back you should have controlled your temper and come home and told your father straight away.'

'Maji, you know I don't have a temper.'

'Only when you are very angry,' she says, 'which means that you *do* have a temper. No?'

She's tough to argue with, my gran.

But seriously, I don't get angry much. It takes an exceptional circumstance, which is what this was, a *very* exceptional circumstance.

Relief arrives on Friday after school when Sandi and Dread come over and give me the lowdown on what's been happening at school. Apart from me missing a ton of work that I'm going to have to catch up on, nothing much has happened. School has somehow managed to carry on without me. And Greaves is still being Greaves.

'So what's happening with Amelia?' I ask. I know Dread's seen her a few times since the party, but he's been keeping shtum about it. 'What's with all the secrecy?'

'*I* know what it means,' Sandi says, knowingly.

'You do? Just because a guy doesn't go on and on about a girl, it's supposed to mean something?'

'It does with you. It means you like this girl *a lot,*' Sandi says.

Dread doesn't do silence. He's got way too much to say and he rarely has a problem saying it. He's in the debating society and when they're up against another school, you can see them cowering when he takes the podium. He can rip any argument apart, any point of view. He knows practically every statistic on everything, which leaves most people, including teachers, reeling. As a challenge, he took the Leave stance in our school debate on the EU referendum that's coming up in June (we all know if he could vote he'd be voting to stay). He was the Brexit King and he won the debate hands down, demolishing his opponent's arguments. And then he wished he hadn't done it because if you're smart enough you can pretty much get anyone to come round to your point of view if you use the right arguments and you're prepared to twist the stats – and voting Leave wasn't the point of view he wanted to promote!

So silence is not his thing. Amelia has definitely got under his skin.

'Come on, spill, Dread. I saw you heading up to the girls' school after school yesterday,' Sandi says.

'We're just hanging out,' Dread says. 'No biggie.'

Sandi and I exchange grins, because we both know that when Dread says something is no biggie it's guaranteed to be *very* big.

'So, is she coming out with us on Saturday?' I ask.

Dread shrugs nonchalantly, as only Dread can. 'Maybe.'

'Maybe?' Sandi and I repeat, grinning.

'Yeah, all right, she's gonna join us later. Happy now? But don't go all soppy and stupid about it, OK? Otherwise I'll tell her not to bother coming because I've got two sniggering juveniles as my best mates.'

'Would we embarrass you like that?' I ask him innocently.

'Let me think,' Dread says, pretending to think about it for about two seconds. 'Just remember this – payback can be a bitch. One day, and knowing you two it definitely isn't going to be any time soon – you may grow up a bit and manage to pluck up the guts to ask someone out, and I'll be there, waiting. Just remember that.'

'Ooh! I'm scared now!' Sandi laughs.

Judging from the expression on Dread's face, namely the scowling and glowering, he really is serious about

Amelia. He's the first one of us to actually take that giant leap and ask someone out rather than just hang out with them. Which reminds me of Ree. I kind of liked her, not that I'd ever say that aloud in present company. But then I made such a fool of myself when I met her I doubt she'd ever want to hang out with me. Plus she was uber-cool, which sadly I'm not.

'Oh yeah, Davy said if you can't make it over to his, he'd email you the video so you can see how he's broken it down,' Sandi says.

'No!' Dread immediately says. 'No emails!'

'Why not?' I ask. 'Doesn't mean I'll use them.'

'Are your parents still consultants at the hospital?' Dread asks. It's a rhetorical question, so I don't bother answering him. 'Cos they need to get you in that MRI machine double quick and check your brain out. I think your cerebrum is shrinking.'

I shake my head at him. 'What are you on about?'

'You seriously want to leave that kind of electronic trail leading back to you?' Dread says. 'Man, you got a lot to learn.'

Dread is also a sucker for conspiracy theories. He sees them everywhere, and he's super-sceptical about practically everything unless it has a mountain of irrefutable scientific evidence backing it up. The guy basically reads too much of everything, so has a hard time believing anything.

Sandi and I roll our eyes. But maybe he has a point.

No, not about my cerebrum shrinking. But about leaving an electronic trail that could come back and bite me when I'm least suspecting it.

The problem for me is that when I go back to school on Monday, Greaves is going to be gunning for me, and she's going to be even sneakier about it. *And* I'll be on report.

I've got the diamond ready to flash at Rawson, but it's fast losing its sparkly lustre. I've spent a lot of time thinking about it – two whole suspended days of time thinking about it – and I've realized that Dread's right. Unless I drop Tom in it, Greaves will claim I cheated.

I admit I'm no saint, but one thing I've never done in my life is cheat. I've never really needed to, for a start, and the thought of getting caught breaks me out in a sweat. Can you imagine the humiliation?

Tom says he has no problem being dropped in it, but he hasn't thought through the repercussions the way I have. She's bound to mark him down as a *sympathizer.*

Sympathizers get the same treatment. Anyone who's ever stuck up for someone like me has received the same punishment, so over time less and less people are willing to come forward or step up. I'm not exaggerating. History is my witness – it's full of blind eyes and deaf ears and turning the other way.

And when I explain all this to Tom, what's the betting he backs down? I wouldn't blame him if he did because this is not his problem. And will Rawson even believe that Tom came across my missing paper while putting his back in Greaves's folder when she was out of the room? And then took it without telling her and gave it to me? It's not typical Tom behaviour, so the chances are, no, he won't believe him.

I might be in danger of overthinking this. Dad says you can never overthink a problem, and he's usually right. This time, though, all the thinking has got me precisely nowhere. Either Tom will stand up for me, or he won't. Either Rawson will believe us, or he won't. And either way, Greaves will win, because in the grand scheme of life, a teacher's words count for far more than the words of a kid who has been suspended.

So I'm worried that by the time I get to see what magic Davy's done with the video, I might already have been expelled.

'Then just make sure you're not!' Dread says. He's all sympathy, is Dread.

CHAPTER 15

'Man, that taste of freedom is sweet!' I declare as soon as we're through my front door.

'It's only been three days,' Sandi says, 'and it's pissing it down and it's bloody freezing. Why did we have to come all this way to get you anyway? We should have met at mine. I could have got us a lift.'

Sandi hates to walk anywhere he can be driven to. 'Where's the fun in that?' I ask.

'This is fun?' Tom says.

'Cabin fever's rotted the last of his brain cells,' Dread says, zipping his hoodie right up over his mouth and pulling his hood over his head, so only a flash of the whites of his eyes is visible. 'See you there,' he says, before taking off.

'I'm not running!' Sandi shouts, but Dread's already halfway up the road.

Dread is a sprinter. His fastest time is just under eleven and a half seconds in the hundred-metre sprint.

That's ridiculously fast, but despite Mr Adams the PE teacher's best efforts, he won't be press-ganged into joining the county team. Dread says it's from years of having to sprint for the bus – he detests mornings almost as much as Maji detests slugs, the arch-nemesis of her vegetable patch. I won't say what she calls them, but she uses very coarse Punjabi words, although never in my parents' earshot of course. Dread's heard her, and with his instant-recall memory, shocked me by using them. He can twist his tongue around most languages almost as fast as he can run.

It's raining that February rain, the hard, freezing kind that's more like being stabbed by an avalanche of icy popsicles.

Dread's waiting for us as we duck into the bus shelter.

There's a middle-aged woman waiting there too. She's perched at the far end of the bench and shuffles right to the edge when we join Dread. Somehow, I don't think she's making room for us to sit down. Maybe she's worried we're carrying an infectious disease. Ebola has reared its ugly head in the news, but doesn't everyone know that it's not airborne?

No, I think it's more about what we look like: four *youths* with our hoods up, looking like juvenile offenders. Hooded youths equal danger for her because, well, we're bound to be looking for trouble, or a free mobile phone at the very least. It doesn't matter that it's raining and that's why our hoods are up. We're a threat. Another case of the minority giving the majority a bad name that paints us all the same tarnished shade.

The others haven't really clocked her or her nervous glances in our direction, because they're too busy larking about. It's Saturday night and it's Dread's birthday. I'd like to tell the woman that it's OK, that we're not going to mug her or anything, because we're regular kids, not muggers. Muggers come in all colours; blacks and Asians don't have a monopoly on it. But she'd probably run a mile if I went over to her to explain.

I spot old Mrs Trent, my neighbour and Maji's walking buddy, heading towards the bus shelter. She's carrying a heavy bag so, being the nice polite guy that I am, I jog over to take it from her. The woman on the end of the bench is on her feet immediately, shouting, 'Oi! You leave her alone!'

Mrs Trent looks baffled. 'What's the matter with that woman? What's she shouting about?'

'I think she thinks I'm going to steal your bag.'

Mrs Trent pats me on the arm and says, 'Don't mind her. It takes all sorts, I suppose. Thank you, Jeevan. Give me your arm, I'm feeling a little wobbly tonight.'

We walk slowly to the bus shelter. 'Are you going home?' I ask her, wondering if I've got time to help her back home before the number 88 bus comes along.

'No, love, I'm catching the bus into town. My daughter's meeting me after she finishes work, and then I'm stopping with her until Monday.'

The woman on the end of the bench gives me a half-smile, almost apologetic, but I think I can be forgiven for not wanting to return her smile. She reminds me of Greaves – she presumes to know me because I'm obviously Asian. The skin colour kind of gives it away, but she knows nothing about me. Greaves might have laughed at Green's retelling of my Christmas tree story, but I bet she thought I was taking the piss with it, that it was all made up. Well, OK, some of it was, but not the fact that we have a real Christmas tree every year.

So, lady perched on the edge of the bench, you don't know me, but I'm like you – I'm a human being. Don't treat me like an alien, OK? I don't even scowl at her. I'm more of a smiler, and she stole my smile.

'Are these your friends, Jeevan?' Mrs Trent asks.

'Yes. We're going into town for Dread's birthday.'

'Oh, that's nice. Happy birthday, Fred!' she says. Mrs Trent's a little deaf, but she gives me back my smile.

Dread doesn't correct her. He grins and says thanks.

'Going to paint the town red, boys?' she asks. 'You certainly picked the night for it. Raining stair rods, it is.'

I'm guessing stair rods is Mrs Trent's version of frozen popsicles.

'We're going to an African restaurant in the city,' I tell her. The city's only half an hour on the train and our curfew is eleven – well, mine is.

'Sounds nice, dear. I like a bit of spice. Your grandma's curries might give me a bit of heartburn nowadays, but that doesn't stop me eating them!' She laughs. 'Don't stay out too late now, will you, Jeevan? It's not such a safe place these days, especially for nice young boys like you and your friends.'

'Don't worry, if I'm not home by eleven, Mum will ground me for ever!' I've known Mrs Trent since we moved here when I was four. No matter how many times my football went into her garden, and sometimes it was several times a day, she'd always throw it back. Sometimes she'd bring it over herself, which is how she became buddies with Maji. I've no idea how they get on as well as they do, what with Maji's broken English.

The bus pulls up and Dread takes Mrs Trent's bag while I take her arm and help her on to the bus. The woman on the end of the bench is already on the bus.

'Such nice boys, aren't they?' Mrs Trent tells her as she sits down opposite her. She winks at me.

Seems Mrs Trent's not half as deaf as she makes out.

The Shake Bar where we're meeting Amelia is packed when we arrive. She's perched on a stool near the door. Dread is grinning at her like a total idiot, and she's grinning back at him in exactly the same way. Beside her is Ree. The pink highlights in her hair are purple tonight, and she looks no less terrifying than the first time we met at the party.

'Hey, Jeev,' she says, giving me a hug, as introductions are made. I clumsily hug her, wondering why I can't just act normal around her. 'You disappeared at the party.'

That's my cue not to make a fool of myself. 'I went looking for this guy,' I say, nodding at Sandi. 'And then we split.'

'Oh, yeah, I remember. You had PMS,' she says, grinning.

I'm rocking those brain cells hard for what PMS could stand for and I'm coming up blank. 'Pre something? Post something? Post Mocks something? I give up.'

'Post Mocks Sleepiness. How did you do anyway?'

'OK, I guess.' I think about telling her about the stuff going down with Greaves. 'I'm not so worried about the mocks,' I begin, and then I stop. It's too long a story and I'm afraid it will bore her.

'Could have fooled me.'

'What do you mean?'

'You look stressed out.'

'Do I?'

'It's OK if you don't want to talk about it.'

'It's complicated.'

'Oh. OK.'

'I've been suspended for three days and my parents have grounded me for a month.'

'No! Seriously?' The look on my face must tell her how serious I'm being. 'What did you do?'

Why does everyone instantly think it was me who did something wrong? 'It wasn't my fault. I'm having some . . . problems with a teacher,' I say abruptly. I can't talk about it with her without explaining the whole thing. We pile on to the train and even though she comes to sit beside me, we're bantering as a group so she doesn't get the opportunity to ask me any more questions.

On the journey into the city, Sandi and I discover that Amelia is the female version of Dread. What are the chances? It's like they went on some kind of dating website, input all their details and credentials, likes and dislikes, music tastes and favourite foods, and the computer came up with their names as the perfect match. They even order the same dishes in Jollof Queen.

Have I mentioned I love spicy food? Anything that involves a plate of rice and chicken with spices thrown in gets my vote. The spices here are spicy in a different but interesting way to the spices Maji uses when she cooks. Mum doesn't cook Indian food much – she likes eating south-east Asian food when we're out: Vietnamese, Chinese, Thai and Japanese, but she only ever seems to cook Italian at home, and I swear my dad must have been an Argentinean in a previous life. Just serve him a side of cow and he's happy – but never in front of Maji. She thinks the cow is, and always will be, a sacred being. *Beef* is practically the only banned word in our house, apart from the usual swear words, so if there are ever any steaks in the fridge, they're taken out of their packaging straight away and referred to as *lamb* from then on.

So my steaming plate of Jollof rice and chicken,

which is what I've ordered, arrives and I dig in with my fork and shovel a mouthful in because I'm starving and still freezing from walking here from the train station in near Arctic conditions. And it blows me away, mind, body and soul! Maji's got a free and liberal hand with the chillies when she's cooking, so I'm not new to the havoc a chilli can wreak in your mouth, but I'm *seriously* burning up. I've got sweat fountaining up through my scalp and pouring down my face in rivulets.

Usually I'd turn to yoghurt to dampen the fires, but there's no yoghurt and there's no bread, which is the next best thing, so I down a glass of water, which is like pouring oil on a raging fire, and I'm coughing and spluttering while everyone else is cracking up. I can't utter a word for a good ten minutes apart from a croaky, 'Water!'

The forensic expert at the table investigates; oh wait, there are two of them now. This could get confusing. Well, one of them checks what I ordered on the menu while the other sifts through the rice on my plate.

Amelia looks up from the menu and says, 'Number 24 on the menu. You ordered the Jollof rice with extra *scotch bonnets*,' while Dread says, 'And you've eaten one of them whole. Not the best idea you've ever had, Jeev.'

Ree removes the remaining two culprits from my plate to hers and takes a bite out of one of them. 'Yeah, they're hot,' she confirms. She's not reaching for the water and gulping it by the jugful, nor has she lost her voice. Told you she was scary!

Still, once I get the feeling back in my mouth, I can reliably inform you that Jollof rice and chicken is pretty tasty – just check they're not serving whole scotch bonnets cunningly concealed in the rice first!

'Cheers for going through Chemistry with me, guys. I owe you,' Tom says to Dread and Sandi. 'Think I've got Chemistry sorted. Physics is something else, though.'

'You've got loads of time,' I say. There isn't anything that Dread and Sandi don't know about the GCSE Physics curriculum and beyond.

'Can't believe you snuck into Greaves's folder and thieved Jeev's paper out of it,' Sandi says, through a mouthful of ice cream.

'Bet you wouldn't have done it, Sand,' I say.

Sandi pretends to take umbrage at my comment – for about a second. 'Too right I wouldn't have!'

'Considering Jeev is going to land you in it, least he can do is pay for your food,' Dread says.

'Thanks, Dread. Like I'm not feeling guilty enough about it,' I say. 'Course I'll pay, Tom.'

Put on the spot, Tom goes red – his go-to colour when he's embarrassed. 'No need, Jeev.'

'What's this?' Amelia asks.

So we tell her and Ree about the controlled assessment – how Greaves gave me a C without marking the second paper and then said she'd *mislaid* it, and then about the infamous chair leg incident, and Amelia sides with me, declaring she just can't believe someone like Greaves actually exists in this century.

I'm getting to quite like this Amelia.

Ree points her spoon of ice cream at me. 'Why make a fuss now? You can get the controlled assessment re-marked later. You should've just let it go.'

'Yeah, but that's not the point.'

'So what *is* the point?'

'Forget it.'

'No, come on. Explain, Jeev. And another thing – did you ever think that she really might have been afraid of the way you were "brandishing" the chair leg?'

'No way was I brandishing a chair leg! I'm not like that.' Ree obviously doesn't get it. I expect Tom to jump in here and speak up for me, but he's picked this moment to head to the loos. I'm gutted that Ree thinks I'm overreacting. 'The point is that I can't let her get away with marking me down on purpose and telling lies about me.'

'I get you, Jeev, but life's full of shitty people like that. Think about it – teacher versus pupil, who's gonna win? Teacher every time. She'll trample all over you. You got to move on is all I'm saying, otherwise we'll be wiping bits of you off the pavement.' She digs her spoon back in her ice cream to make her point.

She sounds like my parents. But she's right about one thing – the whole situation is dragging me down.

CHAPTER 16

On Sunday afternoon we're all back in my room, me, Sandi, Dread and Amelia, Tom too, which is great but for one small, but slightly concerning, problem. From the pointed looks they're giving each other, Mum and Dad might seriously be reconsidering the ground rules of my grounding. Strictly speaking, I'm not allowed to go out, but I am allowed to have a friend over. Having four friends in my room is pushing the rules to breaking point.

Especially as we're having such a laugh that it sounds like there's a party going on in my room.

Plus there's a *girl* in my room, which is so unusual that both my parents, not to mention my grandma, are extremely conflicted about it. Mum and Dad haven't actually said anything about it – they like to think they're way too cool for that. But my gran doesn't hold back.

When Sandi and I went down to the kitchen, she told me exactly what she thought. Luckily, only Sandi understands Punjabi and knew what she was saying. He came to my rescue, smoothing things over Sandi-style – by sweet-talking my gran. My gran adores him because he's 'such a good Punjabi boy'. She's always going on about how hard he works and how helpful he is – you get the picture! And she says it in a tone that suggests I'm nothing like him. It so gets under my skin. She loves to compare everyone's kids. I don't know if this is an Indian thing. Maybe it is. Then again, come to think of it, Dread's mum is always comparing Dread to his cousins, but it's usually to warn him that if he doesn't carry on working as hard as he does he'll either end up being shipped back to Nigeria or stacking shelves in Lidl. Not that that's likely!

Anyway, Sandi very brilliantly diverted Maji's troubled thoughts about the girl in my room to the far more pressing issue of the shortage of Alphonso mangoes.

'What's the big deal about Alphonso mangoes?' I ask naively.

'Don't you know, Jeev? The Alphonso is the *king* of mangoes,' Amelia says as she walks into the kitchen. 'Can I get a glass of water, please?' she asks me.

Maji is on it in an instant. 'Let me help you,' she says, taking a glass from the cupboard. 'Yes, they are the king! Jeevan, why are you not knowing this? You like mangoes, Amelia?'

'They're my all-time favourite fruit,' Amelia replies.

Maji beams at her.

I discover, from the assorted mango aficionados around me, that this year there's an import problem with Alphonsos – 'fingers along the chain needed extra oiling'. Alphonsos are not due into the country until late April, but the season is so short – it ends in June, or whenever the monsoon rains start – that you have to get them as soon as they hit the shops, the Indian shops, of course. And they're not cheap either. But quality rarely is, Maji says, which is news to me. Since Poundsaver opened in town, Maji rarely shops anywhere else.

Anyway, Maji's taken a real shine to Amelia, and the upshot is that Amelia can come round any time she likes. Somehow, I don't think Maji would be saying the same to Ree. I think they'd rub each other up the wrong way. Or is that me I'm thinking about? She put me on the spot in the restaurant last night. She made me doubt myself – and just as I was thinking . . . or hoping . . . On the walk home last night, it was Sandi who pointed out that Ree seemed interested in me. 'She's got a funny way of showing it then,' I'd said, while thinking – seriously? I know I've said it before, but she's way out of my league.

Maji likes to call me her Shammi, who, if you haven't heard of him, was an Indian actor when Maji was young, so, yeah, a very long time ago. He was the Elvis of India, or so Maji says, with a swoon. If you google him you'll see that, apart from our identical surnames, there's a vague passing resemblance between us, but I'm stressing the *passing* and the *vague* here. I guess I'm trying to say that I'm not all that bad-looking. But I've acted like an idiot around Ree, so I shoot down any further thoughts of her – I've got enough problems going on.

Back in my room, Dread says, 'You should get grounded more often, Jeev – your room's massive compared to mine. So, are we getting thrown out?'

Dread drew the short straw in his house – he got the box room. 'This was Shanti's room and she still put up a fight to stop me moving in to it when she went to uni!'

'Girls, huh!' Sandi said, shaking his head, which earns him a glare from me to shut it.

'No. We're safe.' My parents are hardly going to chuck my friends out, because they know I need the distraction. I've been pacing the house all morning like a caged animal, getting told off for wearing holes in the carpet by Maji, told to go and find something useful to do by Mum, challenged to a game of chess, which I lost within seconds, by Dad.

Why all the fretting? Because tomorrow is D-Day.

I'm going into school with my mum and dad, which is bad enough, for a meeting with Rawson, which is even worse, and I have no idea how it's all going to go down, but the worst-case scenario is that at this time tomorrow I could be sitting at home looking for a new school.

'Jeev, that's just not going to happen, man,' Dread says for the tenth time. 'Tell him, Amelia.'

'They won't expel you, Jeevan. The whole class

witnessed what happened,' Amelia explains patiently. 'Isn't that right, Tom? You were there. Can Jeevan's behaviour be construed as being expellable?'

'It's our word against hers.' Tom goes red as Amelia pins him with her bright green eyes. 'Um, no. Course not,' he mumbles.

Amelia turns back to me. 'See. And as for Tom finding the *missing paper*,' her index fingers draw the inverted commas in the air, 'taking into consideration the *anonymous note*,' more air quotes, 'which I'm sure you have a copy of?' I nod. 'Then it's clear that something is very amiss with that lady. I suggest that we take more aggressive action. Even if your Mr Rawson believes Tom about finding the missing paper, Greaves can easily claim that it was an accidental oversight on her part. So there's only one thing for it – the note has to be forwarded, anonymously of course, super-fast to someone who gives a fuck.'

Amelia is so well spoken that it's almost shocking to hear her end her stream of consciousness with that word. We're all taken aback – except Dread, who's obviously been bitten by the love bug so bad that he can hardly string a sentence together.

'And here's where you're in luck – my cousin Clara works at the local rag,' Amelia continues. 'She's bored out of her head, waiting for that big story that'll get her into the major league. This would be right up her street. She's had it with covering weddings and funerals, and interviewing local C-list celebrities opening supermarkets and running through hoops of fire for some random charity in the vain hope that they get picked up by the national press and make it back on the A-list again.' Amelia rolls her beautiful green eyes. 'I mean, give me a break. They're has-beens for a reason. Right?'

I'm wondering when she's going to pause for breath, but Amelia doesn't seem to need to.

'She'd jump at a story like this – local teacher, in a position of authority who believes herself to be above the law, immune to prosecution, with the lives of so many kids in her hands, the power to make or break them. She's violated one of the main tenets of a teacher's code of conduct. She's actively discriminating against a section of society with complete disregard for the consequences to them. Racial discrimination in this day and age, really?'

'There's no proof of that, Amelia. That's Jeevan's theory,' Dread says. 'All we really know for a fact is that she hates him with a vengeance.'

'Even more reason to do something about it. We need to get to the truth. Give me a copy of the note now and I'll get it to Clara. By Tuesday it'll be in the newspaper's online version, and by Thursday, it'll be in the newspaper delivered through your door. By Friday your Headmaster will have had to launch a more official inquiry.' She sits back and smiles.

Amelia's like a whirlwind; she's swept us all up and swirled us through the air. I swear we're all still spinning. Dread says she wants to be an international human rights lawyer, and I can totally see it.

But I'll say this – she has the smarts and the contacts, and she's pretty too. I feel a sudden pang of guilt for thinking about Amelia like that and a mental image of Ree pops into my head. I still haven't found out whether she's originally from South America or Spain. You can't tell by her English – she speaks like the rest of us, without an accent. I kind of even like her pinky-purpley highlights. I can imagine her response to Amelia's fiery monologue. 'Seriously?' she'd say. 'You guys need to go get a life.' *Focus, Jeev – stop thinking about Ree.* What was I supposed to be doing? Oh, yeah, the photocopier.

Dad's got a state-of-the-art printer photocopier scanner thing, so it only takes me a minute to take a copy of the copy. Dread and Sandi meet me on the landing as I'm heading back to my room.

'What's up?'

'We stay quiet about the video,' Dread says quietly.

'Don't say a word about it, not yet anyway,' Sandi adds.

'The note's one thing. The video is a whole different ball game,' Dread says.

I can't say that I'm not tempted to tell Amelia the whole story about the video and get her to pass it on to her cousin. I'm already wondering what Amelia would do if she found out about its existence. It strikes me that there is one difference between Dread and Amelia, apart from the very obvious: Dread thinks everything through as thoroughly as Amelia, but he is far, far more cautious and considered in what he says and what he does than his new partner in crime. Together, they make a formidable team.

But Dread and Sandi are right about not telling her yet. The thing about involving the press is that you lose control of your story, and I can't let that happen. Whatever I think of Greaves — and I'm thinking about my sneaking suspicion here: the suspicion that she's really and truly got it in for me because of the colour of my skin (yeah, I know, that's a serious thing to say out loud) — Mr Green is a good person. Yeah, I know he cheated, but still, he's a brilliant teacher. I don't want him to be collateral damage.

CHAPTER 17

We only have to wait a minute before we're ushered into Rawson's office the next morning. The room is sauna-hot; someone needs to crank open a window or at least stop the radiators from pumping out megawatts of hot air.

'Drs Kapoor, please take a seat.'

Rawson has always struggled with the correct way of addressing two doctors simultaneously.

'Jeevan.' Rawson nods at me and points at the less comfortable hard chair. 'Can I offer you a drink – tea or coffee?' My parents decline. 'Well, I know you are very busy people, so I'll come straight to the point. As I said on the phone, belligerency and threatening behaviour are not acceptable modes of conduct. Jeevan disrupted his English Literature class, he was unable to control his temper, and his teacher felt threatened and intimidated by him. Hence the two-day suspension, which quite frankly should have been a far longer suspension, but

I was mindful that the GCSEs are not too far off and there is still a fair amount of curriculum work to get through before then.'

'Mr Rawson,' Dad begins. 'Jeevan has given us his version of events in class that day and we feel that the facts have been misrepresented to you. You know he is a good pupil. Almost all of his teachers, with the exception of one, would agree with this, and he has done very well in all of his mocks, with, again, the exception of one – English Literature – where a paper was mislaid by the teacher.'

'I don't disagree, Dr Kapoor. Until a few weeks ago, Jeevan was a model student, which makes what has happened recently all the more disappointing, entirely inexplicable and frankly very troubling. Clearly there is a problem.'

'Yes, that is exactly why we are here, Mr Rawson, to talk about the problem, and to attempt to find a solution.'

'Jeevan appears to have behavioural problems in his English Literature class. I wonder if there is something else that's troubling Jeevan?'

What's he on about?

'Perhaps there is an issue, something outside of school that we may not be aware of, that is upsetting him?'

'Of course not!' Mum retorts. It's not quite a snap, but it's not quite one of Mum's considered responses either.

'I completely understand if you don't wish to talk about it here, Dr Kapoor, but the school does have access to an educational psychologist who Jeevan might find it easier to talk to. She will be more than happy to see you as a family too.'

Dark, murderous clouds have gathered on Mum's forehead, threatening an explosion of thunderous proportions, but she just about manages to hold it in check.

'There is clearly only one problem and that problem is his teacher, Mrs Greaves,' Mum snaps impatiently. So far, she's not doing a great job of dealing with Mr Rawson in the calm, cool rational way she expects me to.

'Yes, Jeevan does appear to have fixated on Mrs Greaves. She is of course an excellent teacher, well regarded by her pupils and held in high esteem by her colleagues.'

I know what Rawson is leading up to with this.

The brick wall is going up hard and fast and Mr Rawson is taking shelter behind it. Mum and Dad are trying to hold their tempers in check. I think they finally understand what I've been up against.

'Is that so? Because we were under a very different impression about this particular teacher,' Mum says.

'Yes, I'm sure Jeevan has made his feelings about her abundantly clear to you. Mrs Greaves has talked to me at length about Jeevan and she feels that it is possible Jeevan may have a problem with her, and with older women in general, because, how should I put this? Well, in her words, she feels that perhaps there are certain differences in his background that may be playing a part in Jeevan's behaviour towards her,' Mr Rawson continues. 'I'm certainly not agreeing with her views on this; however, in the absence of any other possible explanations, and bearing in mind that Jeevan has been sent to my office on three separate occasions for bad behaviour in her class, there may well be issues that we should discuss.'

The man seems totally oblivious to the rising wrath of the two Drs Kapoor seated before him. Underneath their outward composure, they are absolutely livid, although Mum is much closer to losing it.

'I think you may find that it is actually the *other* way round, Mr Rawson,' Mum says bluntly.

Uh oh. Mum's lost it now. She and Dad had already decided not to directly accuse Greaves of marking me down even though I'd told them it was so smack-you-in-the-face-wake-up obvious. But apparently it's not, at least not to Rawson, despite the heads-up with the note I sent him. Still, Dad gives Mum a sharp look and tries to maintain his uber-cool reasonableness.

'What we're trying to say, Mr Rawson, is that the assumptions you are making are totally erroneous and therefore merit further dialogue and, perhaps, could well do with some input from other pupils and teachers as to their experience with this particular teacher.

Furthermore, I'm not entirely clear exactly which "differences" Mrs Greaves is referring to. Is she referring to "cultural" differences, by any chance?'

I wonder if Dad spent some time on the phone to his brother, my uncle Raj, who's a lawyer, because the way he's talking I'm wondering if he's about to stand up, adjust his robes and say, 'So I put it to you, Your Honour . . .' and start calling witnesses for the defence.

It's lucky I've already subpoenaed them.

'Well, not exactly, Dr Kapoor. I think it's more to do with the fact that Jeevan finds it impossible to treat Mrs Greaves with the respect that she merits. Mrs Greaves has been with us for a number of years and she is a highly valued member of staff at this school,' Rawson continues, but Dad cuts him off.

'Be that as it may, she has made serious allegations against my son, which will go on his school record.'

'He broke a chair and was holding the chair leg in a threatening manner,' Rawson reminds them.

'And again, I say that it's imperative you speak to the other pupils regarding this particular matter. The chair broke. Jeevan simply picked the broken leg up off the ground. There was certainly no intention on his part to use it.'

'Nevertheless, the fact remains that his teacher felt threatened by him. So I'm afraid that this suspension will automatically go on to his school record, Dr Kapoor.'

'I absolutely cannot allow that to happen until the

matter is fully investigated, and if we must take further action, we will,' my dad insists. 'Jeevan's record has been impeccable since he joined the school five years ago.'

So far, the bulls have eyed each other across the arena, now their heads have dipped and their hooves are pawing the ground. Their nostrils are flaring, their breathing is hot and noisy, and steam is pouring out of their ears. Any second now, they're going to charge at each other. I'm shrinking further and further into my seat. I don't want to be here. I want to be anywhere else but here. This is so unfair. I hate Greaves.

'Impeccable until recently, Dr Kapoor. I will not have a pupil threatening a teacher. Not in my school!'

'Jeevan would never behave in such a way! Talk to his classmates, talk to his other teachers.'

The bulls have charged and locked horns. I wish Rawson had done something about the anonymous note, because if he had, this particular bullfight would not be happening. It would have been a cinch for Rawson to pull up all the records, ask for Greaves's register, where she records everyone's marks, and check out our school reports going back a few years – most of it's on his computer. I gave him the heads-up. All he had to do was access the information.

Amelia's cousin, Clara, from the *Tribune* now has the heads-up too – and I bet she won't be sitting on *her* hands. She'll be careful about how she phrases it, but it'll be way too big for Rawson to sweep under the carpet – no matter how big his carpet.

'I have a report from Mrs Greaves detailing exactly what occurred in the classroom last week and on the previous two occasions, which I believe to be adequate,' Rawson states.

'That is simply not good enough,' my dad replies. He's starting to lose his patience now too.

And I'm seeing red too. Rawson knows what happened one of the times – I was three minutes late for Greaves's lesson and she had a go at me, but not Harry, who was also late. Rawson seems to have conveniently forgotten that he gave me a get-out-of-jail card in the shape of a library pass. I'm suddenly scared, because it feels like I'm being well and truly stitched up. I shouldn't need any evidence, missing exam papers or X-rated recordings; I shouldn't need to catch a teacher red-handed in order to get some justice.

I stand up, out of my seat, ready to defend myself, but my mum puts her hand on my arm.

'Sit down, Jeevan.'

She gives me a look telling me she's got this, that I don't need to fight this battle.

'Before we go any further, I'd like to give you this,' Mum says to Rawson, leaning forward and handing him my exam paper.

'What's this?'

'It's the "missing" exam paper. It's the one that Mrs Greaves claims to have mislaid,' Mum says.

'So Jeevan had it all along, did he?' Rawson asks sharply.

'Actually, no,' Mum replies with deadly calm. 'Jeevan did not have it. While Mrs Greaves was bringing Jeevan to see you last Wednesday, Jeevan's classmate came across the paper in Mrs Greaves's folder when he was looking for his own paper. As you can see, she didn't even bother to mark the paper before she gave him the D.'

Mum sits back and smiles sweetly at Mr Rawson.

As the chess grandmaster said to the novice: check.

CHAPTER 18

I did tell you I wasn't a great chess player, didn't I? And I'm certainly no grandmaster. Because what happens next is nowhere near checkmate.

Rawson sits back and flicks through my paper. When he looks up, he zooms in directly on me. 'Which classmate?' he asks.

Now I'm on the spot, as I suspected I would be, but it still doesn't make things easier. I don't want to dob Tom in, like I said – I'm not a snitch, but, unlike before, this time it matters. 'I'd rather not say, sir.'

'And why is that? It's in your best interest to tell me. Otherwise,' he says, twiddling with the end of his moustache, 'how do I know what you're saying is true, Jeevan?'

'Jeevan would not lie about such a thing,' Mum interjects in true I'll-defend-my-child-against-the-world-Indian-tiger-mum fashion.

'You *must* tell Mr Rawson who it was, Jeevan,' Dad says.

I shake my head. I need to protect my source. 'I'm sorry. I don't want him to get into trouble.'

'Trouble is exactly where you'll be headed if you don't tell me, young man,' Mr Rawson says. 'I don't think you fully comprehend what's at stake here.'

Oh, I think I do.

Sorry, Tom.

'Tom,' I finally say.

Mr Rawson leans forward, presses the intercom buzzer and asks Mrs Dere to locate Tom and Mrs Greaves and ask them both to come to the school office immediately. 'I will return shortly,' Mr Rawson says, rising from his chair. 'In the meantime, can I offer you a drink while you wait? Tea? Coffee?'

Horns have been unlocked and the bulls are back in their corners – for now.

My parents decline the offer of a drink. They both pointedly check their watches, a not-so-subtle reminder to Mr Rawson that they have work to get to, important work in which they deal with real life-and-death issues on a daily basis.

'I'll try not to be too long,' Rawson says, getting the hint.

As soon as he's out of the office, I remember how important it is for human beings to breathe. This is turning out to be far harder than I imagined it would be. Right at this very minute, Tom will be in the line of fire, his integrity challenged, and I'm beginning to freak out a little about whether he might just prefer to duck and run for cover than have to face a two-pronged attack from Rawson and Greaves.

But in the end, it won't matter if he tells the truth and is believed because Greaves will say what everyone would say when confronted with the undeniable truth. She will claim it was a 'purely accidental mistake, an understandable oversight,' because 'she's human like anyone else'. The last point is as questionable as the first, if you ask me.

And as for the D grade she gave me on the paper that clearly hadn't even been marked? Well, I know exactly how she'll justify it. Because she is nothing if not predictable.

'Based on Jeevan's work over the past year, his controlled assessments, and the fact that his work has not been of an acceptable standard, I felt that awarding him a higher grade in the mock examination would do him no favours. He needs to realize that he has to pull his socks up, and a D grade is my way of helping him see that.'

Greaves sits back in her chair, her expression dripping with sympathy and understanding, allowing no one in the room any shadow of doubt that everything she does is for the benefit of the misguided child who she is rooting so hard for, despite his antagonistic behaviour towards her.

No one in the room is in any doubt – except me, that

is. I know how fine an actress she is. After all, I have the evidence.

Rawson is definitely taken in by her. Mr Green too. Unfortunately, my parents also seem to be taken in, at least momentarily, because they've forgotten all about the email. All appears to be lost. But not quite.

I take out the piece of paper I printed out last night and hand it to Mr Rawson. 'My parents had the paper marked by a friend of theirs who's a lecturer in English. He gave me an A.'

That seems to wake the room up.

'Ah,' Rawson says, once he's read through the email. He hands it to Greaves, waiting for her to explain this away in her own inimitable style.

She gives it a cursory glance and smiles at us benevolently. 'I am so pleased that he has such high hopes for you, Jeevan,' she says, 'and I certainly agree with him when he talks about your potential; it's what I've been trying so hard to help you reach. Your parents' friend,' she nods at my parents, 'may well be a lecturer in English, but he is a little out of touch with GCSE English, with the curriculum and with the particular requirements of the exam mark schemes.

'It's only to be expected, of course, because he works at a very different level. I think we can all agree that university is not like school. Creativity, originality and free thinking are encouraged at university, as well they should be. They are indeed the hallmarks of university education, but it is here in school that the foundations are laid. Unless you have a complete grasp of the subject matter at this level, it is impossible to build upon it in any successful way. Jeevan may well have *potential*, and occasionally makes valid points in his work, but in my view, he is trying to run before he can walk. I'm afraid to say that not only is his discipline severely lacking, this attempt to seek praise for work that is quite unsuitable at GCSE-level is a sign that he thinks his level of attainment is, shall we say, somewhat higher than those who know better.'

Those who know better – like me, she means. The *like me* she leaves unsaid as she smiles kindly at us all. I'm pretty sure I'm the only one that can see the malevolence glinting behind her perfect mask of kindly reasonableness. She's actually enjoying this.

'Perhaps the paper can be marked by another member of the English Department from within the *school*,' my mum proposes. 'Just to settle the matter.'

'Dr Kapoor, do you think that's really necessary considering the pressure, and the workload, teachers are under?' Greaves replies. 'What do you think, Mr Rawson? We are still marking, grading and going through examination papers for the rest of the school as well as the mocks. At the same time, we're trying to press on with the curriculum. Time is far too short to be even contemplating such time-consuming distractions at this stage. The GCSEs will be upon us before we realize it.'

'Be that as it may, I am afraid I will have to insist upon it,' Dad says. 'As I said before, Mr Rawson, I want the whole matter *fully* investigated. Jeevan does not deserve for this to mar his school record.'

'Perhaps we can come to an agreement over that, Dr Kapoor. We only have Jeevan's best interests at heart. What do you think, Mr Rawson?'

She's playing it well. She's putting Rawson in the hot seat and making out that it's nothing to do with her.

'I mean, as long as I have Jeevan's full cooperation in class from now until the exams, I am willing to overlook last week's incident. As I said before, Jeevan,' she's looking right at me now, with an unbearable saccharine-sweet expression that's taken everyone in – everyone except me, and it's even given me a moment of doubt about her motives, 'whatever you think, or believe, I'm here for you.' She reaches over and places her hand on my arm, and I struggle and don't quite succeed at stopping myself from flinching at her touch. 'Do you understand, Jeevan?'

I certainly do.

'Well, if you *are* sure, Mrs Greaves.' Rawson looks completely bemused at this turn of events. 'I suggest we monitor the situation, and keep an eye on your progress, Jeevan, so I'm going to keep you on report for the time being. I think once Jeevan has apologized to Mrs Greaves, he can go to his next lesson. There's no sense in his missing any more lessons than he already has.'

They're all looking at me, waiting. So *that's* the price I have to pay. You may well think it's a small price. After all, it's a simple apology. It shouldn't be hard to get the words out, but they are lodged so deep in my throat it's going to take a heavy-duty crowbar to lever them out.

Clearly, Mum and Dad aren't going to take this any further with the school. They got the suspension off my record, so job done as far as they're concerned. They don't like confrontation and they don't like escalating unpleasant situations. They're the pour-cold-water-on-it kind of people generally, and they like nothing better than reaching an amicable solution. I used to be like that too. I used to be the laid-back, not-go-looking-for-an-argument, play-the-peacemaker, douse-the-fires, let-things-go kind of person. But not now, and not when Greaves's shenanigans in the woods have inadvertently handed me the ammunition to fire right back at her.

And it's not just any ammunition; it's not mere bullets or hand grenades, or even a cluster bomb. What she gave me is a *nuclear* bomb.

The problem with detonating a nuclear bomb is the inevitable fallout. It has a devastating and catastrophic effect that can be felt for hundreds of miles around and for centuries afterwards . . .

I've only got a couple more months left of the fifth form. Study leave begins straight after the Easter holidays, which start at the beginning of April. It's now the beginning of February. So I've got about eight weeks left of having to suffer Greaves, four hours a week, which works out as approximately thirty-two hours.

Thirty-two hours until freedom. I won't be staying on in the sixth form, that much I know without any doubt.

Thirty-two hours.

It's not a lot. I could pull a sickie on a few of the days I have double English. That'll bring it down to maybe twenty-six hours.

Twenty-six hours.

My parents are looking hard at me. They won't want to be seen to be obviously pushing me to apologize, not out loud anyway, but their eyes are saying it all. Rawson's also staring hard at me. If his eyes could speak, I'm sure they would be saying, 'Take the get-out-clause and run!'

Yet the whole of my being revolts at having to apologize to Greaves. I swallow my pride and force myself to say the toxic words.

'I apologize for my behaviour, Mrs Greaves. It won't happen again.'

She says nothing. She's waiting for more. Oh crap, this sucks big time. 'I don't know what came over me. I'm very sorry.' I now know what it feels like to be forced to eat dirt, and believe you me, it leaves the foulest taste in your mouth.

'I accept your apology, Jeevan. I hope you've learnt a valuable lesson. I'll see you in class this afternoon.'

Make that twenty-seven hours. I forgot to count today's lesson.

She sticks a few more knives into my back on her way out of the office. 'We'll go through this paper and I'll help you with all the questions you misunderstood.'

Now I feel like I have so many knives sticking out of my back that I'm kind of shocked I haven't keeled over.

CHAPTER 19

It's all over school by lunchtime like an infectious rash that's so highly contagious everyone in my year has caught it. Even some of the little brats from the year below have caught it, and it's still spreading like a bush fire. How has the epidemic manifested itself? Like a mutant form of Tourette's – mutant because unlike Tourette's it involves not a single swear word, indecent remark or offensive comment.

So what's all over school? Me and my infamous, soon to be legendary, apology. It's got the whole school apologizing. Ironic, isn't it? My apology, or at least a not-so-hilarious variation of it, is fired back at me everywhere I go. Trust me when I say that no one wants the most humiliating eat-shit moment in the history of their lives immortalized in this way.

'I'm *so* sincerely sorry, Mrs Greaves.'

'Please accept my humble apologies, Mrs Greaves.'

'I grovel at your beautiful, if slightly over-large, feet, Mrs Greaves.'

'I promise not to be a naughty boy again, Mrs Greaves.'

'You can smack me any time, Mrs Greaves.'

'Spank me, Mrs Greaves, I've been sooo baaad . . .'

You get the gist.

It was my unbelievably bad luck that the Headmaster's office door was ajar during the entire humiliating episode, and the kid waiting outside Mr Rawson's office to see him was none other than James 'Gabby-mouth' Gabbs, who went and gabbled it to everyone he knew during break, and those kids then gabbled it to everyone else *they* knew after break, because it's far more entertaining than reading about the structure of plant cells for the thousandth time, so that by lunchtime it is everywhere and there is nowhere for me to hide.

I wolf down my sandwich and make my getaway from the lunch hall to a chorus of, 'Sorry, did we hurt your feelings?' and enough canned laughter to cover a whole series of *The Inbetweeners*. I know it isn't malicious, well most of it isn't, but it still hurts. I've got thick skin – no, not because brown skin is thicker, duh. Although if it was thicker I'd have no complaints because at the moment I could really do with the extra protection. Imagine if we all had crocodile skin; maybe not – no one's going to look good with reptilian skin. Say the hide of a mighty beast like an elephant. Actually, just *being* an elephant would be awesome, with that memory, that size, that colour. No one messes with an elephant . . .

Jesus, Jeevan, seriously? Get a grip!

My subconscious must be telling me something. Something about being trapped in the powerful jaws of a crocodile, a crocodile called Greaves. The only creature big and mighty enough to escape such a predator is the elephant.

'What you've got to remember, Jeev, is that it's not personal. They're only taking the piss,' Dread says.

'Forgotten it already,' I say, nonchalantly. Now I'm an elephant with Alzheimer's.

'I texted Amelia to hold off on the note thing.'

'What? Why?'

'Man, cos *you're* not thinking straight, someone's gotta look out for you. Think it through.'

I try to think it through. But nothing comes to my totally blank, minuscule brain except that Greaves is going to be off the hook again. I'm pissed at Dread for having texted his girlfriend without asking me first. Clara-the-journalist could have hit the big time with that note; it could have been her Watergate – OK, so Greaves-gate doesn't have quite the same ring. But the cover-up will stay covered up, and that doesn't make me a happy camper.

'Why would you do that? Give me Amelia's number, Dread.'

Dread shakes his head. 'Where's your head at?'

'It's been a bit challenged this morning. Remember?'

'OK, I'll spell it out for you: "Embittered Pupil Accuses Teacher of RACISM"; "Suspended Pupil SLANDERS

Respected Teacher", et cetera, et cetera, et cetera. Get it now?'

Dread's right. The timing couldn't have been worse. If the note thing had come out a couple of weeks ago, my name wouldn't have been associated with it in the way it now absolutely, definitely, without-a-shadow-of-doubt would.

'Embittered just about covers it,' I say. 'There's got to be a way round it though, hasn't there? We could get Clara to say she's had the note for a few weeks. That would put me out of the picture.'

'We could ask her,' Dread says doubtfully. He mulls it over for a minute. 'But that involves asking her to lie and the chances are that she might not take the note seriously. She may think we're getting her involved in a little spat between you and Greaves rather than investigating possible systemic prejudice.'

'Systemic prejudice' – I always knew that Dread had a way with words. But the 'possible'? Dread's on the fence as to Greaves's guilt. I feel let down that he doesn't one hundred per cent believe me. Ree's in his camp too. What does that say? That I'm in the wrong?

'You know it's more than a spat, Dread.'

'It doesn't matter what I think. There's no real proof, Jeev. So no talking to journalists, OK?'

I groan. 'OK, so get your brain working on it, Dread. I can't let this go.'

'No worries. I'm on it. Wait a few weeks. The dust is

sky high. Once it settles, we'll make our move. You still grounded?'

I nod. 'Morose' doesn't even begin to cover the way I'm feeling right now. 'Probably for the rest of my life, if Mum gets her way.'

It's History straight after lunch and by then my mood has sunk from morose to the deepest darkest most wretched depths. I'm trying to talk myself into getting a grip – it's only one teacher, one subject. If I drop one grade then it's not the end of the world for me, and in the scale of things it really doesn't matter because I'll probably do just fine.

But it *does* matter.

Mr Green's lesson doesn't disappoint. He's on the ball: all our History papers are marked, graded, dissected and commented on, some are ripped apart, not literally of course, with pointers given, sample answers provided, all with his characteristic humour and sarcasm.

It takes my mind off the last lesson of the day, the one I'm dreading, when the whole class will be watching me. Imagine thirty pairs of eyes on you, analysing your every move, every breath you take. But it's the thirty-first pair of eyes that *I'll* have to watch out for – the eyes of Mrs Greaves – because those eyes will be firing lethal daggers into my back with such astounding speed and precision you'd think you were in a Jackie Chan film.

And I haven't seen sight nor sound of Tom all day either. I wanted to apologize to him before English, and find out what he said to Rawson and Greaves – and what they said to him.

Mr Green sets a short Sources paper for the class to do in pairs. He likes discussion, collaboration and interaction in his lessons. 'You might actually remember more of it if you've had to argue your case or your point, defend a position and justify your view. Or at least that is my hope,' he says. 'And if there's one thing we teachers are good at, it is living in hope. I don't want to look back on these last two years and think: well, that was a complete waste of time – and neither do you! If I'm bothered then you should be bothered. Got it? Good. Get on with it then.'

Mr Green's coming towards me. 'Jeevan,' he says, stopping by my desk. 'An exceptional mock examination paper – the best in the year. Produce the same quality of work in the real thing and you'll get that A star.'

I wonder if he's saying that to boost my morale. 'Thanks, sir.'

'Don't rest on your laurels, though. Complacency will lose you the star. Stay focussed. You missed an important lesson last week, so I'll go through it with you now.'

He goes back to his desk at the front of the class and I follow. If you miss a lesson you're expected to catch up with it in your own time, so this is highly unusual – even for Mr Green, one of the most bothered-about-us teachers in the school.

'Before we start,' he begins, 'how is it going?'

I know what he's referring to. I shrug. 'OK.'

He raises an eyebrow. 'OK? Really? I was under the impression that things were definitely *not* OK, Jeevan.'

'They could be better.'

'Yes, indeed they could. I am frankly astonished at what I've heard about your behaviour during your English lesson last week.'

That makes me look up. Is he actually saying he believes Greaves? No. That's impossible. Not him. Anyone else but not Mr Green. But then I remember that episode in the woods that day, and me thinking exactly the same thoughts then. If I hadn't caught it on camera, I wouldn't have believed it myself.

'Shame we're not allowed to use our mobile phones in class because things would definitely be better for me if we were,' I say. 'The camera doesn't lie.' It's come out a little strong, so strong that it might even be considered bordering on the belligerent. I wonder if he'll send me to the Head. All it would take is for me to stand up and accidentally knock my chair to the floor, for it to break, me to pick up the chair leg, and he could claim that I was answering back, being belligerent, throwing chairs around and threatening him with a chair leg. He could hardly claim he was 'feeling intimidated' though, because he's built like a rugby player.

He gives me an appraising look, but I don't look away. I've done nothing to be ashamed of, nothing at all. Unlike some people.

'Jeevan, Jeevan, Jeevan,' he says, sighing. 'I don't need a recording of what took place in the class. I don't actually believe you're capable of the kind of behaviour that you have been accused of. I've talked to the Head and let him know my feelings on the matter. I think it's all been a case of rising tension, stress and misunderstandings. Cut Mrs Greaves some slack – she's been under a lot of pressure.'

I blink in shock. I shouldn't be shocked though because Mr Green's all right. I've always said so. What I'm shocked about is that he's trying to have her back as well as mine!

'What I don't wish to see is the situation escalating to the point where it affects your GCSEs. Did you discuss the possibility of moving to a different class with the Head?'

'No. I didn't think of it at the time.' Damn! My parents didn't think of it either, and they've usually got everything covered. 'We were too busy trying to keep the suspension off my school record.'

'And you managed that?'

'Yes. Mrs Greaves agreed to it. But my paper won't get marked by any of the other English teachers because Mrs Greaves says they're too busy with *other* high-priority stuff. So the overall C grade stays.'

'Ah, I see. Yes, she's right, of course. You have to remember that it's only a mock exam, Jeevan. You'll do fine in the real thing.'

Yes, I'm disappointed in him. He doesn't get that it's not about that any more. It's gone way beyond. Her power and her capacity and appetite for making my life difficult are growing. She actually believes her own lies. That's a dangerous state of mind.

I'm going to trust him and tell him what's really going on with Mrs Greaves – and see what he says.

I lower my voice. 'It's not just me she marks down,' I say. 'It's all of *us*.'

'Us?' he asks.

'Yes. Kids like me – the non-white kids, Mr Green.'

It takes him several long moments to respond. 'Ah. I see. That's a pretty big accusation to make, Jeevan.' He's lowered his voice too.

'I know, sir. But it's true. You just have to look at the way we're marked – and not just in my year.'

'How sure of your facts, are you, Jeevan? Is this not just part of the clash you're having with her, a way of getting back at her for what you see as unfair treatment?'

'No, sir, it's not. And I'm sure that's what she's been doing.'

He's looking at me carefully, and again takes his time before responding. 'In that case, I would suggest to you that the parents of all the kids who feel this way write to the Head, lodging an official complaint.'

Yeah, like *that's* going to happen.

Mr Green must realize that too. Who wants to put their name to a letter like that? Not any Indian parent

I know. And certainly not my keep-under-the-radar parents. They feel they've fought and won the battle that needed to be fought. This would be going a whole step further, and I'm not sure they'd be up for that.

CHAPTER 20

We file in to the last lesson of the day, English Lit. Whoopi-do! Greaves is standing at the front of the class with a scary smile on her face. Gloating doesn't come close to describing it. In her hand, she's got a sheaf of essays ready to hand out. She eyeballs me. What's the betting I'm getting another C?

Tom's in his chair already and I sit down beside him. We exchange smiles – his rueful, mine apologetic. We don't have time for more than that because Greaves has rapped her hand on her desk and called for silence. She calls Harry up to hand out all the essays. Harry is one of the Favoured Ones, even though he's walked in a few minutes late – again.

My essay has so many red marks on it you can barely read what I've written. So has Tom's. His face has fallen. We both flick to the back of the second sheet where the two Cs are sticking their tongues out at us and shouting, 'Na-na-na-na-na!'

It's no surprise to me, but it is to Tom. The look on his face makes me wince.

He's been tarnished as a sympathizer.

It was inevitable. As soon as he reached inside that folder, found my missing paper and delivered it to me, his fate was sealed. I had nothing to do with his decision. I hadn't asked him to look for it while Greaves was out of the room; I hadn't asked him to steal it for me.

So why do I feel so responsible?

I don't bother going up to the front of the class to ask Greaves about my essay, what all the red marks mean, because a cursory glance tells me that they're all meaningless and bear little or no relation to what I've written. I guess it's pretty much the same for Tom. He's got his head bowed over his essay trying to decipher Greaves's notations, but you need an Enigma machine to decode that stuff.

'I'm sorry, Tom.'

He looks up through his mop of sandy hair. 'What for? You didn't do anything.'

'I kind of landed you in it.'

'No, you didn't.'

She's speaking, or rather shouting, in our direction. 'Did I or did I not specifically say NO talking? Why you both feel you can disregard my instructions, I do not know. Silence means silence. Do you understand?'

Tom's gone beetroot-red. 'Sorry, miss,' he mumbles.

To say that Greaves used to like Tom would have

been the understatement of the century. Tom was the epitome of the perfect Anglo-Saxon, fair-haired, blue-eyed boy as far as she was concerned; his lineage practically goes all the way back to King Harold – OK, maybe not quite that far back, but you get my drift. But because he's now been marked as a sympathizer, he's ended up with an arrow in his eye just like King Harold, speaking metaphorically, of course.

Thirty pairs of eyes have swivelled in my direction. There's a hushed silence – the kind that only happens when everyone holds their breath at exactly the same time, which is so rare I'm not even going to try and work out the probability of it happening.

Everyone's waiting. Greaves is waiting. Nothing's going to happen until I've uttered my second grovelling apology of the day.

Except I'm having real trouble getting the word *sorry* out of my mouth. Someone sniggers behind me, setting me on edge. I've had probably the most humiliating day of my life in school ever – even if you count the time I peed my pants when I was four. I'm about to say something, something I really shouldn't, something that will get me into a whole lot of trouble, when the classroom door opens.

'Mrs Greaves, so sorry to trouble you in the middle of your lesson. Can I have a quick word?'

It's Mr Green.

Greaves's face undergoes a massive change. Two

little beetroots have coloured her cheeks as she sashays towards him.

I've been forgotten, for now.

She steps out of the class to just beyond the door. Thirty pairs of ears are straining to eavesdrop, but their whispered exchange is too brief for anyone to catch a word. I've got a full view of Greaves's face from my desk. Her lips are moving, and I'm no lip-reader, but I think I make out one word. I'll know later if I'm right about it.

When she returns to the classroom, she's not quite herself. Whatever Mr Green said to her has left her flustered and distracted, although not so distracted that she's forgotten about me and Tom, *the bad boys*. We all know how laughable that is because there's bad and there's *bad*. Greaves could never hack it in an inner city school.

'Harry – can you sit beside Tom, please? Jeevan – move across to Harry's desk, please,' Greaves says.

Everyone's watching.

I'm surprised she hasn't asked for that all-important apology from me. I was ready for it as well, but I'm not about to offer it up of my own volition. So I collect up my stuff, taking my time; I'm not in a hurry. This lesson is a load of bull. I'm going to learn nothing new, nothing useful, nothing of any value or relevance to the English Lit GCSE, which is the sole reason for me being here. No, wait, I am learning something of value; it's a Life Lesson.

I'm learning that patience, forbearance and the moral high ground aren't easy companions.

I'm on the moral high ground, the forbearance I'm working on, but the patience bit just keeps slipping away from me. You might say they're the same thing. Patience: the capacity to accept or tolerate delay, problems or suffering without becoming annoyed or anxious. Forbearance: patient self-control; restraint and tolerance.

I've shown huge forbearance – I've still got that ticking time bomb on my laptop – so that's self-control and restraint right there.

But my patience, the capacity to tolerate what this teacher keeps throwing at me without becoming outraged, is where I'm having the major problems.

During the lesson, we read passages aloud and there's a cursory attempt on her part to analyse the scenes from the book we're studying, but to be honest, we make a better job of that than she does.

What's got her so flustered?

I only manage to talk to Tom after the lesson when we're safely away from Greaves's classroom.

'So what happened this morning?'

'It was bad. I thought any minute now and they're gonna call my parents! I told Rawson I took the paper from Greaves's folder. But he kept on and on about it, asking me again and again if I was sure. Like I would lie!' Tom says, slamming his locker shut. 'Anyway, I said yes

I was one hundred per cent sure, and I didn't budge. So, yeah, it was tough.'

'Thanks, Tom. I can't imagine how tough,' I say wryly.

'You wouldn't believe it.' Then he catches on to my tone. 'Yeah, sorry, course you know. Then Mrs Greaves comes along and that's when it went from bad to shit-myself-terrible.' Tom's voice fades. He's fidgeting and I've got a nasty feeling rising up from my gut.

'So she started saying how she's noticed that I've been hanging out with you a lot.'

'Yeah? So what if we hang out?'

'And how you always kind of talk me into things. She said I had to stand up for myself and not let people tell me what to do.'

'What? She said I *make* you do things? Like how, like what? And why would I do that?' I'm shocked to my core.

'Because you're *controlling* – her words, not mine, Jeev,' Tom says hastily. 'She said you know how to persuade me, what buttons to press, and how you'll make sure I won't have any other friends unless I do as I'm told.'

'Fuck's sake! She's saying I'm a bully? Me, a bully?'

'And that wasn't the worst thing – Rawson backed her up. He told me to think very carefully about my future in the school. "Bullies are to be given no quarter here," he said. He's told me I have to go and see him tomorrow morning – after I've "given careful consideration to the whole matter".'

'What did you say to that?'

Tom shrugs. 'I told him I wasn't lying. I was telling the truth. No one put me up to anything. I told him the exam paper was in the folder and all I did was take it out and give it to you. I stuck to my guns. But he still wants to see me tomorrow.'

'He's playing the big bad wolf, Tom. It's all a load of bluster. Ignore it. Everyone knows I'm not like that. She's not going to get away with it. I'll sort it out, OK?'

'Who's going to believe any of us, though? I mean, Greaves is a teacher. We're done for.'

'Come on, Tom. It's going to be fine.'

'How?' Tom's looking really upset, not actually crying, but not far off. I need to help him to buck up.

'She might *think* she's above the law,' I tell him. 'But she's about to find out what happens to people who think that way.'

Tom doesn't seem reassured. I watch him head out of the gates to the bus stop. I check my watch. I've got some major thinking to do. But before that, I'm going to find out if my lip-reading was up to scratch.

CHAPTER 21

Even on the wildest of wintery days, when it was mind-numbingly cold and dark as night at half past four in the afternoon, the tangled, slippery path has never deterred me. I can run through it in less than two and half minutes if I sprint.

It feels wilder today. I haven't been down here in ages. I've been taking the bus to the next stop and skirting round the park and the woods along the street, which takes much longer. I don't ever have that sneaky cigarette any more. What was all that about anyway? Oh yeah, it was my stupid little rebellion – meaningless on so many levels.

A rebellion has to be *against* something; it has to be visible to whoever or whatever you're rebelling against, doesn't it? Or is it enough that *you* know you're rebelling, so whether anyone else knows doesn't really matter? The rebellion can be totally inside your own head, I suppose.

But just because you think you're a rebel doesn't make

you one, and what I'm thinking now is that having that one cigarette was, if I'm totally honest, a bit pathetic, a case of me being just another Rebel Without a Cause.

Well, I've got a cause now, a real one. I don't want it, and I don't need it. I'd much rather go back to when everything was simple – when having that one sneaky cigarette was the sum total of my rebelliousness.

But instead, here I am, shivering in the woods, hiding from plain sight, wondering whether my lip-reading skills, or lack thereof, have led me down this particular garden path. I'm waiting. I've been waiting half an hour now and I can no longer feel my fingers or toes. It's February, so at least it's not dark at this time. There's an occasional glimmer of sunshine, but the sun is hanging low in the sky, its watery light fading fast, and losing its battle against the incoming clouds. I'm losing my battle too. I keep telling myself that I'll be OK because I've got ammunition. But ammo is useless if you're not going to use it.

And then there they are.

They're heading my way again and I'm hit with a strong sense of déjà vu.

'Nicola, for God's sake, will you just listen to me?'

'I *have* been listening, Daniel, and if you could be bothered to listen to *me* then you would know that I totally disagree with you.'

'So you don't think you're being unfair to the boy?'

'No. I don't.'

'How can I make you see what you're doing?'

Greaves stops. 'Enough of him. It's been a long and trying day. I've had a lot to deal with. I don't think I can take any more.' Her eyes crinkle as though she's fighting tears.

'I'm sorry. I know it must have been hard, but—'

'No buts.' She tosses her hair over her shoulder, catching a strand, which she twists between her fingers. 'It's over. I can move on now. That's what I need help with. Will you help me?' And then she smiles up at Mr Green. 'We could go somewhere else. Find a nice cosy pub with an open fire and get a drink or two.'

Mr Green shakes his head, as though he just can't believe what she's like. He's got a lot to learn about her. 'This is important. The kid is sinking low and I hate to see it. He's a decent boy and he works damn hard. He looked utterly depressed today.'

Greaves's mouth twists into a grimace. 'Oh, he's depressed, is he? Poor little mite. Well, it's not enough simply to work hard, as you well know. If there's not a lot going on *up there*,' she points to her head, 'then no amount of work is going to get you the results. And, well, the boy's certainly not quite up to scratch, even if *he* seems to think he's Shakespeare reincarnated. Hardly surprising, I suppose. English isn't his first language, after all. I've tried my best with him, I really have, but he's become unmanageable, and now he's disrupting the rest of the class. As for Tom Picher, well, he's well and truly under that boy's thumb. I can't tell you how disappointed I am in Tom – he was one of my best students. He's changed, and not for the better I can tell you.'

'Of course English is Jeevan's first language!' Mr Green laughs. 'I think you're wrong about all of it. There's no harm in him, none at all, and I've told Rawson as much.'

Greaves's smile is scary. 'Oh, Daniel, that's what I love about you – you like to see the best in *all* the kids, but we all know that you are just a softie and perhaps a little too lenient with them, particularly with, you know, kids like Jeevan.'

'*My* teaching style is not what's under scrutiny here. I get results and that's all anyone's interested in.'

'Yes, you do, and no one can say that you don't try your best with all the kids. This particular problem is different and I would very much appreciate it if you didn't meddle in it. You know nothing about how that boy behaves in my class, you did not see how difficult – how threatening – he was.' Greaves's voice has gone all wobbly. She sniffs, as though she's crying.

Greaves has put on her little act again.

'He was coming at me with a wooden chair leg. I was terrified out of my wits – you should have seen his face.'

'He wasn't. He wouldn't do that. Your fear was all in your head.'

'*In my head?* The whole class saw what he did!'

'I know. I've spoken to some of the kids.'

He has? I had no idea. But Greaves doesn't give in.

'And today – even after his so-called apology, he was up to his tricks again, and if you hadn't come into the class when you did, I don't know what would have happened.' She's bawling her eyes out now.

What? What tricks? I'm at a loss.

'Oh Nicola, please stop crying. You've got yourself all worked up about nothing.' Mr Green pats her arm sympathetically, but Greaves takes this as a sign of affection and pushes herself on to his chest. It's obvious he doesn't want to put his arms around her, so he steps back a little and continues to pat her shoulder.

The déjà vu is now at epic proportions.

'Nothing? What do you know? He's not like that with you. He's got a problem with me.'

I can see that Mr Green is having major problems trying to reconcile the Jeevan he knows in his History class with the Jeevan Greaves is talking about. So am I.

This is *exactly* what Dad has warned me about. Keep your head down, he said, and don't draw attention to yourself from those who don't need an excuse to behave unfairly towards you. And if you raise your head above the parapet, be prepared for the consequences. I should have paid more attention to Dad. I hate to admit it, but he knows what he's talking about.

'There are only a couple of months left before the exams. If you can't handle him then just move him to a different class.'

'And give him what he wants?' she says, with sheer disbelief. 'Why the bloody hell should I allow that? *I'm* the teacher – *I'm* in charge, not that Asian kid, with his jumped-up, know-it-all attitude! Who does he think he is? And as for his smug parents, lecturing me – who do they think they are?'

For the first time, her mask has slipped.

'For God's sake, Nicola, calm down.'

'Calm down? I'm not going to calm down! I'm telling you – you can't let those coloured kids win. Look at them all – acting like they bloody own the country!'

I'm truly and utterly gobsmacked. Stunned. If I couldn't feel the cold dampness seeping into my bones from hiding out here in the woods, I might think I'd taken a wrong turn and walked into a fascist rally or secret KKK meeting – they love to hang out in the woods too!

Mr Green's stunned too – he's staring at her with utter contempt. 'Listen to yourself. How can you believe that pile of shit? So Jeevan *was* right about you – as was that anonymous note.'

'And if I had got a look at that note, I would have known if it was your star pupil who'd written it! Devious little runt! Stand up for him if you feel you must, but I will most certainly be taking this further and making an official complaint against him.'

'What? Rawson told me that the suspension has been struck off the record now that the boy has apologized to you.'

'Call that an apology? It had to be *dragged* out of him.'

'What, so you think you've lost face? For God's sake, he's only fifteen years old.'

'He needs to be taught a lesson.'

'In what? Because he's Asian and doing well? Just like his parents? That bothers you, makes you uncomfortable? I get it now – you're trying to put them in their place?' Mr Green laughs, but it's a sardonic laugh, and he's shaking his head incredulously. 'I really didn't take you for that kind of person.'

'What kind of person would that be? The kind you can use and discard? Make promises to and then break them?'

'Oh for God's sake! It was just the once!'

'It was twice, actually, *and* you were going to leave your wife!'

'I wasn't! Your delusion just doesn't know any limits, does it? I'm sorry to have to say this, but this was a bloody big mistake,' he retorts, pulling no punches.

Greaves's hand flies to her mouth. 'How could you say that? You're so cruel!'

'I'm cruel?' Green says, incredulous. 'I say it because it's true.'

'But I meant more to you. I know I did.'

That woman is *seriously* off her head.

'Drop the act. You know what it was – a one-night stand, which you tried to prolong. I admit I was wrong to let it get that far and I'm sorry if it caused you any

185

distress, but that's the end. If you believe anything else then you seriously need help. I didn't ask you here for any other reason than to talk about why you're intent on destroying a kid I happen to care about.'

'That's a lie. You asked me here for one thing – just like last time.'

'You're delusional.'

'*I'm* delusional? I didn't expect this of you. But, then, I suppose I shouldn't have expected much. How *is* your wife now?'

'She's doing better, so just leave her out of this, all right?'

I detect a note of concern in Mr Green's voice. I reckon Greaves is not above a bit of blackmail herself, so he's right to be worried. She's perfectly capable of making his life a misery. I should know.

I can hear Mr Green's heavy sigh from here. 'I simply wanted to see if there was any way I could help you with Jeevan. Is there no way things can be smoothed over?'

I know why Mr Green's tone has become placatory – he's terrified Greaves is going to drag his wife into it. But judging by the look on Greaves's face, his belated attempt at damage limitation has come way too late.

'It has gone far beyond that, far beyond your control. I'm warning you now – back off! Or your wife may receive her own little note.'

OH MY GOD! Did she really say that?

'Nicola—'

'I *will* be making an official complaint in due course. The boy's parents may think that they've been oh-so-clever removing the suspension from his school record. Let them try and remove an expulsion.'

I swear she's almost gleeful.

'He's done nothing that warrants expulsion. Rawson won't do it, and if he tried, the boy's parents would fight it.'

'Let them try.'

I'm watching and listening and it feels like I'm in some kind of strange play about someone I don't know. It doesn't feel real.

Mr Green's face is rippling with repressed anger; it's like a bunch of snakes are fighting to get out and wrap themselves around Greaves, so that they can twist and trap all that nastiness inside her and squeeze it out of her pores. He clenches and unclenches his fists, visibly struggling to keep his cool. I don't know how he does it, but he does. 'You know, I was fond of you. I thought you were lonely and misunderstood. But I was mistaken, very much mistaken. Goodbye.'

He turns away, but she grabs hold of his arm. 'Daniel! Daniel! Wait! I'm so sorry, so sorry. It's the only thing I could think of doing.' Greaves is desperately clinging to his arm.

'For Christ's sake, let go of my arm, will you?' Green is trying to shake her off, but the limpet is firmly attached. Actually, she's more like a Rottweiler – once she's sunk her teeth into you, she ain't letting go. Mr Green's lucky she didn't go for the jugular, otherwise he'd be dead meat.

'You don't understand. Please, wait . . .'

He doesn't wait for her, but she goes chasing after him.

I head in the other direction, towards home. The play is over. Normally, there would be a round of applause right about now. The actors would come out for their curtain call, all smiles and bows.

But this is not a play. It's my life, and somehow it's taken a funny turn – funny peculiar, because there's definitely nothing to laugh about.

Expulsion. That's her aim.

She won't get away with it. Will she? She has a knack of making people believe her, of twisting the truth and making it work for her. Mr Green's spoken up for me, but it was Greaves's word that counted for Rawson.

Good job then that this jumped-up *coloured* kid remembered to press Record as soon as they started talking.

CHAPTER 22

I like to see the funny side of things, to have a laugh and treat things like a joke. But that's impossible when you know there's someone out there who hates you so much just because you're supposedly a *jumped-up Asian kid* that they're prepared to tell the worst lies about you. The more I try to stick up for myself, the worse it gets, and the worse *she* gets. She's like a cruise missile: target locked on and homing in. Is it too late for evasive action?

Unless I act soon, her campaign against me will carry on. Now it's reaching its conclusion. For her, that equals my expulsion. For me, well, I've got two ticking time bombs: one I've tried not to think about, and one that I need to think about.

Faced with someone who seems to think that I, and others like me, have no right to do well, what other course of action is open to me but to upload the vid and let the whole world know who she really is? Because it's definitely no longer just about me. It's about all the others, too.

Greaves has made me see that. I just want things to go back to normal. I want my old self back. You remember him, don't you? That Jeevan who's fun-loving, caring, thoughtful, studious, all-round nice guy, normal, a bit boring, a bit of a nerd. Hey, we can't all be perfect.

I want to be me again.

'Jeevan! Be careful!'

'Sorry, Maji.' I've managed to miss the cups and pour tea all over the worktop. I grab a cloth and mop up the spilled tea, but end up spreading it across a greater area.

'Here, give me the cloth. Let me do it,' Maji says, bustling around me. 'Sit.' She puts the cups on the table and opens a packet of biscuits. 'Eat.'

'I'm not hungry, Maji.'

'Why? What's wrong with you?'

'Nothing. I'm fine.'

'So eat.'

I take a chocolate digestive and dunk it in my tea to appease her.

'All week you have been like this, Jeevan. No smiling. No chitchat. Tomorrow is Friday. Only one more day of school and then it is the weekend.'

School. It's like a tornado raging around me, howling and churning up the ground as it whips me up into its vortex. My foundations have been swept away. Maji is a tough cookie, but even she's struggling to hold on to me.

'Tonight I will be talking to your parents,' Maji continues. 'No more of this grounding nonsense. It is making you too sad, and I do not like to see my Jeevan so sad.' She ruffles my hair. 'You're a good boy, Jeevan. Do not worry about this thing at school. All will be well. And so many As in your report – you make us so proud, like Shanti.'

And my grandma, as usual, is the first to have my back. 'Thanks, Maji.' I give her a hug before I head to my room.

So many As. And the blip – the C.

I wish I didn't care. I wish I wasn't so obsessive about it. But wishing for things doesn't make them come true.

I have unwritten essays piling up, Maths, Latin, Biology and Physics homework to tackle, but I'm too distracted to concentrate. The threat of expulsion I overheard Greaves make has been hanging over me all week, dragging me down. I don't know when she'll launch her next attack, what pretext she'll use to bring me down. She said she's going to do it soon, which might mean tomorrow. I'll have to take a sickie just to miss double English. It means I'll miss several other lessons that I can't afford to miss. My other teachers will start getting pissed off with me. I'm going to start falling behind. It's all too much. How am I going to ace my exams with all this shit going on?

Someone knocks on my bedroom door.

'Yeah?' I call.

The door opens and Sandi strides in, grinning at me.

'Hey, bruv,' he says. 'Thought you might like company.'

Fifteen minutes later, there's another knock, and this time it's Dread. 'What's up?' he says, coming in with a bag of chin-chin, deep-fried sweet Nigerian morsels of lethalness, which he throws in Sandi's direction while parking himself on my bed.

'Oh, man, my favourite!' Sandi beams.

'They'll make you fat,' Dread says. 'I keep telling Mum not to make them, but you know my mum. She thinks I'm skin and bone.' He shakes his head in despair.

Dread is tall and slim in a toned-muscled way despite the fact that he's not a gym buff and has never been near a set of dumb-bells in his life. I guess it's in his genes, like his speed in the hundred metres. There's a super-sprinting gene – Colin Jackson discovered he had it – that some people including West Africans and West Indians have, which is why the line-up for the hundred-metre sprint at the Olympics does not in any way resemble the hundred-metre sprint at our school sports day. So Dread always wins it.

'What's new, Jeev? You given up talking this week?' Dread asks. He never beats about the bush. I wish he would sometimes.

'Nothing much. How's Amelia?' I ask. I'd like to ask him about Ree too – yeah, I know she doesn't seem to get me and she winds me up the wrong way, but I kind of like her, I think. I stay quiet, though. It would raise too many flags with Dread and Sandi, and that would *not* be a good thing. Unless I was serious. Which I'm not. OK, OK, I'll shut up about her now.

'She's good. Haven't seen her since last weekend, but she said she's sorry about all the shit going down for you.'

'Yeah, her and me both. Why haven't you seen her? Thought you two were joined at the hip now.'

Dread looks away. 'Trouble at home. Not mine,' he adds quickly. 'We were over at her place and her parents came back early – we were just listening to music. They were a bit surprised to see me there.' Dread shrugs. 'For some reason, Amelia hadn't got around to telling her parents about me.'

'What, so they told her to dump you? So she *dumped* you?' Sandi asks through a mouthful of chin-chin.

'Don't be stupid. She hasn't dumped me.'

'But how can she *forget* to tell her parents about you? Oh, did *you* get angry with her and dump her?'

'No, Sandi, I haven't dumped her.'

'So, what's the problem?'

'Man, you don't give up, do you?'

Sandi grins. 'That's me. So what's the script then?'

'There is no script.' Dread holds up his hand to stop Sandi persisting with the never-ending stream of questions. 'OK, just to shut you up, I'll tell you. Ever since they found out about me, they've been inviting me over *all the time*. Every family lunch, every family outing to the theatre or cinema – you name it! Me and Amelia ain't got no time to ourselves. We can't breathe. They're suffocating us! So we're keeping a low profile for now. OK, Sand? Heard enough?'

'OK, jeez, I was only asking!'

'Now back to you, Jeev, and your sorry problems. What's going on? You ain't looking green with hollowed-out eyes for no reason.'

I told you Dread doesn't miss a trick. So I tell them about my new recording and what I've caught Greaves saying. They're not going to believe it.

Sandi can't utter a word for a full two minutes. 'She really said that?' he finally asks.

I nod. 'I was right about her all along.' I try to resist saying I told you so, but not very hard. 'Told you so!'

I know, I know, that was childish and pathetic, but it was also deeply satisfying.

'OK, OK, for once you were right and I was wrong. But I'm just gonna remind you that you had no proof before,' Dread says.

'You did record it, didn't you?' Sandi asks.

I allow a smile to rise to my lips. 'You better believe it!'

They cheer and we all high-five.

'So, are you gonna play the recording, or what?' Sandi says impatiently.

I access the file on my laptop, check the bedroom door is firmly shut, and hit Play. I haven't watched it again since I recorded it.

'Man, you were so right about her,' Dread mutters as we're watching it.

'*Can't let the coloured kids win?*' Sandi shouts out as soon as the recording ends. I have never seen him this angry.

'Keep it down!' I hiss. The last thing I need is my gran walking in.

He drops his voice. 'She actually bloody says that! You can't let her get away with this. Budge, Jeevan, let me upload it to YouTube right now!'

'Calm down, Sandi,' Dread says. 'We need to think this through.'

'What's to think through? When Rawson sees it, he'll know exactly what Greaves has been up to,' Sandi says. 'You've got all the ammo you need.'

'God, Sandi, don't you get it? I don't want to drop Mr Green in it.'

'And now that Greaves has threatened Green, it adds all sorts of complications,' Dread says. 'Man, oh man . . .'

'Look, Mr Green's a big boy and he'll have to look out for himself. You,' Sandi says, jabbing his finger at me, 'are going to get EXPELLED if you don't use the recording! Get it?'

'You think I don't know that?' I sit down on my bed, my head sinking into my hands. 'I don't know what to do any more.'

'It's obvious what you should do—' Sandi starts.

Dread cuts him off. 'Jeev, we've got this. OK? Don't stress it.' He turns to Sandi. 'Let's get this over to your mate Davy, and see how he's divided up the other one. He can do the same with this one.' Dread turns back to me. 'Like it or not, it might be time to drop a bomb.'

CHAPTER 23

If it were that easy to drop a bomb, wouldn't bombs be dropped more often?

Yeah, OK, I know, bombs are dropped almost every day – but only in war zones. Most of them we don't even get to hear about.

I'm not trying to make a comparison between life here and life in a war zone – that would be impossible, and stupid. Everything's relative to your own experience. Shit goes down here too, but on a different scale.

I know my life's been normal. I'm not poor, or disabled, or challenged in any way. My life's not especially tough or full of hardship. I've had it easy, I know that. I could have been born into a family in a war zone, but I wasn't. I've been lucky. For me and my mates, colour, nationality, religion – all those things that can get people so excited – were never an issue. And, until now, I've not given much thought to racism, because I thought discrimination was something that happened to other people. Not to me.

But it's happened to me now and I'm struggling to understand it. To understand Greaves and the sheer hatred she feels for me. Why is she like that? What makes her hate me so much? Is it really simply the colour of my skin that's so disturbing? Does she really believe that it's impossible that we could be similar in so many ways?

And even if we weren't similar, would that be such a big deal?

Someone shake me. Please. Fling a bucket of water at me, throw off the bedclothes, ring a bell next to my ear, anything. Just please wake me up and get me the hell out of this nightmare.

But there's no one here. It's midnight. Sandi and Dread went home hours ago. Maji goes to bed at half past nine like clockwork. Mum and Dad are fast asleep – they're on the early shift tomorrow, so they'll be getting up at three.

It's just me.

I boot up my laptop and slip my Beats over my head. I've almost forgotten where I've buried the bomb – sorry, the two bombs. I hit Play, and watch the first one, trying to work out where Davy could have spliced it. How much of Mr Green has he managed to edit out? Was it even possible to do that? There's *a lot* of Mr Green – some of it's OK, some of it's a bit iffy, and some of it's just plain bad.

Collateral damage. That's what Dread called it. 'It's

just too bad, Jeev. You gotta look out for yourself now.'

I'm still struggling with it. I've been struggling with it ever since I recorded the damn things. But much more so now. Back to all those bombs being dropped in war zones – there are innocent people being killed all the time. Collateral damage has become acceptable because shit happens in war. The bomb-droppers say it wasn't their fault, and when it's proven without doubt that it was their fault, they're forced into apologizing and justifying their actions. But by the time that happens, people have already moved on. And the dead remain dead and, over time, they are forgotten too.

But I can't do that. I won't let Mr Green become collateral damage.

So my conversations with myself for the last few hours have gone something like this:

You have no choice.

There's always a choice.

She's taken that choice away from you.

Then take it right back.

It's wrong and you know it.

There's wrong and there's an even worse wrong.

That still doesn't make it right.

But it doesn't make it your fault either.

It's my fault if I use it.

It's your get-out-of-jail card. Anyone in your position would use it.

Not everyone. I'm not everyone.

Get a grip, man – you're about to be expelled!

They won't expel me. They can't.

Yes, they can, and they damn well will.

My mum and dad won't let it happen.

They might not be able to win this one.

But I haven't even been that bad.

According to her, you have.

But everyone else knows the truth.

Yes, but she's the master of spin.

Even spin-doctors get caught out.

Not this spider.

Mr Green will back me up.

He would, except he's already caught in her web.

But he won't let me go down.

She has him by the short and curlies.

There are other teachers who'll back me up.

Can you see them lining up?

They can't all believe her.

Told you, she's the grandmaster of spin. You'll be out on your ear.

And that's what it comes down to – her threat. Was it idle? Was it just to get Mr Green's back up? Was it just her wishful thinking? Can she talk Rawson into agreeing to it? Will Mum and Dad be able to fight it, appeal it, fix it like they fix their patients? They're good at fixing people. Is this fixable?

Will they believe me when I tell them that none of it was my fault? I was never disruptive, belligerent or threatening – I've never owned those kinds of adjectives. They've never belonged to me.

You see the nightmare I'm stuck in?

Show me a way out, someone, please.

CHAPTER 24

The first thing I do when I get up is groan. You know that expression, 'like death warmed up'? Well, let me tell you – the expression is all wrong. I feel like death, but there's nothing warmed up about it. I'm cold, shivering and shaking, and weak. It can't be just down to the meagre three hours of sleep I scrounged out of the eight I need to fully recharge my batteries.

I crawl feebly down the stairs and unplug my phone from the charger, wondering which one of my parents to text. Mum is bound to come over all mumsy – she'll want to analyse all my symptoms and suggest various remedies, but Dad will just tell me to buck up and get to school and see how it goes, and if I really don't feel well later then I should go and see the nurse and if she thinks I should go home then and only then should I head back home.

Needless to say, I pick Mum to text.

Not feeling well, Mum. Threw up this morning. Think I

might have a tummy bug. Don't worry – I'll catch up on all
the schoolwork I miss. Drinking gallons of peppermint tea
and reading my History notes. See you later xx

Mum texts back immediately, asking if I need her to come home. She says she can be back in an hour if it's an emergency, and do I have any stomach cramps? And then she goes into a set of detailed questions about the state of my bowels, which doesn't need repeating. I respond with a definitive *no* to everything. But I do say that I'll let her know how I am by lunchtime. I add kisses to each text because I know she likes that.

Maji's already left – she's doing a morning at the *gurdwara*, the Sikh temple today. The daughter of a friend of hers has had a baby boy, so there's a scripture reading at the *gurdwara* that will go on for the next twenty-four hours. Lots of people will be in and out of the temple, which means a ton of food will need cooking. We're not Sikhs, but that doesn't matter at all to Maji. Service to God and people is what it's all about for her. So my gran will roll up her sleeves and muck in – or, knowing Maji, she'll be making sure that everything is cooked to her exacting specifications. She also has a very sweet tooth, so she'll make sure there's plenty of sugar and butter in the *prasad*, the blessed food that we all get a handful of, despite her diabetes and cholesterol!

So I have the whole day to myself. Someone, probably Mum, has taken away my controllers for the PS3, which shows you how much my parents trust me not to play

FIFA while the grounding is still in effect. Well, I guess they were proved right as I've just switched the box on! I switch it off again.

Without Maji at home, the house is dead quiet. She usually either has the TV on at full volume – she loves daytime TV – or has the radio tuned to her favourite Indian channel which plays ancient Bollywood songs on a permanent loop, interrupted only by adverts for Sari, Sari, where you can find spring collection saris, 'direct from India, fashionable and affordable; or three-for-two offers on all the lentils and beans at Mangala's Cash and Carry; or Hurry to the Sweet Mart for the best in indulgence. Go on – treat your loved ones today!'

I don't know what to do with myself now that there's no one here checking up on me, and not having to pretend I'm ill only makes it worse. I'm kicking my heels around, doing nothing, completely unfocussed despite the fact that I have a ton of homework to get through before Monday morning.

I eat another round of toast before I tackle some homework. An hour and a half later, with two pieces of homework done, I'm drifting again, so I head back to the kitchen for lunch. There's cheese in the fridge, so I make some sandwiches and sit in front of the telly to eat them. I've just finished and put my plate in the dishwasher when the front door opens and Mum comes rushing in.

'So how do you feel?' she asks, placing her hand on

my forehead and checking my temperature before she's even taken her coat off.

'Much better, Mum. I told you I'd text you if I felt any worse.'

'I know what you're like, Jeevan. You would have said you felt fine even if you were much worse.'

'No, I wouldn't. It's only a tummy bug and I feel tons better already.'

'Well enough to go to school? I can drop you off if you like,' Mum says, calling my bluff.

'Yeah, but by the time I get dressed and we get out and drive to school, there'll only be one lesson left and then it'll be time to come home. Is it worth it?'

Mum gives me a look. 'It depends – is it English Lit?'

I go for honesty. 'Yes.'

'Then, no. It's not worth it.' I love my mum. 'I was finishing early today anyway. Your grandmother asked me to show my face at the temple for a couple of hours, so I promised her I would try. Your dad's meeting us there later. Would you like to come with me?'

My turn to give her a look. 'I'm grounded, remember?'

She smiles. 'Oh yes, so you are, but I don't think the grounding includes visiting the *gurdwara*. Sandip's family are sure to be going there later too.'

I see where she's going with this, and I like her style. I rarely go to the temple, any temple, if I can wriggle out of it. Maji is always desperate for me to show my face every so often at the Hindu temple, but even she doesn't

205

count once a year as *occasional*. She sighs and tuts her disapproval every time I say no to a temple visit. She'll be beaming if I show up today – even if it is at the Sikh temple, and if Sandi is there then at least I'll get as many brownie points as he's bound to get from her.

'If I get another homework out of the way, and still feel OK, then yes.'

'I'll give you an hour and then we'll leave.'

Which means that by the time we get there, it won't be too long before Sandi arrives. An unexpected silver lining to the day.

'Oh, please, Aunty, let Jeevan come back to ours for a while,' Sandi says, employing his best pleading voice.

We've been here almost an hour and a half, shown our faces and made all the oldies happy, especially Maji, who loves showing me off, her favourite grandson. I'm banking on Mum and Dad not wanting to bring up the suspension and the grounding in public, and as this special request hasn't come from me, it might just work.

'Well, it's just that he hasn't been feeling well today, Sandi,' Mum says. She strokes my hair. 'Which is why he couldn't go to school. I think it's better if he goes home and rests.'

Damn. Mum's way too good at this.

'But he looks fine now. Doesn't he, Maji?' Sandi says, turning towards my gran. Sandi's pretty good at this game too.

'You were not well today, Jeevan? Oh my poor boy, why? What is the matter?' Maji asks, concerned. 'Sonia, you should have let him stay at home instead of bringing him here.'

'Oh, I'm fine now, Maji,' I reassure her.

'If you are sure you are all right, *beta*, then go with Sandi. His father will bring you home later,' Maji says.

Mum's been outmanoeuvred, and she's not happy about it at all. She smiles at Maji then at me, but I can tell it's forced. 'Be sure to ring us, Jeevan, and one of us will come and fetch you.'

I could hug my gran, and I do before setting off with Sandi's family.

Back at his house, it's not long before everyone's busy and paying us no attention.

'Time we made our move,' Sandi says.

I follow him out and we head next door to the flat above the shop where Davy the techie lives.

Missing English Lit today means I have twenty-three Greaves-hours to get through before we're on study leave before the exams. Twenty-three hours to avoid expulsion and a nuclear explosion.

But first things first – I need to make sure my ticking time bomb is ticking properly.

CHAPTER 25

Davy's in a pair of ripped jeans and a crumpled T-shirt. His hair is dishevelled, and he probably should have shaved the week before last. He looks like he just crawled out of bed, but I'm guessing that he hasn't as it's about half past five. He yawns and rubs his eyes. Maybe he *has* just woken up.

'Hey, guys. Come on in. Excuse the mess,' he says, gesturing at the heap of clothes in the corner of the room, the mugs of half-drunk coffee and empty packets of biscuits and crisps littering the coffee table, the desk and the bookshelves.

So this is what a student pad looks like, or rather this is what it looks like if you have your own place and you're in your third year at uni. My sister Shanti rooms in her college at Oxford, and it's *nothing* like this. Yeah, I know she's a girl, but she's also super-obsessive about tidiness and cleanliness. If Dread ever tried dusting for prints in her room, he probably wouldn't find a single one. At the most, he'd get a couple of partial prints, and not a single strand of hair either. Her room's cleaner than an operating theatre in a hospital.

I suppose I'm somewhere in between Shanti and Davy – I'm definitely not obsessive but I'm not a complete slob either. Mind you, it might be different if I didn't have Maji and Mum on my case about keeping my room tidy.

'Mum said to pop in later for dinner if you're not doing anything. She's cooked way too much again,' Sandi tells Davy.

'Himani's coming over later – OK if she comes too?'

'Yeah, Mum meant the both of you,' Sandi says. 'She still can't get her head around the fact that Himani can't cook.'

Davy grins. 'So *that's* why she always goes into all that detail about how she's cooked every dish.'

Davy is so distantly related to Sandi that neither of them really knows how, but when Sandi's dad found out that Davy's shared flat fell through in town, he offered him the flat above the shop at a discount. Himani, Davy's girlfriend, lives in a shared house with a bunch of girls, but she spends a lot of her time in Davy's flat.

'OK, let me just get my laptop,' Davy tells us. He heads off to the bedroom.

I perch on the sofa, but Sandi grabs the bin from the corner of the room and starts clearing the debris off the coffee table, so I get up and take the mugs through to the kitchenette. I open the fridge out of idle curiosity. There's half a pint of milk, a slab of cheese, some tomatoes, a couple of eggs and a solitary potato. Not much cooking happens here, which is no surprise when food is always on tap at Sandi's next door.

Davy returns with the laptop and we sit on either side of him on the sofa. 'Right, it's loading up,' he says. 'This is the original. Do you want to see it again? No? Good. I've cut it into three sections.'

My heart is in my mouth now. I'm not sure why I'm feeling so nervous. Maybe it's because I never intended to use the damn thing – or even show it to other people. Mr Green's a generally good guy, so for people to see this and laugh at him and ridicule him makes me feel bad. I'm even feeling uncomfortable about Greaves being compromised.

When Davy clicks on his YouTube link my stomach almost falls out on to the floor.

'I thought – you haven't – I mean, Jesus, have you loaded it on to YouTube already?' I say, panicking.

'Take it easy, Jeev. It's on private view. I haven't published it. Look, are you sure you're OK with this?'

I shake my head. No, I'm not OK with it, not any of it. I stand up and pace round the room. I want out of the whole sordid thing. Why did I record it? What came over me? Did I know then that I'd need some kind of ammunition against Greaves? No, I didn't. I knew she hated me; she's always had it in for me, always marked me down, always scoffed at my essays and ridiculed my answers in class. But I had no idea about the *depth* of her hatred.

This can't be about revenge, though. I don't want revenge. I just want things to be normal, the way they are with all the other teachers in school. You know, they teach you, you learn, you do your homework, you contribute in class, if you can, and if you can't then you don't.

'Jeev, you OK, man?' Sandi asks.

'No. Yeah, I think so. I'm not sure. I've watched the whole thing through loads of times and I just can't see how it can be cut up to keep Mr Green out of it. I mean, it's totally impossible, isn't it? He's in the whole thing, for God's sake! With her! If it was anyone else . . .'

Davy pats the sofa next to him. 'Chill, Jeevan. I'll talk you through it all first, OK?' He turns the sound off on his laptop and angles the screen away from me. 'And then I'll play them out loud – if you want. If you're not happy with the way they are then I'll give it another go.'

Davy turns the screen so I can see it too. 'OK, so I've chopped it into three sections in case you want to upload just one or two sections like the sex bit. That's the one that's going to get you all the hits on YouTube. I've pixellated and blurred his face, which wasn't that easy as he moves around a bit. But don't panic. There's some brilliant software out there now, and I reckon I've done a pretty good job.'

I'm nodding. It sounds like it might be OK – if it's shaming Greaves that I'm after.

'Right. The first bit is very interesting with that anonymous note stuff. Your Mrs Greaves, she's something else, dude, the way she's got Green wrapped around her little finger – the dumb-ass falls for her act hook, line and sinker! "I love the kids, and I love my job. It's all I ever wanted. It's all I know, Daniel,"' Davy says, in a high falsetto dripping with fake sincerity.

He doesn't do a bad job of imitating Greaves's voice. 'It might be obvious to us – but will it be obvious to other people? Like the Head? I don't know,' I mutter.

'Of course it is!' Sandi says.

'I'm not so sure.'

Davy has done a good job. Mr Green's face is well and truly blurred. There's only one problem. Well, two, actually. The first is that if you know Mr Green you'd probably be able to identify him from his body – even though he's not wearing one of his usual sharp suits but a fleece and old jeans. The second is related to the first: even if you might not be able to tell the identity of the man from his clothes and the way he looks, you would definitely recognize the voice as belonging to Mr Green. 'Can you disguise his voice?' I ask.

'Anything is possible, mate,' he says. 'Now the next bit is the sex scene. It's pretty short. They're still talking as they head closer to where you're hiding. It's obvious that she's seriously got the hots for him cos she's practically *dragging* him along.'

'Yeah, she may be dragging him but he goes with her, doesn't he?' I say.

'That was his choice,' Sandi says. 'You didn't make him go with her. He could have said no.'

'He didn't know I was hiding behind that holly bush,' I point out, 'with a camera recording his every move.'

'It's a park, a public place! And what they're doing is just so wrong. They're teachers! They should have known to get a room. I mean, why take that kind of risk? It's mad,' Sandi says.

'Maybe he thought nothing would happen if they met in a public place. Anyway, the second clip is basically them at it,' Davy says. 'There's a lot of moaning going on – it's all the lady teacher, your Mr Green is pretty silent. You kept the camera off him mainly, although you do catch a glimpse of his face now and then. But there's no mistaking her. She's very clear.'

'And the third clip?'

'You've got Mr Green lighting up a cigarette. Greaves tells him off for breaking his promise to her and for smoking. He tells her not to worry because the cat sure ain't gonna complain. He's a funny guy, your Mr Green,' Davy says.

'He's got his moments,' I reply.

'Then it's all the personal stuff – about his wife, and it ends with him saying he'll back her up.'

'Forget about that – we've got something even better

now – and this stuff is red hot!' Sandi says.

'Don't tell me you've caught the Headmaster having sex in the woods now?' Davy says. 'Man, do you hang out in the woods just in case you catch some dogging action?'

I scowl at him.

'Show him, Jeev,' says Sandi.

I take the memory stick out and pass it to Davy. 'Just take a look.'

Davy plugs it into his laptop and presses Play. He's shaking his head all the way through it. 'Jesus, what the hell is she doing here in England? She needs to get herself over to one of those Deep South states in the USA – there's plenty still like her over there. She'd fit right in.'

'Can you edit Green out of this one?' I ask him.

'Jeevan, if you're going to make a habit of catching people on candid camera, do me a favour and get yourself a decent camera, will you? He's in every shot. Even when she's doing her KKK impression, you zoom in on Green's face to get his reaction. And then you got her threatening him, but you're focussing on his face again.'

'It doesn't matter,' Sandi says. 'When she goes on about coloured kids and not giving in to them? That's the bit we need to post on YouTube!' he says excitedly. 'We should do it now – it's got all the incriminating stuff that proves she's had it in for you since the beginning.

We could even splice it together with one of the clips from the first video when Greaves says that Rawson wasn't overly concerned about the allegations in the anonymous note. Even Rawson doesn't come off that well, remember? Man, he's going to regret saying that to Greaves.'

'I remember,' I say. I can actually remember all of it, every single word, every single expression and every single action. It's imprinted in my memory with indelible ink; even Tipp-Ex couldn't paint over the ugly marks it's left on my mind.

'We can publish that one clip by itself to start with, can't we, Davy, now that it's all divided up?' Sandi asks.

'We can. As I said, everything is possible. I'll need a bit of time to work on the second video, though. But I still reckon the first one is the one you want out there. That's the one with real shock value.'

'Mr Green would be in it up to his knees if that one went viral, which it will if we post it on YouTube and add links to it on Twitter, Instagram and Facebook,' Sandi says.

'But you can't really tell it's him,' Davy says.

'But it's still got his voice,' says Sandi.

'Sandi, shut up for a minute, will you?' I say in exasperation. 'Sorry, dude, but I need to think.' My hands have been getting clammier and clammier, which oddly enough is what happens when you get cold feet.

'What do you want to do?' asks Davy.

CHAPTER 26

It feels like a loaded question, but it's not.

In all honesty, I don't know what I want to do.

'How would you divide the second video up?' I ask Davy.

He shrugs. 'To me, it's best kept whole. It's simple, yet powerful, and it's got way more impact. It packs a killer right-hook. So I'd hate to mess with it. You'd lose context. With the first video – then it has to be the sex scene that is uploaded. Green doesn't come out of it that badly, if you ask me.'

It sounds like Davy has forgotten that this isn't one of his assignments for uni that we're talking about, but my life – and the lives of two teachers.

I swallow hard. This is the moment of no return, I think. The moment it's all been leading up to. To press Publish, or not to press Publish: that is the question.

Davy and Sandi are looking at me, waiting for an answer. I wish Dread was here to run through all the final pros and cons with me one last time, but he's not. It's down to me. What would he say if he were here? The last time we talked about this he was all for me seeing what Davy had done to the video with a view to posting it on YouTube. What would he say now?

I don't know. It shouldn't matter, but it does.

In the final analysis, taking everything into consideration, would he say that it's just plain wrong? I know I'm justified because *she* started it – she wronged me, big time.

I can almost hear Dread's voice.

'A wrong is a wrong when you *know* it's wrong. And you know this is wrong, Jeevan. Doesn't make it a right just cos you think you're justified.'

'But doing nothing when I know someone's doing all these wrongs to kids like me makes me just as guilty, doesn't it?'

'But doing something wrong to get revenge for the other person's wrong – well, that makes you just as guilty.'

'But I'm justified.'

'OK, so justify the justification, cos you know what? Anyone can use that line to justify anything. Ask Mr Green – he knows all about History. He'll tell you how many people have justified what they've done even when they knew it was dead wrong.'

OK, shut up now, Dread-in-my-head! I don't need to hear your voice of reason, because you're not the one with the threat of expulsion looming over you. That would be me. I take a seriously deep breath before I say the words I've been fighting almost since I pressed the Record button. 'What the hell, publish it.'

'Seriously?' Sandi asks. 'Just like that?'

'What do you mean? You're the one who keeps telling me to stick them up on YouTube. All I've been doing 24/7 is agonizing over those stupid bloody videos. They're my last resort. They might be the only things that'll save my skinny brown arse. So NO, it's not *just like that*!'

Sandi puts his hands up. 'Chill! I just didn't think you'd go through with it in the end.'

My head sinks into my hands. Sandi has me all confused. When I said I didn't want to use it, he said use it, and when I give the green light to it, he says no.

Davy gets me, though. 'Look, the other teacher in the video, the bloke, Mr Green, you're worried about him. Right?'

'Yes. Last thing I want to do is land him in it. He's done me no harm, he even tried to stick up for me. So even though you've blurred his face, it's still too obvious it's him, and no one else has a voice like that.'

'OK. I'll make his voice totally unrecognizable. What I can also try to do is blur more of his body, not just his face,' Davy says.

I'm nodding. 'Yeah, that would be good. Can you see what you can do with the second video too?'

'Yeah, sure. It'll be harder to edit the guy out of it, but I'll give it a go.'

'Cheers, Davy. I'll give you my number. Call me when it's done. The sooner the better though, cos I'm getting kind of desperate.'

'Understood.'

And that's where we leave it, for now.

I call Dread as soon as I get home.

'Dude, I'm busy. Leave me your thoughts,' his recorded voice message tells me. I guess he's out with Amelia. So I leave him my thoughts, and within a minute he's called me back.

'So you were too sick for school, but you went over to Sandi's and watched the videos?'

'I wasn't sick, Dread. Well, I *was* sick – sick of Greaves's double English lesson, what she'll say, how she'll goad me, have a go at me, try to provoke me. And what she might accuse me of if I just *breathe* the wrong way.'

'Man, I feel your pain. It's not right,' Dread says distractedly.

'I'm this close to getting expelled.'

'Nah, that won't happen. We'll make sure everyone gets wind of what's been going on, so she won't be able to get away with it. We've got your back, Jeev.'

'She'll find a way. Trust me.'

'Mate, don't take this the wrong way, but I can't talk about it now. I'm out.'

'With Amelia?'

'Yup, and Ree. I filled her in on what's going down

with you and Mrs Greaves, and she gets it now. Don't stress, she's safe, OK. Look, we're going into the cinema to watch this Moroccan movie that's just won loads of awards. I'll come by tomorrow, OK?'

'Yeah, sure. Thanks, Dread. Enjoy.' What's the betting they're the only teenagers in the whole of the UK watching a Moroccan film? And Ree's with them? Maybe she was interested because she went to Casablanca at Christmas. I would have gone with them – if they'd asked me. I watch Indian films with Maji. They're subtitled, thank God, otherwise I'd only understand every few words. My Hindi sucks. Maji blames my parents for not teaching me when I was younger. Their argument is that they had no time and as long as I can get by in Punjabi, what's the big deal?

But that's not what I'm really thinking about. It's Dread's words 'she gets it now' that take up more of my head space and, for some reason, I'm wondering how Maji will take the pink/purple hair.

Which makes me do a double take.

I must be thinking of asking Ree over. Maybe I will. Or maybe I'll engineer for it to happen by letting Dread know it's OK for Amelia to ask Ree over when they come to mine next – you know, just so it's not obvious that I kind of like her. That would be easier and more likely to happen, because let's face it, I'm not going to ask her out, am I? Why would I risk the rejection?

I can't think about Ree. I'm stressed enough.

Music, that's what I need, while I play catch-up with my homework. Then I find a book to read. One of the reasons I love English Lit – correction, used to love English Lit – is because I'm a book geek. Reading's my third favourite hobby after *FIFA* and playing actual football. I play for the school team; well, I'm only in the seconds but football is football whether you're in the Championship or the Premier League. Back to books: they're why English Lit is, sorry, was, my favourite subject at school. That's a bit of an admission, but we all know I don't always do the cool thing. I'm not a pack animal, more of a lone wolf.

OK, maybe not quite such a lone wolf. Dread is a reader too, but he'll read anything and everything he can lay his hands on: non-fiction, fiction, newspapers, blogs, magazines – anything that's lying around anywhere within reach. I've even seen him glancing through the pile of junk mail sitting by my front door when he's been waiting for me. He read *Remains of the Day* in Year Eight, which he borrowed from my mum. My parents have stacks of books – I don't think they've ever got rid of a single book since they were kids – and Dread has read way more of them than I have. Our school library was recently renamed the Information Hub (that was one of Rawson's bright ideas), and books became more sidelined. I pity all those kids coming through the school now – they're going to miss out on so much, like the *Noughts and Crosses* series, which blew our minds.

I hope they make it into a film. If you can't read it then you need to watch it because it really makes you think. I wonder whether Greaves has read it. Maybe I'll give it to her as a leaving present when she gets me kicked out . . .

We've already filled in our options for what we want to do for A level next year. They're dependent on getting the right grades. My school requires at least a B in the subject you want to continue at A level, but we all know that the school prefers As (don't we all?), and because it's a grammar school and is selective, it can pretty much demand what it wants. It's all down to 'merit'. Supposedly. Every year there's an influx of new pupils into Year Twelve, and a smaller number of us are asked to leave, in other words we get chucked out, because we haven't got the grades, or because our teachers don't think we'll achieve enough of the right grades at A level. Well, they can't have us ruining the school's amazing stats in the league table.

I've a feeling that if Greaves doesn't manage to get me kicked out now, which is still moot, then she will do all she can to make sure I don't come back to the school for my A levels.

Sandi and Dread are staying on at the grammar. They'll get the grades easily; they're both doing sciences and the school has a brilliant science department.

I've got a few options: I could start looking for a new school or college to do my A levels in now, but most of them are miles away. It'll suck big time all round, not just for me but for my gran too. She's used to having me around, and she hates having to give herself her insulin shot.

Or I could wait and see what happens when I drop the bomb. Because if it isn't me who'll be leaving the school, it'll definitely be her.

Again, there are choices there too. Humiliate her, or out her as a racist? I know which one Davy wants to go with. Sandi doesn't care which one. Dread thinks the second video – and so do I. But I want to see what Davy can do about editing Green out of it.

The way I'm feeling right now, I'm tempted to go with the first video just out of spite. I'm not spiteful or vengeful generally, but these are exceptional circumstances, and exceptional circumstances call for an exceptional response. So for the greatest impact and the highest level of satisfaction in the bringing down of Greaves, it has to be the X-rated video.

There's only one small drawback. Despite what Davy says about being able to disguise Mr Green's voice, I'm sure everyone will still realize it's him. So it would drag Mr Green into the mess, which is not what I want to do.

So maybe we should go with the second video, which is just as good and actually better, because it shows Greaves for what she is without embarrassing Mr Green too much.

Choices, choices – they're giving me brain-ache.

There is a third option, I suppose: to do nothing.

CHAPTER 27

Maji's gone to bed, nine-thirty on the dot as usual, and Mum's out for dinner with some mums from school, leaving me and Dad chilling and watching TV.

Dread's mum picked my mum up in a taxi at half past seven. Mum will come back a little tipsy, although she always denies she's had more than two glasses of wine when she's been out. I think she's worried that coming home drunk is not quite the right example to set. Not that Dad has any problem with it.

Mum will also come home armed with such a long list of questions for me that it'll almost feel like an interrogation. She'll have tons of gossip, too. She'll know all about whose kid is going out with who, who's been in trouble, or who hasn't done one bit of work and did so badly in their mocks that they'd better pull their socks up. I swear the mums spend more time talking about us than anything else. Some night off.

The big story will be Dread and Amelia. Dread

hasn't introduced Amelia to his mum yet and, Dread told me, it's really rankling with her. Mum will have to own up to the fact that Amelia was actually over at our house with Dread. I can almost guess how the conversation went.

'So *you* met the girl? Can you believe it, I've never even seen the girl! Come on then, tell me what's she like,' Dread's mum will ask.

'She's very nice. Very polite,' Mum will reply vaguely.

'All I know is she goes to the girls' grammar. Dread has hardly told me anything about her – he's usually so open. I'm getting worried it's serious.'

'No, they're only fifteen!' Mum will reply.

'Dread turned sixteen the other day – and that boy has an opinion about everything – you know what he's like. Usually I can't shut him up. But he won't even *talk* about the girl, and when I ask him to tell her to come over for dinner, he shakes his head and all I get is, "Yeah, thanks, Mum, when she's not so busy." I mean, what does that girl do that she stays so busy? Everyone's got to eat sometime.'

So I'll definitely get asked about Amelia so Mum can give Dread's mum the lowdown. Except I won't be telling her much more than she already knows because, well, because it's Dread's business.

Mum is bound to tell all the mums about the meeting with Rawson and Greaves. I'm guessing that'll be the oh-my-God-gasp-out-loud-gossip of the night. I never thought that I, of all people, would end up being notorious enough for other people to gossip about. And I could end up becoming even more interesting if I get expelled. I don't go looking for the limelight, and now that the spotlights are on me, hot and glaring and blinding, all I want to do is shift them to something else, or better still to someone else. There is one easy way of doing that – except it's not that easy, which is why I'm seriously thinking of asking Davy to delete the first recording. That's the conclusion I'm coming to.

Davy told me that he would use an online proxy service through which he would join Facebook or Twitter or whatever, and create a new fake account and then upload the video anonymously. 'No one will know who's loaded it. It'll never come back to you,' he'd assured me.

But things have an odd way of coming back to you.

I go back to watching the TV. Dad's got a magazine open on his lap – a dense-looking medical journal called *The Lancet* or something, but it looks as though he's decided it's way too heavy for a Friday night. The ten o'clock news is on. I'm only half watching it. Brexit talk takes up the bulk of the news. There's a Leave campaign and a Remain campaign who are having a daily running battle to win supporters before the EU referendum on 23rd June. I'll have finished my last GCSE exam the day before. I'm dimly aware of another bombing somewhere in the Middle East where there's a real war going on. I catch the feel-good story at the end, which, I have to admit, is pretty amazing. Somewhere in East London a unicyclist managed to get himself stuck underneath a double-decker bus – I swear I'm not making it up. It's one of those facts that are stranger than fiction, which people only believe when there's proof in black and white or on camera in glorious Technicolor. A big crowd had gathered around the bus and somehow managed to lift the bus up so the cyclist trapped underneath could get out.

The whole of the ten o'clock news should be like that – can you imagine? Half an hour of feel-good stories about people helping other people, each story more heart-warming than the last as people outdo each other with acts of kindness. Only in the final two minutes of the news programme would we be reminded about how low human nature can sink.

It would be a different world if people were outdoing each other on the goodness scale.

But human nature doesn't seem to be like that because over the course of millions of years, or at least ever since we've had TV, the feel-good story remains a short story.

But we need those short stories because tales of death and destruction and war and famine are still very much the main events.

Oh God, I sound seriously down, don't I? Don't worry. I'm not depressed or suicidal or anything like that.

Although I have to say that I never used to understand how people could get so down when they seemed to have pretty normal lives. But look at me – from the outside, my life looks normal, but crack open the lid and you'll see the raging maelstrom in my head. And that's where everything goes down, inside your head, where no one else can see it.

My head feels like it's spinning round and round on my neck like that girl from *The Exorcist* who's possessed by the devil. I know I should go to bed but I'm nowhere near ready to sleep. Dad switches the channel over to a stand-up comedy show like he's read my mind and realizes that I need some laughter to lighten my mood. Well, he *is* a doctor.

'How easy do you think it would be for me to move to a different English class, Dad?' I ask him when the programme ends. Despite getting my fill of jokes from a couple of my favourite comedians for a whole hour, it's not been enough to distract me from my problems.

Dad looks at me, deliberating. 'It's not going well then, I take it?'

'No.' I don't elaborate.

I'm fully expecting him to launch into one of his you-must-try-harder pep talks. Instead, he simply says, 'Then I'll call the Headmaster on Monday and talk to him about it. Let's see what we can do.'

'Thanks, Dad. Think I'll head to bed now.'

Dad catches hold of my arm as I'm leaving the room.

'Sit down for a minute,' he says. I sit down beside him. 'I know you're trying.'

I don't reply.

'There was a time not so long ago when you would have made a little quip about that,' Dad says. 'You know *trying*, as in being . . .' His voice trails off. 'Never mind.'

'Yeah, I get it,' I say, giving him a lame smile. 'Sorry, Dad, it's late.'

'What if it is not possible for you to move class to a different teacher?'

I shrug. 'Then I guess I'll be stuck with Greaves until the end of term.'

'No, what I mean is that if there's not so much of the curriculum left to cover, and you think you can manage it without going to her lessons, then I might request that you go to the library instead.'

Now my head is seriously spinning. I hadn't even considered that option. 'That would work. That would definitely work. There's not that much left to do, and then we'll just do practice essays and look at past papers – I can source most of those online, and all the mark schemes too. I can easily manage, Dad, no problem. Will Mr Rawson allow it?'

'He may object in the first instance, but I'll phrase it in such a way that he'll have to think very carefully about it.'

'Thanks, Dad.' I give him a hug before heading up to my room.

God, thank you for my dad, I think, before I fall asleep.

The next morning, we're all at home. Dad's making breakfast for everyone, which means Mum definitely came home tipsy. She's sitting at the counter with a steaming mug of tea in one hand and a slice of toast slathered in raspberry jam in the other, looking slightly jaded.

'Morning, Jeev,' she says, setting her tea down and drawing me in for a hug. I give her a kiss on the cheek. 'How are you?'

'Good, thanks, Mum.'

'Dad was telling me you want to leave Mrs Greaves's lessons?'

'Yeah, if it's possible to move classes then that's great, but if I can't then I'll go to the library and finish the course myself.'

'I'm very concerned that you won't be taught the last bit of the curriculum properly.'

'Don't worry, Mum. I'll be fine. I've done most of it myself anyhow. Seriously, I won't be missing anything. Dread and Sandi are in Mr Parker's class, so I can always get their notes.'

Mum nods. 'OK. If you're sure.'

'I'm sure, Mum.'

'So, umm, Femi was telling me that she hasn't met Amelia yet. Why hasn't Dread introduced her to his mother?'

I knew it! Mum didn't even beat around the bush this time but went straight in with the interrogation. 'Dunno, Mum. Not my business.'

'But why? She's been over here.'

'I really don't know. And, anyway, you're not Dread's mum.'

'So it's serious?'

I sigh. 'No, it's not serious, not as far as I know.'

Mum's grinning at me. 'OK, OK, no more questions, I promise. Sit. Eat.'

Dad's cooked one of his mega fry-ups with sausages and bacon, eggs, mushrooms and tomatoes. There are even some veggie sausages for Maji, so she won't complain about being given just the tomatoes and mushrooms the way she complained at Christmas about just being given the vegetables. And no, we don't have a cat, but yes, we did have a Christmas tree at Christmas. It's called poetic licence, being creative, although I'm not sure Greaves appreciates my creativity.

But now we know that it very much depends on *who* is being creative.

I dig into my food, feeling properly hungry for the first time in ages.

It feels as though things might finally be looking up for me.

CHAPTER 28

Dread and Sandi are in my room the next afternoon, and I'm surprised that my parents haven't raised an eyebrow or made any sarcastic remarks about how well the grounding's been working out. I think they realize that these are exceptional times – that and the fact that Maji had a word with them.

'Why are you making my poor Jeevan suffer like this?' I overheard her saying to them. 'He is a good boy. You must stop this nonsense now. We must do something to help him. This is not his fault – someone has given him the evil eye. I will go to the *mundir* and ask *Panditji* to perform a special ceremony for him. He will break a coconut and get rid of these bad energies that are strangling my poor Jeevan.'

'I thought they broke the coconut to break false pride and ego,' Dad says. 'To reveal the pure person beneath,' he adds knowledgably.

'But isn't the coconut broken just to wish someone

good luck in their new house, or their exams? Like a blessing or something,' Mum counters.

I can just imagine Maji's despairing look at her son and daughter-in-law, and she uses the moment for a little dig too. 'Yes, yes, for all those things too. If you came to the *mundir* more regularly, you would know these things.'

I can almost see Mum and Dad rolling their eyes.

'The coconut is God's fruit. *Panditji* will break the coconut according to what one wants to ask of God from the ceremony,' Maji explains. 'It was very neglectful of me not to have done this for Jeevan before his exams. No matter. I will arrange it now . . .'

I'm not entirely clear whether the grounding has been withdrawn until further notice or just considerably relaxed. I told you my gran's got my back, didn't I? Although I'm not sure how breaking a coconut will help.

'So those are the choices. What do you think I should do, because I'm going round and round in circles like a demented dog trying to catch his own tail,' I tell Dread and Sandi.

'You look like one, too,' Sandi says.

'Thanks! I feel like I haven't slept in months.'

'Yeah, well, it's clearly addled your little brain,' Dread says. 'Wait and see what Davy's got for you. Looks like he might be able to work a little more magic on the sex video. But I still say, go for the one where she's being all racist. It's the one that'll grab Rawson's attention.'

'Yes, but it also lands Green in it. I focus in on his face way too much, too, especially when Greaves is going all KKK with her "coloured kids" spiel. Davy says it'll be really hard to edit him out and keep all that other stuff.'

'Don't listen to Dread, man – go for the X-rated one. That'll grab *everyone's* attention. It'll go viral in minutes, no, in seconds,' Sandi says. 'You've got to! Keep hold of the other one as backup.'

'Guys! You're doing my head in! I need to know which one? If any!' I say in frustration.

We go round and round it again until I've had enough. 'Right, that's it. No offence, Sandi, but I think I'm going with Dread on this one.'

'Your funeral,' Sandi says, shrugging. 'Don't come running to me when you end up on your arse outside the school gates.'

'Dad offered to talk to Rawson about moving me to an English class with a different teacher. And if Rawson agrees, then I might not have a problem.'

'I wouldn't bank on that happening, Jeev. The other classes clash with your options,' Dread pointed out. 'That's why me and Sandi don't have Greaves. There's only one other English Lit class you might get into – Mrs Stevens, but cos you do Spanish, I'm not sure.'

That reminds me – somehow I have to find a way to ask Dread where Ree's parents are from without raising any flags, no mean feat where Dread is concerned. His antennae would be on full alert. My money's on Spain or Latin America. Maybe I could ask Ree for help with Spanish conversation so that I'm ready for the oral. Or I could just ask her out without trying to use a ruse, as scary as that might be. What I actually need to do is get her out of my head, where she seems to be taking up a lot of room lately!

'Yeah, I thought so. Dad also said if I can't get moved then he's going to request a library pass for the rest of the term, so I don't have to go to Greaves's lessons.'

'Your *dad* suggested that?' Sandi says, shocked. 'Get out!'

'Yeah. I know! So I'm thinking we should ring Davy and tell him to forget about all the fine-tuning I've asked him to do cos it's a waste of his time.'

'No, wait. Let him do the changes, and let your dad meet Rawson, and then see,' Sandi says.

'I'm not going to use them, Sandi. They're too dangerous.'

'Not if they're done properly,' Sandi replies.

'Mistakes can still happen, bro,' Dread says.

A knock on the door shuts us all up. It's my gran with a plate piled high with treats.

Maji made *shakkapare* this morning. They're the Indian version of chin-chin. Both are as evil as each other on the deep-fried, sugar-coated front, and they're both really good in a bad, bad way. I know how she likes a secret taste of one or two with a cup of tea herself, despite the fact that it's probably the worst thing ever for her.

Sandi envelops her in a hug and tells her he wishes his grandmother could cook as well as her, which makes Maji beam happily and makes *me* roll my eyes. She puts her hand on his head, like she's giving him a blessing or something. 'You are very welcome, Sandip,' she says. 'I'll put some in a tub for you to take home.'

Dread's phone pings with a text message as my gran closes the door. Then it pings again, and again. He almost looks embarrassed, almost but not quite, as he reads his messages. He spends a couple of minutes composing his responses, then puts his phone away.

Sandi and I are looking at him expectantly.

'What?' he asks, raising his eyebrows.

'Amelia?' Sandi asks. 'Have you been back round her house again?'

'Yeah, it's all cool now. Think her parents realized they were cramping our style – after Amelia laid it out for them. Anyway, there's a party tonight if you're interested. One of her friends, big house up on the hill, no parents, but no one's allowed to put it up on Facebook or the house goes into lockdown. I think she's got some heavies on her front door just in case of gatecrashers. But Amelia said it was cool to ask you two.'

'Wish I could,' I mumble. 'I think I'm still grounded and I'm not going to tempt fate by asking my parents if I can go to a party. Besides, I think I need to sleep tonight.'

'We've got loads of family coming over for dinner, so

it's a no for me too,' Sandi says. 'But you and Amelia go and have fun,' he adds, 'and think of us stuck at home, bored out of our heads while you're out partying all night long.'

'Hang on a minute while I get my violin out,' Dread says, 'because you're making my heart bleed.'

My phone pings with a text message. Dread, who's sitting nearest my phone, picks it up and reads it.

'Hey, it might be private,' I say, trying to grab it.

'Jeev, you've got nothing to be private about.'

'Thanks a lot, Dread. Just because I don't have a girlfriend doesn't mean – oh forget it. Who's the text from?'

Dread looks up from the phone. 'Davy.'

'And?'

'You're not going to like it.'

'What do you mean? Give it here.'

Dread's shaking his head. 'All he says is *PUBLISHED*, like that in capitals.'

'What? No! I didn't say he could do that! Shit! Let me see.'

I grab the phone. True enough, all the text says is *PUBLISHED*.

I'm shocked. I was thinking it might take Davy a few more days to fine-tune the videos, get hold of the software to disguise Mr Green's voice. Then he was supposed to text me to come over and look at it before deciding what to do.

But no.

He's only gone and bloody put it out there without asking.

And now it's done.

'Jeev, you're going green. Breathing might be a good thing, dude,' Dread reminds me.

'Which video?' I manage to say.

'I'm hoping it's not the first one,' Dread says. 'No one needs to hear that woman moanin' and groanin'!'

Sandi's already accessing YouTube on my laptop. He's on the website now, searching for it. 'What's he called it? Do you remember?'

'No. I don't know. I can't remember,' I say, wracking my brain.

'Think!'

'I don't know!' I snap at him.

'He wouldn't use your name, would he?' Sandi asks, and then he answers his own question. 'No, of course not. That's too incriminating.'

'Davy knows her name, right? So try Greaves?' Dread suggests.

Sandi types it in. 'Yes! Got it! But I can't tell which video it is. It's hard to tell from that image.'

His finger is hovering over the Play button, poised to press it.

'No, wait!' I say.

Dread and I move closer to the screen. I don't even know who he's tagged, if anyone, but the video is ready to share anywhere now. I'm so mad at Davy for doing this. He knew how conflicted I was about it.

Maybe that's why he did it. He knew I'd dither and agonize over it, so he took the decision out of my hands.

I look at the screen. 'Oh my days! It's already had thirty hits,' I whisper. Thirty people have seen it already! 'How's that even possible? No one knows about it apart from us.'

'And it's only been online for about a minute,' Sandi says. 'Someone going to press Play?'

No one speaks. A hushed silence has fallen in the room. We're staring at the screen, but the screen is still suspended on the blurred image. Dread and I are standing over Sandi's shoulder; even Dread's forgotten to breathe. I reach over, move the cursor over to the Play button, and take a breath. Then I tap Play.

CHAPTER 29

The sound blares out – way too loud.

'Turn it down! Quick!' I hiss.

'I don't know how,' Sandi shoots back.

I depress the Sound and the Pause buttons and click on Full Screen before taking the video back to the beginning.

'OK,' I breathe. 'Ready?' It's a question for me more than it is for Sandi or Dread.

'Go for it,' Dread says.

I hit Play.

It's the sex scene in the woods. It's the one that's going to put Greaves into the deepest, darkest hole, make her a laughing stock, a figure of ridicule. She deserves it, doesn't she? After what she's done to me, I should be shouting out YES! I should be telling everybody that it's about time someone brought her down several pegs.

But did that someone have to be me?

So I'm watching the video and instead of it feeling

like a 'Yes! Gotcha! moment, I'm feeling apprehensive and conflicted.

In the scene playing out on my laptop, Greaves and Mr Green are heading closer to where I'm hiding behind the holly bush. Even though I've watched this so many times, it feels different. For a start, Mr Green is a blob of blurriness. I peer hard at the blob, wondering whether you can tell it's Mr Green. Davy's made his voice sound several octaves lower, too. But I can still make out his voice – no, not his voice, but his tone, his way of speaking. Or is that because I already know it's Mr Green?

And then they're doing it. The blob's not blobby enough. Mr Green's forehead dips out of the blurry blob for a microsecond, you briefly see his hairline, catch a glimpse of his beard. Mr Green's hands are in and out of the blob, and then his left hand comes out of the blob long enough for me to see the wedding band on his finger.

'Oh my God! Did you see that? Did you see his wedding ring? Can you tell it's him?'

'Calm yourself, Jeev. It's so fast, no one will notice it. They'll be too busy watching the main event,' Dread says. But even I hear the note of uncertainty in his voice.

We carry on watching the video to the end. It lasts five minutes, which is longer than I thought it would, and way too long in my opinion. It's quick, I suppose, considering what they were doing, and pretty gross considering where they are doing it, and as to who Mr Green's doing it with? Well, that's just so grim there isn't a word to describe it.

There's a major flash of Greaves's lacy red knickers, her thighs as she pulls her knickers up and then a lot of wriggling as she attempts to pull up her woolly tights. This is not good; it's not good at all.

I'm cringing.

She buttons up her blouse and rearranges her cardigan. Her coat is on the ground because she'd whipped it off to lie down on. The blob that is Mr Green is lighting up his cigarette – you only see the smoke rising around the blob that Mr Green has been transformed into. Greaves is dusting the leaves and muck off her coat before putting it on, grinning her head off like she's had the most lush romantic time instead of a sordid quickie. And then the video ends abruptly – just before Greaves utters her next words, which I know off by heart.

'Daniel! You told me you were giving up. Another broken promise.'

At least it ends there, before she says his name. Phew. That would have pointed the finger directly at Mr Green, and then the whole school would have known exactly who Greaves was with. It's one thing making Greaves a laughing stock: it's a whole different matter making Mr Green one. He made a mistake and he realized it pretty early on, though not nearly early enough.

'Davy's done a decent job on it,' Sandi says. 'You can't

tell it's Mr Green at all, and no one's likely to guess, are they? I mean, who would even *think* it could be him? Not me. It could be any old bloke, and most people will think it's someone from outside school.'

I notice Dread doesn't say a word.

'Dread? What do you think?'

He's chewing his lip thoughtfully, and that's not a good sign. 'Yeah, it's a decent job,' he says finally. 'A little rushed, perhaps. You can see Mr Green's hand, the wedding band, which isn't great. You catch a glimpse of his forehead, which isn't great either, but it doesn't necessarily make him identifiable. The thing is, we all know who it is, so it's hard to watch it without seeing him in the picture, blurry blob or no blurry blob.'

'Yeah, I know what you mean,' Sandi says. 'I'll message some people and tell them to watch it. Just to see, you know. They're gonna be shocked to see what Greaves has been up to! Bet you they won't guess who the man is, though. I mean, look – he's all blurred. The video's gonna go viral!'

I'm barely paying any attention to Sandi, who is getting his phone out. Dread's fallen back into silence. There's more he's not saying, I can sense it. I wait while he mulls it over some more. He thinks we've missed something. I can't tell what it could be. Sandi's right – unless you knew it was Mr Green, there's no way you could tell it's him. I need to call Tom, tell him to log on to YouTube and say we've found a video with someone who looks like Greaves in it, *doing it* with some bloke in the woods. If Tom can recognize Mr Green from the blob, then we're definitely in trouble, but if he can't then Mr Green stays safe.

'Right, that's done,' Sandi says, putting his phone away.

'What? What's done?' I ask him, but Dread interjects.

'Did we, um, did any of you hear Greaves say his name?' he ventures hesitantly. 'I don't know, but I think she actually says "Daniel" at some point.'

Oh God.

As soon as Dread says that, I know he's right. Somehow, we've all missed it – bloody Davy included.

'Take it back a bit,' I tell Sandi.

'Where to?' Sandi says.

'I don't know! Get out of the chair – I'll do it!' I shout at him.

'Calm down, Jeev.'

'I can't! OK? Oh God, I'm in so much trouble!'

Sandi is barely out of the chair when I'm on it. I slide my hand across the keypad, scrolling back through the frames on the video, and then I press Play.

And there it is. 'Oh, Daniel,' Greaves says, in raptures.

Shit! Shit! Shit!

I knew it. I knew this would happen if I left it to someone else. Greaves says his name. *She says his bloody name!*

'Oh crap!' Sandi says quietly.

'And then some,' Dread says. 'The blurring is still pretty good though. People might not pick up on her saying his name. She sort of whispers it breathlessly. It could sound like David, or Nathaniel, or – anything, really. Don't panic, Jeev.'

But it's too late for that. I've gone into a mega meltdown. 'Call Davy, Sandi! What the hell was he thinking? He's supposed to be a pro! Tell him to take it down. Unpublish it, or do whatever he has to do, but tell him he has to do it right now!'

Sandi's already got his phone out and is scrolling through his contacts list. His face looks ashen. 'OK, it's ringing. Hello? Hello? Davy? Damn! Voicemail.'

'Keep trying!'

'Guys, the hit count is going up fast for some reason,' Dread says.

'What? How? No one even knows it's there.' I refresh the page; Dread's right. It was on thirty and now it's on sixty. Don't people have lives? Do they sit on YouTube all day and scroll through anything that might be remotely interesting despite it being completely unrelated to them in any way whatsoever?

'Um,' Sandi mutters. 'That might be my fault.' His voice has gone very quiet, which is a very bad sign.

We round on him.

'You didn't,' Dread says.

'I did.'

Dread knows without even having to ask him what he's done. But just from their tones, I know it's going to be the worst thing possible. 'What have you gone and done, Sandi?' I ask him.

'I didn't put it on Facebook or anything. I – I just mentioned that someone thought they saw Greaves on a YouTube video. I can make up a name – anyone's name, because no one will know who saw the video first when it's spreading this fast,' he finishes lamely.

'It's gone up to a hundred and forty hits now,' Dread proclaims.

'Why is it spreading this fast, Sandi?' I ask tersely. 'Tell me!'

He looks anywhere except at me, and I know without any doubt that there's only one place where it could have gone viral this fast.

He's only gone and stuck it on WhatsApp. Sandi's got over half the school on his WhatsApp, and half the kids in all the other schools in the area too.

We're talking hundreds of kids in his contacts list – and it would only take one of them to post a link to the video on Instagram and Twitter to make that hole I'm sinking into drag me into the deepest darkest unexplored bowels of the world. The way things are going, I'll disappear into them soon and never be seen again.

'You stupid bloody idiot! Why did you do that?'

'I'm sorry, OK? We all thought it was safe then. I said I'd message some people to have a look at it – you heard me.'

'I didn't, and messaging doesn't mean bloody posting

it on WhatsApp for the whole world to see!'

'You heard me, didn't you, Dread?' Sandi's tone has gone all plaintive.

'I heard you, kind of. It's too late now. We need damage limitation,' Dread says.

'Call Davy!' I yell at Sandi. 'Tell him he has to get it off YouTube now.'

'Three hundred hits,' Dread says. Ten seconds later he says, 'Three hundred and seventy hits.'

CHAPTER 30

Whenever someone asks my mum how old she is, she always replies, 'It's not how old you are, but how young you feel.' She'd never admit it, but she hates getting older. 'At least we Asians have one advantage,' she says. 'We don't have to waste any money on all those anti-wrinkle creams, anti-aging serums and Botox injections.'

I'm not in the least bit vain, but I'll tell you this for nothing: ever since the day I pressed Record on my phone in the woods I've noticed loads of lines on my face, and a frown so massive that even Dread has noticed it.

'Man, my sister's got some straightening irons – you sure you don't want to borrow them and iron out them furrows? They're so deep I could skateboard through them, kick up, and do a triple somersault.'

'Triple somersault? Give it a rest. You don't even *own* a skateboard.'

'Dude, I'm gonna get myself one right now,' he says. I throw a book at him.

Dread's right – I'm not looking my best. I feel more haggard, more ancient than even the ancient mariner.

It's not just the weight of responsibility for what I've allowed to happen that's hanging like a noose around my neck, or the images that I've allowed to become public, but the crushing weight of being responsible for potentially jeopardizing Mr Green's future too.

Like the ancient mariner, I am doomed to be forever haunted by what I've done. The souls of Greaves and Mr Green will rise up wherever I go, their faces fixed in expressions of horror and loathing, and even if I flee to the ends of the earth, I will never be able to escape them.

I know, I know. I do realize that I'm being a bit over the top. But it's the guilt that's the killer.

'How come she doesn't feel like shit for treating me so bad? The way I am about the video going viral and what it's going to do to her?'

'Are you serious, Jeev? Who cares what she thinks or feels? She's a racist and she's out to get you. And now you're fighting back,' Dread explains patiently.

'What now, then?' I ask the guy with all the answers.

'Damage limitation,' Dread replies. 'We get hold of Davy and get the video taken down.'

The trouble is, you can't undo something that's already been done.

'OK,' Sandi says, putting his phone away. 'I've got through to Davy. He's taken it down. You can check if you like. He said he's sorry, but not to stress about it, because it's not illegal to record something that happens in public, and it's not illegal to post it on the Internet either. That's what YouTube is all about.'

'That's not the point!' I snap back.

'I know. Sorry, Jeev,' Sandi says lamely.

'Check this out,' Dread says. He points to the screen. He's on Facebook.

'Crap!' I say.

Davy may have taken the video down, but the damage has already been done. A link to it has been copied and posted on Facebook by someone from another school and it's had ten shares already.

'Is it on Twitter?' I ask.

Sandi checks his Twitter feed on his phone. 'Yeah, it's there.'

'Instagram? Snapchat?'

Sandi doesn't even bother to reply.

It seems as though everyone is bloody everywhere, and so is the damned video. There is no escape from it.

I feel bad for Greaves, with her red lacy knickers being displayed for everyone to mock, and trust me, there's a lot of mocking going on. But it won't be half as bad as I feel for Mr Green when it comes out that it was him in the video. At least that hasn't come out yet.

'It's only a matter of time before people realize that Mr Green's first name is Daniel and put two and two together,' I say anxiously.

'Not necessarily. I don't think I knew his first name was Daniel before all this.'

'Seriously?' I say. I don't remember if I did or not now.

'How many teachers' first names do you know?'

He's got a point.

'And who would put Daniel Green in the woods with Greaves? Dude, unless he comes out and publicly admits, "Yes, that's me making a complete fool of myself," it just ain't gonna happen. Remember how long it took for us to believe you?'

Dread's got a point. I'm praying – yes, I'm that damn desperate – that he's right.

I don't care what Dread says, but I still need to go back to my original question, because it's important for me to understand it. Everything that's happened comes back down to it. Why doesn't Greaves feel bad about the way she's been treating me?

A few years back, I asked Dad why Uncle Raj went to grammar school but he didn't – when they'd both passed their eleven-plus exams.

It was a sore point. 'I've told you all about it before. Is this to distract me from the game? Don't be so devious, Jeevan. Play your next move.'

'OK. I'm thinking.' Our game of chess was almost over – we both knew Dad had got me cornered. 'Yeah, but was there really a *quota*?'

'Apparently. I'm sure it doesn't happen nowadays,' Dad said. 'How many of you are there at your school?'

'There's got to be about a thousand boys in total, and probably about fifteen or twenty Asian kids in each year. There are a few African boys, and a few more who I think might be from the Caribbean. And Dread – but he's half.'

'Well, in my day, out of a thousand, there were maybe three of us. At the very most.'

'In each year?'

'No. In the whole school.'

I was shocked. I couldn't imagine being the only one in a whole year, never mind the whole school – that's like not having Dread there, or Sandi, my best mates. But that's how it was for Uncle Raj. 'Maybe it was because there were less black and Asian kids in the area. Or maybe their English wasn't good enough.'

Dad gave me a look. 'My first language may have been considered to be Punjabi, but my father always spoke to us in English – and he spoke it "like a native", as you know.'

I smiled, because they were Granddad's exact words.

'I speak it like a native too, and so do you.'

'But you still haven't explained why Uncle Raj went to the grammar and not you.'

'Your grandfather was told, unofficially, by the Headmaster of our middle school, that the quota for black and Asians had already been reached, so I had to go to the comprehensive school.'

'Never! Why didn't Granddad fight for you?'

'There was no point. That's how it was back then. We just accepted it and got on with it.'

'But that's so unfair!' said the naive twelve year old that I was then.

'Jeevan, it was a different time. It didn't stop me, and if you had not passed your eleven-plus, it would not stop you. It's all based on merit now, so don't worry your brain about old stories. Worry about how you're going to get out of this game of chess with your king still standing.'

That was a few years ago, when I started at the school. Now I'm in Year Eleven.

Dad said it's all changed now. It's all down to merit, so he taught me that to get ahead, you've got to work damn hard.

But he didn't tell me that in reality, for some of us, it doesn't always matter how hard we work because some things in life are stacked against us. Some things haven't changed since he was a kid growing up here.

And what if you're not a clever-clogs smarty-pants, or not naturally gifted in some way, or if you're just a regular kid and your teacher takes an instant, but deep and abiding, dislike to you for no apparent reason whatsoever, where does that leave you?

You might still be OK.

I would have been fine in the long run. I wouldn't even have known about half the stuff Greaves thought if I hadn't been in the wrong place at the wrong time.

But the point is now I *do* know, and because I know, it changes everything.

It's not my behaviour she finds threatening. It's the colour of my skin. I'm not a kid in Year Eleven doing his GCSEs, thinking of doing English Literature at A level and at uni, I'm just a coloured kid who shouldn't even be *thinking* of doing any of those things because I'm jumping up out of the hole where I belong.

And because I'm not a human being as far as she's concerned, it naturally follows that I have no feelings that can be hurt. If you treat people as somehow being less than human, turn them into creatures that need to be kept in their place, controlled, what do they become?

Cockroaches.

Yes, believe me – you can get away with saying that on TV and in the papers and on every single social networking site. I heard it with my own ears. It's perfectly acceptable to stamp on nasty little cockroaches, obliterate them, nuke them to oblivion and let them die on boats, because cockroaches are not human beings to people like Greaves. Her type believe that they have a long and powerful history. They feel personally responsible for dragging the natives kicking and screaming out of the Dark Ages into the new age of civilization. (Yeah, some of the natives might have got a bit crushed in the process, but that collateral damage was inevitable and all done in the name of the greater good.)

'She really believes that people like her put the

GREAT into Great Britain; that they are right and they have might by their side.'

Dread shakes his head. 'Man, oh man, you seriously need to chill! There is such a thing as overthinking the whole thing, Jeev, and we've all done History at school, so we know what's what. Listen, dude, I *get* that you're angry, and I know you're down about all this, but it's just one stupid teacher. This ain't you.'

No, this is not me.

'And I've said sorry like a thousand times, Jeev. You know Davy was only trying to help. You gotta get over it,' Sandi adds.

'How can I when it's going to be all over the school tomorrow? Greaves is going to be a laughing stock and Mr Green's going to get unmasked.'

'About time! Well, not for Green, maybe,' Sandi says. 'I might not have had Greaves for English, but my brother does, remember? Sukh's *told* me what she's like, and she's no different towards him than she is to you. So, boo-bloody-hoo, Jeev. You're not the only one she's been picking on.'

'I know. That's my point.'

'So she's finally getting what she deserves – it's called karma. Sometimes people just get what's coming to them. The video can't be traced back to you, so you're not in the picture. And you still have a problem?' Sandi says.

'Guys,' the calming voice of Dread interjects. 'We're

all agreed that she doesn't deserve any special treatment, and that you, Jeev, are not incriminated in her downfall in any way, so please will you both just chill out? And this is the black man talking here, so don't give me no lectures about how bad you guys got it, when me and my lot have had it a whole lot worse.'

That shuts us both up. Technically, Dread is only half black, but technicalities never get in the way of people like Greaves. The thing is though, Dread knows he's untouchable. He is probably the only kid in school who'll sleepwalk into twelve A stars for his exams and then four A stars for his A levels. He's no goody two shoes, but that doesn't stop Rawson holding him up as his star pupil destined for greatness or, if not greatness, then at least Oxbridge. Every school wants a Dread – it's good for their PR *and* their league table stats.

'Look, the school might never find out about the Greaves video, anyway,' Sandi says. 'It's not like any of the teachers follow us on Twitter or Instagram. They'd have to do a special search for Greaves on YouTube to discover the video, and I can't see any of them even thinking of doing something like that. And what then? What if none of this comes out? Where will that leave you? I bet you anything you'll be calling me up and asking me to get Davy to post it back up on YouTube again.'

'I bet you I won't, Sandi. I'd like to bury this so deep that it'll never see the light of day again.'

'Oh, they'll get to know about it eventually,' Dread says. 'The powers that be will find out. It may not be straight away, but these things have a way of surfacing. Scandal always worms its way out of the woodwork – and if it doesn't, there are plenty of people who'll give it a helping hand. Someone will blab about it. You wait and see.'

I'm hoping against hope that Dread is wrong.

But Dread is rarely wrong.

CHAPTER 31

Monday morning rolls around way too fast. I should have taken another sickie. I could have pretended I was having a relapse. And I *am* feeling sick – so sick to my stomach that I don't think I'll be able to eat anything ever again, which must mean I'm *very* sick. But I can just imagine what my parents would have to say about that. Mum might have raised her eyebrows; Dad might have wondered what was going on; both would have been pretty certain what it was all about even if neither of them said it aloud. And then they would have sent me to school.

So I drag myself out of bed and stumble down the stairs.

Maji is making porridge in the kitchen – she's loaded it with almonds and raisins and topped it with a heavy drizzle of honey. It smells so good that I dig in and immediately start feeling better. Maybe it won't be that bad at school today, I think. Maybe most of those hits on YouTube yesterday were from people completely unconnected with the school.

I know, I know, there's wishful thinking and there's living in cloud cuckoo land. Personally, the idea of living somewhere that is unrealistically, idyllically perfect suddenly sounds like heaven to me – as long as I skip the dying part.

But there's no skipping the dying part. The minute I get to school, I start dying. The place is buzzing so loud that you'd have to be deaf not to hear it.

Small pieces of me begin to shrink and shrivel up with that thing called guilt, and no matter how much Sandi and Dread tell me to buck up and stop feeling responsible, I'm finding it hard.

'Did you see it?' Alex asks Dread.

'Yeah, totally disturbing. Messed with my head, man.'

'I know! Completely gross!'

'I saw it too!'

'And me. Man, it's *so* bad!'

'Worse than bad.'

'Sicker than sick!'

'I put it on Twitter and people told me to take it down, it was so bad!' Gabby-mouth says. 'Then they only went and retweeted it! It got about fifty retweets – it broke my record.' He laughs gleefully.

So *that's* who's on Twitter. I should have guessed.

Mind you, it's got to be a real challenge for Gabbs to keep to a hundred and forty characters.

'Who caught her?'

'Yeah, that's what I wanna know.'

'Didn't she know someone was recording it?'

'Course she didn't.'

'You think she would have pulled them red lace knickers down if she thought she was on candid camera?'

'You never know. Maybe she's an exhibitionist when it comes to stuff like that.'

'Maybe she thinks they turn men on!'

'Someone needs to tell her she's so wrong!'

'Can't see her in a thong myself.'

'Ewww! That's just disgusting!'

'Oh my God, I think I'm going to be sick!'

'*Is* she in a thong?'

'What's the matter with you? No!'

'Red pants?'

'Lacy red pants?'

'How'd she keep the mud from sticking to them?'

'Haven't you seen it?'

'No, I didn't know about it.'

'I've got it on my phone. Watch!'

Choruses of 'Oh no, no way, she never did,' and then peals of mocking laughter.

'I still want to know who caught her in the act.'

'Who posted it on YouTube?'

'It don't say.'

'Check.'

'I think it's gone now.'

'Yeah, it was up for about an hour, and then it disappeared.'

'Was it someone in our school?'

'Who knows?'

'It must have been – they knew her name.'

'Lots of people know her name.'

'But it was someone from school who told me about it.'

'Our school?'

'I don't know.'

'I heard it from a boy over at the comp.'

'I heard it from a girl at the grammar.'

'I saw Gabbs's link to it on Twitter.'

'I saw it on Facebook.'

'But who's the guy she's with?'

'No idea. Looks familiar though.'

'How can you say he looks familiar? He's a blob.'

'Anyone recognize him?'

'Not me.'

'They've blurred his face.'

'You can still see some of him.'

'Yeah, but not enough.'

'I saw his hand, there's a ring on his finger. He's married.'

'Married? OMG.'

'Greaves is married.'

'Thought she was divorced?'

'Yeah, I heard her husband left her.'

'Wise man. So it's not her husband.'

'Who is it then?'

'Could be anyone.'

'Maybe it's another teacher.'

'Ha-ha. It won't be anyone here, that's for sure.'

'You never know. It could be.'

'It could be a pupil for all we know.'

'Ugh! Don't be gross!'

'No, stupid, there's a wedding ring on his hand.'

'Any of you guys tied the knot?'

Laughter.

'She's been playing about with a married man?'

'She's a very bad girl!'

'Then he's in the shit now, isn't he?'

'Only if his wife recognizes him.'

'How's she going to do that when the video's gone?'

'It's still out there.'

'But she won't see it, will she? It's not like it's got her name on it.'

'Does Greaves's name come up on Google?'

'Search *Greaves* and see.'

'There it is!'

'Click on the link.'

'It's still there, the whole dirty video.'

'She's gonna be in the shit.'

'Only if Rawson finds out.'

'How's he going to find out?'

'Someone's bound to dob her in.'

'Who?'

'Not me.'

'Nor me.'

'Yeah, if she finds out who it was, she'll kill them.'

'Only if she's allowed to stay in the school.'

'Someone *has* to tell the school.'

'What's Rawson gonna do about it anyway?'

'He'll ask her to leave.'

'Bet you he doesn't.'

'He might ask for a quickie down the woods to hush it up.'

'No way!'

'He's not going to sack her.'

'Course not – it's not illegal to have sex.'

'It might be in the woods.'

And so it goes on.

And on.

All day.

No guesses for which one of the sixty-odd teachers in school is the only one to ask us directly what all the buzz is about. Dread is sitting next to me in History, and both of us keep our heads down and our mouths firmly shut and let others do the talking.

'Come on, then, don't be shy,' Mr Green says. 'Let me in on the joke.'

And that's the strange thing – *no one* tells him anything. I'm surprised, very surprised. Even Gabby-mouth, who normally can't even keep quiet about his own farts, doesn't breathe a word.

In the end, Mr Green shrugs. 'Suit yourselves,' he says, and gets on with the lesson. Oblivious.

Mondays end with English Lit and all morning I've been dreading it. Apparently, from what I've heard, Greaves hasn't got a clue that half the kids in school have seen her with her knickers down. But it's only a matter of time. I'm so not with it that when I'm told to go to the Head's office straight after the last lesson before lunch, I am overwhelmed by an oh-my-God-they-know-it's-me moment.

I can't concentrate in Physics; it's hard enough at the best of times, but when the lesson ends, I haven't got a clue what we've covered. All I can think is that I'm in deep trouble and that I shouldn't have bothered to come into school. In fact, I'm seriously considering developing an unidentifiable virus that keeps me at home until the exams when I'll miraculously recover to the point that, against all odds, I somehow manage to ace my exams.

So I take the Walk of Shame again.

It's become a habit.

This time I'm on my own, which is why I get away with dragging my feet. Basically, I'm stalling, my head buzzing with *what* they've found, *how* they could have found it out, and *what* they're going to do. Obviously, they've found out I took the video and posted it up to shame Greaves.

But how did they find out?

Someone must have dobbed me in, or how else could they have found out so quickly? Davy said he used an anonymous site to create a fake account, so nothing leads back to either of us; there's no trail to follow. Nothing at all.

Except there *is* one thing – one person.

The person who links Davy and me; the one who put us in touch.

Sandi.

I can't believe I'm even *thinking* it could have been him. But it's starting to make sense.

Who was the first to tell me to post it straight up on YouTube?

Who sent out all the texts that sent the video viral within minutes?

Who also runs at the first sign of trouble?

CHAPTER 32

He wouldn't do that to me, would he?

Sandi has been my friend since primary school. We're not just friends, but best friends. His bright orange turban was almost as much a fixture in my life as it was in his. I kind of miss it in a weird way, and I can tell he does too. But we both knew its days were numbered.

Like mine are now.

So I know, deep down, that Sandi would never ever tell the school it was me who recorded the video, or that I had anything to do with it being posted on YouTube.

However they've found out, it can't have been him, or Dread, or anyone else. Hang on a sec. Did Dread tell Amelia about the video? But Amelia's on my side – yes, and she was all for getting the anonymous note out in the public domain, wasn't she? Did Amelia tell Ree? I can't imagine Ree'd approve of the video. She was probably disgusted with me for allowing the video to get out there.

Would she have tipped off the school though?

Whoever it was, this is it for me. This is the final showdown.

I'm sure they're going to expel me.

So now you understand all the foot dragging and the mental trauma I'm going through as I haul my sorry ass along the Walk of Shame. I've got no answer for Rawson apart from outright denial. That's what Dread said to do. 'It can't be proven, so deny everything. OK? Don't admit it, act like you're horrified that anyone could even *think* it's you. You don't know anything. Geddit? And if it comes down to it you can plead the Fifth Amendment.'

'If you haven't noticed, we're not actually in the United States of America, and this is not an episode of *Law and Order*. So can you please take this a bit more seriously, Dread?'

'Like I said, deny everything.'

'But what if they say they have proof?'

'Forget it. They don't have a shred of proof because there is no proof for them to have. Davy knows what he's doing. It's untraceable. And what you did, well, that's not illegal anyway. There are no laws against recording the wildlife in the woods. It's not your problem that the wildlife you chanced upon on the day you happened to be out birdwatching was a lesser-spotted shag, which, by the way, happens to be a real bird.'

'A shag is a real bird?'

Dread responds with a despairing shake of his head.

'Ha! I didn't think so.'

'Look it up for yourself – it is, you idiot!'

When Sandi joins us I give him a look.

'What's wrong? Something happened?'

'Jeev has to go to the school office. They must have found out something.'

'What? No! How?'

'Thought you might have got cold feet and dobbed me in,' I say, half-jokingly.

'That's not even funny, Jeev,' he says, outraged, punching me hard on the arm.

'Ouch!' I rub my arm. Serves me right. I knew it couldn't be him, deep down.

It's only when I reach the school office that it hits me – Mum and Dad are coming into school this lunchtime for a chat with Mr Rawson.

So it has absolutely nothing at all to do with the stupid video. Well, in a roundabout way it does, but not in the oh-my-God-I'm-going-to-get-expelled way. I breathe easy again.

'Take a seat outside his office,' Mrs Dere says. 'Mr Rawson will call you in when he's ready.' She gives an almost imperceptible shake of her head, as if to say, *not you again!*

I smile back at her and give a slight shrug. Yes, it's me again, the troublemaker who never knows when to quit.

I sit down on the chair, sorely tempted to get my phone out and see what's going on. It's lunchtime, so there's bound to be stuff happening all over Facebook and Twitter, and several other places, including in real life in the dining hall, where the main action will be taking place.

It's only a matter of time before a teacher overhears the words 'Greaves' and 'YouTube' uttered in the same sentence. It's making me wonder what *would* happen if Rawson finds out.

'If it's not right under their noses, they can easily miss it,' Sandi pointed out. 'They don't see half the stuff that goes on and they turn a blind eye to anything they don't want to see. How many times have they given the wrong person detention?'

'Lots of times,' I respond, and it's true.

I remember when meek and mild Henry Wills threw a snowball at someone in the playground – that constitutes an offence in the eyes of some teachers; it's almost akin to drug smuggling or something. Apparently, this particular law was passed because many years ago, a snowball hit someone in the face. That was enough to spell the end of snowball fights.

Anyhow, standing beside Henry was Ollie, who has a reputation as a troublemaker, but who looks nothing like Henry and is about a foot taller. So it couldn't be said that it was a case of mistaken identity when Mr Fraser gave Ollie a detention. Ollie fiercely denied it was him, because, well, because it *wasn't* him, and Henry actually owned up to being the snowball thrower, but was told to go away.

Personally, my ancient mariner moment would be well and truly history if none of the teachers ever found out about the video. For everyone else in the school, Greaves will never be the same person. *That* I can live with. The question remains: what would Rawson do if he did find out?

He would be forced to ask her to leave, wouldn't he? I'm not so sure now. I hope he would. Let's face it, he's let me down before when I've really needed him, so the chances are it could well happen again.

I look at Rawson's office door. It's firmly shut. All I can hear is the quiet murmur of voices. I'm wondering if my parents are even in there. It's possible they haven't arrived yet and Rawson's in another meeting, or on the phone. I strain my ears, hoping to catch the sound of a female voice, which would give me a clue as to whether my mum's in there. No, the voices are too quiet; a *civilized* conversation is taking place. I hope that means it's boding well for me. I have no desire to be sitting in Greaves's lesson this afternoon.

Can you imagine the sniggering? The innuendoes? She'd have to be deaf and blind not to twig that something was up. I guess I've still got some empathy for her, despite everything.

And that makes me think of something which for some reason I've only just thought of – and it doesn't seem to have occurred to Dread either, or maybe it has but he hasn't got around to mentioning it to me yet. Parents will get wind of the video, some might even watch it.

So if Rawson decides not to take action, they will surely force him to act. No one wants a teacher associated with that kind of scandal teaching their kids, do they?

All of that remains to be seen.

I'm about to stand up and start pacing round the room when the door opens.

Mum and Dad exit Rawson's office. I stand up and take a step towards them as Dad is saying, 'Goodbye, and thank you.'

I'm not getting called in, but from the way Mum and Dad are smiling at me I know that they've either swung it so I've switched English Lit teachers or I've got a library pass. Either way I'm happy.

Breaking the coconut must have worked – or that's what Maji would say. I bet she had to have several broken for me.

I will never have to go to another of Greaves's lessons again.

Result!

CHAPTER 33

I hang around after school, hoping to catch Dread, Sandi, Tom or anyone who knows anything and will give me the latest. I've been secluded in the library, which is working out well for me cos I got a head start on my homework, swot that I am, but even so, I'm still in catch-up mode. When I get home tonight, I'm going to source the rest of the English Lit curriculum so I don't miss out on anything by not going to Greaves's lessons.

There are sample essays, sample answers, tutorials and tons of other stuff, all online. Go and see. YouTube's got some brilliant maths tutorials too (yeah, I know I'm a real saddo, but watch them and you'll thank me later). I discovered them too late for the mocks, but they're there for the GCSEs in the summer.

I see Tom first and he comes straight over, a big grin plastered on his face.

'So?'

He's still grinning. 'You'll never guess!'

'What? Tell me!'

'Greaves got called out halfway through the class. Mrs Dere came and got her, and sent a lab assistant to sit with us for the rest of the class. Greaves never came back to the lesson.'

'And?'

'And that's all we know, all anyone knows, yet!'

'So Rawson must know about the video.'

'Everyone knows about the video!'

'Everyone? *All* the teachers?'

Tom shrugs. 'Well, I don't know about that, but if Rawson knows, then at least some of the teachers must know, and if some of the teachers know, then *all* of the teachers will know pretty soon.'

Dread and Sandi come over and join us by the school gate and we walk down the road together.

'Yeah, we heard,' Sandi says. 'Shame no one was sitting outside the Head's office listening in on *that* conversation!'

'Yeah – where's Gabby-mouth when you need him?' I say bitterly.

'It could have been about something else entirely,' Dread points out.

'Yeah, right,' Sandi says.

'And even if it was about the video, then it could still have gone either way.'

'There's only one way she's going – and that's down

the tube!' Sandi laughs at his own little joke while the rest of us groan.

'So what exactly did Mrs Dere say when she came into the lesson,' I ask Tom.

'"Mrs Greaves, the Head wants to see you in his office immediately." And that was it. There was no please, no thank you. So everyone thought it *had* to have been something to do with the video.'

'Rawson is definitely going to sack her,' Sandi says.

'About time,' Tom says. 'She's got worse. She sets us work at the start of the lesson and then just sits there and does her marking, and that's it. She's not even *pretending* to teach.'

'Thank God for my library pass,' I say smugly.

'Yeah, I'm thinking of asking my dad to go in and ask for one for me too,' Tom says. 'You know, we should get the whole class to do it. That's something Rawson can't ignore!'

'Yeah, brilliant idea, Tom, and I'll get painted as the troublemaking leader of the pack,' I say. 'Leading astray all the poor little lambs in the class – the way I supposedly did with you.'

'Think about it, Jeev. If enough parents complain, the school might have to do something about her. Oh, there's my mum. I've got a dentist appointment – my filling fell out. Let me know if you hear anything, OK?'

'Yeah, I will. Good luck with the driller-killer!'

'You won't have to do anything,' Sandi says when

Tom's gone, 'because, I'm telling you, she's gonna get the boot!'

'Rawson won't sack her, Sandi,' Dread explains patiently. 'That's not how things work. He'll ask for her resignation, and that's what she'll do – resign. She'll cite personal circumstances or family problems or something, and get herself a good recommendation and end up in another school far, far away where no one knows her and her reputation has not preceded her, and there she will undoubtedly keep up the good work.'

'So the whole thing will end up getting hushed up and brushed under that sodding carpet in his office again. Rawson's going to have to clear it out eventually. He's practically swimming in shit,' I say bitterly.

'More like drowning!' Sandi exclaims. 'He'll be looking for a lifebelt soon, a lifeline out of the muck.'

'Look, I'm not saying that that's what's going to happen, Jeev. It's just one possible scenario,' Dread says.

Haven't I said before that Dread is always right? Always, annoyingly, and without fail he is correct in his analysis of any given situation. It's a gift; one I wish I had. Oh, and another one of his irritatingly long list of talents is that he's ace at chess. Yes, Dread is the only person I know to have beaten my dad at chess. They've played several times and Dread has beaten my dad every time, although Dad did come close to winning once, but only close, and I think that's only because Dread took pity on him.

And you know what? There wasn't even any money on the table.

I think I've gone right off chess.

We troop into school on Tuesday morning and the buzz is still there, but not at the same volume as yesterday. The news that Greaves was called out of a lesson to go and see the Head has whipped round the school. No one knows anything beyond that. No one's overheard any of the teachers talking about it, or managed to hover for long enough outside the staff room to catch any snippets of information. And, of course, no one has asked a teacher anything directly. Which one of us would be stupid enough to go up to a teacher and ask, 'By the way, sir, did you see that video on YouTube with Mrs Greaves and some bloke doing it in the woods?'

But today we might find out what it was all about, and whether Dread was right, or Sandi. My money's on Dread, of course.

What actually happens comes as a total shock.

'Quiet, please,' Mr Rawson says, completely unnecessarily because if someone dropped a pin in the hall everyone would hear it.

Half the school – the upper school – are in the hall for assembly, waiting in total, expectant, silence. Rawson is getting ready to make the announcement that we've all pretty much predicted, so no one is coughing or sneezing or shuffling their feet, or even fidgeting, because *everyone* wants to hear this.

Rawson does not disappoint in that regard – there is no preamble from him. He gets straight to the point. 'It has come to my attention that a particularly vicious and insidious attack has been launched upon a member of staff.' Mr Rawson pauses for effect and casts his eyes round the hall. 'This attack has come in the form of a video, which has been made available on the Internet, and has subsequently been very wrongly and libellously associated with a member of the teaching staff at this school.'

And there it is loud and clear – the one scenario even Dread did not predict.

'I have informed the authorities and the police are now involved. I am sorry it has come to this, but I will not tolerate anyone who thinks that they can besmirch the reputation of a respected member of my staff and get away with it. No teacher at this school is in any way associated with the video that has been posted online, and I cannot emphasize that enough. Clearly, someone has seen some spurious resemblance and linked this teacher's name to that scandalous piece of footage on YouTube.

'Well, I will *not* sit back and watch while her reputation is tarnished in this way. No!' He hits the podium with the flat of his hand and everyone jumps in their seats.

Rawson raises his voice and continues his speech, preacher-man-style, like he has right and might, not to mention Lord Jesus himself, on his side. 'Make no mistake – this matter will be investigated thoroughly and the culprit, or culprits . . .' He looks sternly at us, his gaze fixing on various pupils, the usual suspects, before passing over me and then landing firmly back on me.

I gulp hard.

And try not to let my expression waver even a milli-fraction.

My stomach begins to grumble loudly and a few heads turn in my direction. I shouldn't have skipped breakfast this morning. Now I'm feeling so sick I don't think I'll ever be able to eat anything ever again. I clutch my stomach hard, hoping to control the loud grumbles.

'. . . will be brought to justice! Make no mistake about that!'

Rawson nods at someone sitting at the back of the hall. There's a shuffling at the back and heads begin to turn to see who it is.

From the back of the hall, a police officer makes his way to the front and climbs the steps on to the stage. He must have arrived late or else we would have seen him when we filed in earlier.

I hazard a quick glance at Dread, and he's shaking his head, very slowly, very deliberately.

He can't believe it either.

This is so completely gobsmackingly, ridiculously, unbelievably unbelievable.

CHAPTER 34

'Thank you, Mr Rawson. Good morning, everybody, I am Detective Inspector Philbin.' He pauses for a minute to allow the gravity of his rank to sink in. People around me sit up straighter. 'I shall be investigating the matter of the video. If this is, as I suspect, someone's idea of a prank, then let me tell you this: there is nothing, I repeat, nothing, remotely funny about it. One of my officers will be in school over the next couple of days, looking into the matter. We will also be looking at your Facebook pages, your Twitter accounts, and anywhere else we feel like looking. Because this pathetic attempt to link an entirely innocent teacher to such a scurrilous video is NOT acceptable. It has far-reaching consequences.

'So if anyone here has any information, any information at all, regarding the origin of this video, then I urge you to come forward. Thank you.'

Assembly ends very quickly after that. The hum of voices rises to a crescendo as we file out. Everyone knows that it's highly unlikely the police will actually do anything. The fact there's still loads of well dodgy stuff on Facebook and Twitter alone shows you how much the police can really do about it.

Dread backs me up on that. 'Hot air,' he says dismissively. 'They're obviously trying to scare people into confessing something, but what they don't know is that no one in the school did it, so no one's going to tell them anything. If their tech guys could have found the source, they would have done it by now. That's assuming they've even bothered to set their techie guys on to it.'

It's break time and Dread and I are sitting on the wall outside the science block.

'This is small-time stuff for them. It's just to stop anyone from doing it again,' Dread continues. 'And Twitter and Facebook won't care – there's that video-nasty of a baby being dunked in a bucket of water several times that people have asked to be taken down, but it's still there. Apparently, it doesn't break the law or contravene any of their regulations. Man, their rules are lax.'

Dread's confirming what I already thought. But that's not what's troubling me, and he knows it.

Sandi comes bounding over to us, a big smile on his face, so we know he's got something for us.

'OK, hot off the press – Greaves only went and got herself a makeover! Well, she had her hair cut into a short blonde bob. I just saw Sukh and he said we totally won't recognize her now. At first his class thought they had a supply teacher, and then they realized it was her!'

Dread and I exchange a look and shrug. 'She's just trying to put some distance between herself and the woman in the video,' I say. 'It's a clever move.'

'She *thinks* it's clever. We know better,' Dread says. 'There's a whole world of difference between being clever and thinking you're clever.'

'Wait,' Sandi says. 'I haven't finished – the other thing I heard is that the police officer in assembly is the Head's son-in-law! Can you believe that?' Actually, we can. 'So no one's bothered about getting into trouble for reposting the video on their timelines. In fact, everyone thinks we might as well share it on all our pages just to see what happens. They can't put the whole school in detention, can they?' Sandi says gleefully.

I've been struck by a thought – yeah, I know, it's not been happening much recently, but this thought makes me do a double take. 'What if the school really thinks that Greaves and the woman on the video are *not* the same person? I mean, you'd have to be blind not to see it, but what if they *are* blind?'

'Of course they know it's her, Jeev. They don't have to *admit* it though, and they can deny it all they want, and carry on with their line that it's a lookalike that someone's spotted in a video and is now claiming is Greaves for a laugh – a schoolboy prank. She'll simply say she was so upset by it that she was forced to change her appearance so that people wouldn't associate her with a sex tape.

What we can't do is go out there and say what we know to be true.'

'No, we definitely can't do that!' Sandi says, looking worriedly at me. 'You won't, will you? Jeev? We'll get in a whole lot of shit if you do. Davy too! It won't be fair on him, or any of us.'

'I wouldn't do that to you, Sandi,' I say wearily. 'I didn't want the video out there in the first place, remember? But it went out there anyway – thanks to your brain-box cousin Davy, and it looks as though nothing's going to come of it.'

'Apart from Greaves being a laughing stock,' Sandi says.

'Yeah, for about five minutes. But it won't take long for people to forget what she used to look like and think, "How can anyone have thought that was her? Sure, the faces are very similar but everyone knows about Photoshop and how you can do virtually anything to anyone to make them look the way you want, or make things appear the way you want them to." So, ultimately, no damage done to her rep, and she gets to carry on as she always has.'

There is an uncomfortable silence. Dread and Sandi both know that what I've said is true. Just look at all the people who're still merrily in power when a small-time scandal is uncovered about them. Time dissipates the memory of it until eventually it's forgotten. Well, almost forgotten.

'There's still the second video,' Sandi reminds me.

I glare at him. 'If Davy publishes that, I swear I'm gonna kill him! Tell him not to touch it.'

'Just saying,' Sandi says, holding his hands up. 'Seriously, Jeev, you should think about it – it's so incriminating.'

'For Mr Green too, remember? Davy said that when Greaves comes out with all that bad shit, I'm focussing in on Mr Green's face.'

'Not to mention the fact that everyone's gonna know it was Green in the sex tape if the second video goes public,' Dread says. 'The fact that he's a blurred-out blob won't make a difference.'

'Oh yeah,' Sandi says. 'I hadn't thought of that.'

'Do you think Green's watched it?'

Dread lays it out. 'It's all over school, Jeev. We've had an assembly about it, there's a police officer hanging around, and the staff know. Plus, of course, Greaves has had that ridiculous radical makeover. So, yeah, he's watched it.'

'He's got to be scared, hasn't he?' Sandi says.

'Not necessarily. If he's seen it then he knows that whoever uploaded it went to great lengths to conceal his identity. He'll also know that it's likely to be someone in this school who recorded it. He'll also—'

'Stop there!' I cut in. I know exactly where Dread is going with this. 'Don't say another word.'

My head has started to thump with an almighty

headache. I need to lie down – not in the nurse's office, but at home, in my own bed, in a dark room, where I can empty my head of all this. 'Look, guys, I feel like shit. I think I'm gonna head home.'

'What? You're seriously going to bunk off?' Sandi asks.

I shrug. 'Yeah, I guess so,' I say, jumping off the wall.

'Jeev, wait. Where are you going? You can't just leave. You'll get in trouble.'

'Dread, it's all right. I can handle trouble. Haven't you noticed? Me and trouble are like *that*,' I say, crossing my fingers to indicate that trouble and I have been walking along the same path for some time now. We're uneasy but inseparable companions. I desperately want it to go away, but it's stalking me no matter what I do. It's always there. I might as well stop trying to fight it and just give in to it.

I ignore my friends' calls and head across the school to get my school bag, which I'd left in my locker. Just because I'm bunking off doesn't mean I shouldn't get some work done later. My head is pounding, like someone's taken a jackhammer to it.

I need to get away from this place as fast as I can now, because I'm choking up. I never cry, but there are tears in my eyes, well, my eyes are wet and blurry, so I guess I *must* be close to tears, much as I'd like to deny it. I don't want anyone to see me like this. This is just not me.

So, I'm practically running, and storming through the door, slamming it open, and the door slams hard and fast straight into a teacher standing on the other side of it, talking to another teacher. It all happens so fast she doesn't see it coming. It hits her in the face and sends her falling backwards.

'Oh no! I'm so sorry. I didn't see you. Sorry. Are you all right?' I move towards her to help her up, hoping I haven't hurt her, although I realize I must have, because I'd shoved that heavy fire door so hard it almost went flying off its hinges.

The teacher is clutching the right side of her head, tears of pain rolling down her cheeks, but she's screaming and shouting for me to get away from her, and she's calling the other teacher to help her.

At first, I don't recognize the teacher, but the voice I know only too well.

And then I'm breaking up into a thousand pieces because there is no coming back from *this*. No one will think it was an accident.

No one will believe me this time.

'Stay away from me! Get away! Help me, Theo, please get him away from me. He did this on purpose!'

Mr Elias practically shoves me out of the way to help her up.

'Did you see that? Did you see what he did? I told the Head he's a violent boy, but did he believe me? You saw him, didn't you, Theo? He saw me standing on the other side of the door and did this on purpose. I warned the Head about him.' She's leaning into Mr Elias for support, her shoulders heaving as she sobs.

I'm still standing there, waiting for the inevitable.

'It hurts so much,' she's crying. 'Look at my face, Theo! It's not bleeding, is it?'

I know how hard the door slammed into her, but no, thank God she's not bleeding. There is one hell of a livid red mark down her right cheek though. It's swelling up, and I know it'll end up an ugly-looking bruise. Which *I* caused. Accidentally.

'I'm really sorry, Mrs Greaves, I – I didn't see you there. It was an accident. Mr Elias, please, sir, you saw it. It was an accident.'

'An accident? Jeevan, you've tried that excuse one too many times. How could you do this to me? I've tried so hard to help you, given you so many chances,' Greaves says, through copious tears.

'Please, miss. It really was an accident. I wouldn't do that on purpose. Please believe me. I didn't see you there.'

She shakes her head. 'But no more,' she says, her voice dropping to a whisper. 'I can't help you any more.' She turns back into the comforting arms of Mr Elias.

And I know with a certainty born of experience that the curtains are finally about to come down on me.

'Get to the Head's office. Now!' Mr Elias yells.

CHAPTER 35

Yes, you've guessed it. I've been here before – too many times, on my personal Walk of Shame. This time I don't drag my feet. I welcome it with open arms. I want out. They want me out. So bring it on, and the sooner it's all over the better.

I sit outside Rawson's office, waiting, while Mrs Greaves receives medical attention in the nurse's office. Mr Elias is in with the Head. What's the betting Greaves's side of the story gets told, not mine? The way she went on about how she'd given me so many chances would have definitely coloured Mr Elias's view of what actually happened.

And it has. I'm called in, but only briefly, because my parents have already been summoned. I'm sent back outside the office to wait, again. That jackhammer inside my head is like a bludgeon and I've broken out in a cold sweat. I need to get out of this place right now. I can't wait for my parents. I get up and start walking out of the lobby outside Rawson's office. Mrs Dere looks up from her computer and sees me.

'Where are you going? The Headmaster has asked you

to wait, Jeevan.'

'I-I need the toilet,' I stammer.

'All right, but make sure you come straight back,' she says.

I rush down the corridor, hoping I don't get seen by anyone. Lunchtime is over and everyone should be back in their lessons by now. I can't risk getting my bag from the locker, so I head straight for the door out of here – the door to freedom – and as I'm about to push it open, I hear my name.

'Jeevan! Wait! Where are you going?'

It's Mr Green.

'Home. I'm going home,' I say, and I push the door open.

'Wait!'

'I'm sorry, sir.' I step out and head for the gate, head down, shoulders hunched against the pelting rain. I'm out of the school gates when he catches up with me. He leads me under the cover of the bus shelter.

'I was on my way to see the Headmaster. I heard about the incident with Mrs Greaves,' he begins.

'She's told everyone I did it on purpose. No one believes me,' I say.

'Well, I do, and I will say as much to the Head.'

'But you weren't there. He won't listen to you.'

'I'm going to try and help you, Jeevan. Running away from school at this point is only going to make things worse for you.'

'They can't get any worse! Rawson already said I'm going to be excluded until they decide what to do.'

'Are your parents here yet?'

I shake my head.

'Then wait for them. Come on, let me take you back. I'll go and speak to Mr Rawson while you're waiting for them.'

How can I not listen to him? He's trying to have my back – after everything I've done to him. True, he may not have seen the video yet, but it's only a matter of time. When he finds out it was me, what'll happen? I'd hate to see his disappointment in me, and I hope it doesn't change him. Every school needs a teacher like him, so does every kid. So here I am, waiting outside the office, again.

Mr Green is in there with Rawson. The door's shut, so I can't hear what they're saying, but every now and then I hear raised voices. Eventually, Mr Green comes out, and he doesn't look happy. I'm guessing he may have told Rawson that Greaves holds a bit of a grudge against me. I wonder if he's gone as far as to tell the Head that Greaves is an outright racist? He may have, but then it's his word against Greaves, and without proof . . .

Mr Green puts his hand on my shoulder and says, 'Hang in there, Jeevan. Whatever is decided today is not the end of it, OK?'

What does that mean?

The thing is, he knows the truth; I know he knows

the truth, but he doesn't know that I know he knows. What would he say if I told him I have a video that proves Greaves is a racist who has it in for me? Would he tell me to use it? Somehow, I think not. And I can never tell him – or anyone, because then they would find out for sure that I'd filmed the sex video too, and I can never let that come out.

So I'm stuffed.

My parents arrive and I'm called in too. Heated exchanges take place. It's all blah blah blah. I say my piece, but the only people who hear it are my parents, and they don't count in this. No one else is listening to me, so no one else hears what I say.

So I end up excluded from school. It's a temporary exclusion, which may result in a permanent exclusion. Knowing my luck, it will.

The Head means to talk to the school governing body before making a pronouncement. My parents are angry – no, that's definitely a gross understatement. They are *seething*, with plumes of fire and smoke practically billowing from their ears and out of the top of their heads. You can barely make them out for the fire raging around them.

Dad has called his brother Raj to come over later. If Rawson's taking this under advisement, then my dad can equal that and get his lawyer brother in on the act.

I'm the talk of the town.

Dread and Sandi are bound to have heard about it

by now. I can't remember who was in the corridor when I smacked the door into Mrs Greaves because it's all a blur, but I'm sure there were other people around.

My parents drop me home and I wash down two paracetamol before going up to my room and getting into bed. Mum and Dad were silent the whole way back, which is not a good sign.

They promised me a long hard talk when they got back from work.

I toss and turn, and eventually give up on trying to get any sleep. It's ten to four and school's only just finished and already my mobile's been bleeping with hundreds of messages and missed calls. I've turned it off. I've sunk to the bottom of the high seas and there is no lifeboat big enough or strong enough to weather the storm to come out and save me.

'Jeevan? Jeevan?'

Maji's calling me from the bottom of the stairs. Maji was very upset when my parents brought me home. But she was upset *for* me, rather than *at* me. She won't let my parents sit on this without fighting it. But I'm wondering if it's worth fighting it. Isn't it better just to let it go now? Hasn't enough damage been done?

'Jeevan?' Maji calls me again.

I come out of my bedroom and stand at the top of the stairs. 'Yes?'

'Your friends are here. They are in the kitchen having some snacks. Come down, *beta*.'

I groan. I wish they hadn't come. There's nothing they can do to make things any better. The show's over now.

I go into the kitchen and they're all there: Sandi, Dread, Tom and Amelia. Ree's there too, minus the highlights in her hair today.

'Hey,' I say.

'Was it really an accident?' is the first thing Sandi asks me.

'Of course it was, you idiot,' Dread says, with a shake of his head at Sandi. 'An unfortunate accident in a series of unfortunate events.'

'Yeah, but the Baudelaire kids have nothing on you, Jeev!' Amelia says, trying to lighten the mood. 'Well, maybe they do. I'm sure we can still do something about this.'

'Not this time, Amelia,' Dread says. 'Unfortunately, no one believes it's an accident. Except us. I did warn you that bunking off would get you in trouble, Jeev.'

'Yeah, OK, wise guy. You were right and I was wrong. It doesn't matter now.'

'I thought it had to be an accident, but at the same time, you know, it was Greaves, so I wouldn't have blamed you if you'd done it on purpose. No one would have blamed you. I mean, it wasn't as if she didn't deserve it.'

'Sandi!' This time it's both Dread and Amelia who tell him to shut up.

'Jeez! I don't mean it in a bad way,' Sandi says.

Ree's watching and listening, taking it all in. She must think I'm a complete idiot. She's probably right, to be fair.

'So did you get expelled?' she asks.

'Temporarily excluded, whatever that means. By next week, if they're feeling generous, I'll be asked to leave. Otherwise, it'll be a straight expulsion.'

Her mouth forms an O. 'Yeah, it's serious,' I say.

'Oh my God!' Sandi says. 'But what about the rest of the year and the exams? You've still got controlled assessments to do as well.'

Sandi can't get his head round what's happened. To be honest, neither can I. I don't think it's properly sunk in yet.

'Rawson mentioned something about there being examining centres outside the school where I can go to sit my exams, so I won't have to go back into school. And I've done all my controlled assessments already.'

I can tell they're all shocked.

'I knew I should have let Clara run that piece in the paper,' Amelia says. 'It might all be different now. Greaves has got away with everything. She'll carry on doing what she's been doing all these years, and no one can stop her.'

'What are you talking about?' Tom asks.

I forgot he doesn't know half the story. So Dread fills him in on my sneaking suspicion about Greaves being a racist. There's no need for secrecy now. I'm not part of the school any more, and I know that if I so much as step inside the school gates, Greaves would set the dogs on me.

'Hang on a minute. You filmed them?' Ree asks. 'When they were doing it in the woods?'

I shrug. 'I'm not proud of it. I don't know why I did. It just happened.'

'And this video got put online?' Ree's asking.

'Yeah, but—'

'So you shamed that woman and blurred out the male teacher, and the world has seen her with her knickers round her ankles and you think that's OK, do you?' Ree says, glaring at me.

Oh crap. 'That's not what happened. I mean, yeah, she comes out of it looking bad, but I didn't put it online – I never meant for that to happen.'

'But you thought about it and you even got someone to blur out your favourite teacher – as though he wasn't in the wrong too.' She shakes her head at me.

'We all know he behaved as badly as her,' Dread says. 'But there's more to the story.'

'Exactly! I'm not saying he wasn't in the wrong. He was. But I care more about his reputation, because he's a good teacher,' I say.

'Why should you? He clearly doesn't. He thinks he can get away with behaving like that – and you've allowed him to. Just because you've got beef with

Greaves doesn't make it right for you to bring a whole pile of shit down on her head.'

'That's not what it's all about. There's more to it, Ree. Trust me, she's something else.' I'm tying myself into knots trying to explain the whole scenario to her. Why do I care so much what she thinks of me? From the way she's looking at me now, I can forget all about asking her out any time soon, maybe not even in this lifetime. I'll have to wait to be reincarnated – and hope I don't come back as a toad. I might as well let her in on the rest of the story. 'But the second video in the woods shows what she's really about.'

Ree's staring at me like I've already morphed into that toad. 'You filmed them *twice*?'

Oh crap. I must sound like I'm stalking Greaves.

'Go and get your laptop,' Dread says, coming to my rescue. 'Show them what really went down.'

I glance out of the kitchen window. Maji's pottering around her vegetable patch. She probably won't come back into the kitchen for a while now that she's fed and watered all my friends.

I fetch my laptop from my room and set it up on the kitchen island. We cluster round the screen and I press Play.

By the end, Ree and Tom are speechless. When Tom finally speaks, we all know what he's going to say. 'No way! She actually says she can't let the coloured kids win!'

'Shows you what a terrible person she is,' Amelia

says. 'And who still uses the term "coloured" now, anyway?'

'*This* is the clip you should have leaked,' Ree says. 'Not the other one.'

'I honestly didn't leak the other one, Ree.'

'That was my friend who did that,' Sandi says. 'And, yeah, it was my fault it went viral before he could take it down. That's all on me.'

Ree's expression softens a tiny bit.

'You should have shown this to Rawson,' Tom says.

'I know! That's what I keep telling him,' Sandi says.

I slam my laptop shut. 'I can't. Not without dropping Green in it!'

'Then prepare for your funeral,' Sandi says.

If I didn't know Sandi so well, I would be even more pissed off with him than I already am. But I know, irritating and single-track-minded as he can be sometimes, that he's only trying to help me see the light. He is completely baffled as to why I'm bothering to protect Green, to my own detriment. He's not the only one.

'He's right, Jeev,' Ree says. 'Lose that emotional tie you seem to have with this Green guy. It's not doing you any favours.'

'Easier said than done.' I don't want to talk about it any more. No one gets it, so what's the point? I start collecting up the dirty plates and cups and glasses and stack them in the dishwasher.

'And there's no way I'm posting the second video anywhere, and I'm not going to give it to Rawson, and you know what? Let's drop this, OK? I've had enough.'

There's a chorus of, 'Yeah, sure, Jeev. Of course.'

Whatever they all think, Mr Green's gone out on a limb for me despite Greaves's threat, so I should do the same for him. Shouldn't I?

An hour and a half later, they leave, all except Dread who said he'd hang with me for a while longer. I'm glad they came – Ree too. She must have forgiven me because she gives me a tight hug, leaving me bathed in her scent of peaches and vanilla. 'All this sucks, but it will blow over eventually. Hang in there.' I sensed she wanted to say more, but with everyone standing around to say their goodbyes, she backs away.

Hearing their shock and indignation at what's happened to me has stopped me slipping further into that mire of self-pity I've been drowning in lately.

'You gotta show them you can still ace your exams, Jeev. I'll give you all my notes and then some, so you won't miss a thing.'

'Yeah. Thanks, Dread,' I say distractedly. My head's still with Ree.

'No, I mean it. Don't go and flunk them out of spite or anything stupid like that.' Dread clocks the I-don't-give-a-shit-about-exams expression that's written all over my face.

'What's the point?'

'You don't really want me to explain, do you?' Dread asks. 'Because it could get very tiresome and repetitive. I'll just say this: do you *want* your parents to kill you?'

I roll my eyes. 'OK, OK. Point taken. I wasn't going to flunk them on purpose anyhow.'

'You've lost perspective on this whole damn thing.'

'I have?'

'Yeah, you have. It all started with a teacher who kept marking you down, again and again and again. And marking other kids down, kids like us, me not included, of course, but anyone in her class, in her power. And because she did it subtly, people didn't notice it, so she could get away with it.'

'I thought it started with me being in the wrong place at the wrong time.'

'No, it started way before that, and you've been fighting it, in your own little way, for a long time.'

I have. Much good it did me. It only served to get her back up.

'All those essays you wrote trying to show her who you are, what you are, where you're from. She may have laughed when Green told her your story about the cat and the Christmas tree – but she didn't know that was your story until afterwards. And all the other stuff you wrote – well, she didn't get it because she didn't want to.'

'And look where it got me. I should have just not bothered. I should have not tried to be clever about it. I should have ducked under the radar and toed the line –

her well-drawn, completely demarcated white line.'

'That's not what I'm saying.'

'I know what you're saying, Dread.'

I sense he wants to say more, but I'm not in the mood to hear it.

He changes the subject. 'Ree's been asking Amelia about you.'

That gets my attention. 'Oh yeah?'

'I know you like her, Jeev, so no need to play all coy.'

'How – never mind. She's all right – when she's not picking on me.'

'Guess when you only know half a story it's easy to jump to conclusions.'

Dread's right, as if he could be anything else.

'Do you think, you know, she's interested?'

'Man, you're dim. Why else would she ask Amelia about you? Why do you think she was asking all those questions just now? She's making sure you're cool.'

'Think I've blown it then.'

'Whatever. Lighten up, Jeev. What will be will be. We've got your back, OK? I'll come round tomorrow.'

'Yeah, you know where to find me,' I say glumly.

My phone pings with a WhatsApp message, but I ignore it. Sandi's been messaging – *POST IT* – all day and it's getting annoying. He knows I won't. He knows I can't do it. I'm seriously thinking about blocking him. I see Dread out and head up to my room. Miles Davis's *Kind of Blue* feels just about right for what's happening in my head, so I put my Beats on and hit Play, then notice the WhatsApp message is not from Sandi.

Ree's sent me a whole load of GIFs that, she says, are guaranteed to make me laugh.

I think I'm in love.

CHAPTER 36

There's more music to face when my parents and my uncle arrive. But I'm glad they didn't walk in half an hour ago. Mum would have raised both eyebrows if she'd seen Ree giving me a hug, which would have been followed by a whole load of questions that I wouldn't have been able to answer.

My headache had receded earlier, but I know it'll start thumping with a vengeance again. The rest of the evening will be spent trying to salvage something out of the latest mess I've landed myself in. Sure, it was an accident, but that's neither here nor there, as Uncle Raj puts it, considering my alleged previous behaviour in class.

'Jeevan, why, why, why?'

My uncle is shaking his head at me. I've had the head-shaking thing from pretty much everyone I know. It's getting harder and harder to explain that it was a complete accident. I did NOT do it on purpose and I was mortified that I'd managed to hurt someone, even if that someone was the person who's been ruining my life.

'It really *was* an accident,' I repeat. 'But I completely understand why no one believes me.'

'If you don't want the situation to escalate any further, I suggest you don't fight it,' my uncle tells my parents.

They object immediately, just as I knew they would.

'Raj, the point is that Jeevan is innocent, so I'm not having that woman accuse him like this and get away with it!' Mum says.

'Maybe she has unfairly accused him, but the fact is the Headmaster could have called the police and had Jeevan charged with assault.'

'Assault?' my dad says. 'God, that would go on his record, wouldn't it?'

'The police are already in school investigating something else,' I tell them. 'I guess Rawson doesn't want the school involved in two scandals.' Or maybe whatever Mr Green said to Rawson had some bearing after all.

They all look at me. I'll have to tell them the story – they'll find out soon enough anyway.

'Someone posted a video on YouTube of two people doing it in some woods. One of them looks likes Greaves. Well, that's what everyone thinks.'

'And is it her?' Mum asks.

'She says it's not.'

'But is it her?' Dad asks insistently.

They're all waiting for my answer. I suppose I could tell them the whole truth about the sex vid now, get it over and done with, but I chicken out – I'm in enough trouble as it is.

'Yes, unless she's got a twin no one knows about.'

'Has the video been taken down?' Uncle Raj asks.

I nod. 'Yes, it's gone now. It was posted anonymously, but the police are looking into it.'

'Over the weekend, as other parents find out about the sex video, the school may have to take some course of action. It's possible they might even ask this Greaves woman to leave quietly at the end of term. So, I still advise you to let the school decide what it wants to do about Jeevan. Remember, it's only a temporary exclusion. By next week, the situation may have changed.'

'And if they decide they want to exclude him permanently, what then?' Mum asks my uncle.

'Jeevan can sit his exams in one of the examining centres, and because it's Jeevan, we all know that he will come out with flying colours. Don't we, Jeevan?'

I shrug. 'I don't know about flying colours, but I'll do my best.'

'Your best is all we ask for,' Dad says.

'Any school or college will be glad to take him into their sixth form with his results,' Uncle Raj says.

They're talking as though it's a dead cert that I'm

going to be permanently excluded from school *and* that I'll still manage to ace my exams. Dread was talking in the same way. Ordinarily, I might have aced them, but this is *not* an ordinary moment. There is nothing *ordinary* about it. I'm trying to get my head round not ever going back to my school again, not seeing my friends on a daily basis, not being able to complain about the school lunches, not having the benefit of all the great teachers there – especially Mr Green. There are way too many *nots* to list.

I don't want to sit my exams at some random centre. I want to do them with my friends, at school, in the normal way. I want *normal* back in my life.

I've well and truly fallen off the plank. I'm in the deep blue sea and I'm sinking. I'm going to be stuck with the God-awful, miserable life of a hermit crab – and it sucks. All day, every day, stuck inside a prison of my own making, except at least with the hermit crab that's all it's ever known. I've known different.

Within three or four days, Mum and Dad have realized it too. I am no longer grounded, partly because my friends can't always pop over and give me their notes from all the lessons I've been missing, but mainly because they're worried about the state of my mind. To be honest, so am I.

'Mrs Kapoor, Amelia's having friends over for her birthday, a few girls from her school, and she's asked

Jeevan, Sandi, and Tom too. Is it OK if Jeevan goes?'

'Forget it, Dread. I'm not in the mood. Anyway, I think we've got a family dinner thing here.'

Mum is looking at me strangely. 'It's only your uncle Raj and aunty Mina. Your cousins aren't coming, so you should go with Jonathan and your friends.'

'No, it's OK.'

'Oh, but I insist,' Mum says firmly. 'Besides, it'll be boring for you to have to hang out with us oldies.'

Dread's grinning at how easily I've been outmanoeuvred. I'm not finding it half as amusing. The last thing I want to do is to hang with my friends and pretend I'm having a good time. All I want to do, and all I've been doing for the past few days, is the sum total of nothing. I lie on my bed all day, Beats clamped over my ears, volume ramped to the max, playing Miles Davis's *Kind of Blue*, because when it's that loud you don't have to listen to that persistent voice whining and droning on and on inside your head, telling you that you still have the means to achieve the end you want to engineer: the annihilation of a certain Mrs Greaves. The ticking time bomb has never been properly deployed. *Deploy it! Deploy it! Deploy it!* That's what it keeps telling me to do.

Like I've always said, that's not me. Yes, I'd rather be expelled than send another video viral, because it might mean that Mr Green would become collateral damage.

Might? You're protecting him and destroying yourself on

a might, or a maybe or a possibly? Seriously?

But everything I do ends up making things worse. I've had enough! Don't you understand?

But this will put it right for you. Just do it!

See what I mean about the pester power of that pesky voice? It's sounding more and more like Sandi.

And then there's Dread. And Sandi. And Amelia. And Tom. And now Ree too. They're like that annoying little voice multiplied by a thousand. That's why it's better for me to stay at home, where I can drown out all their voices. My head's not in a good place. I'm afraid I'll mess it up with Ree before it's even started.

'Nice pad.'

We've just reached Amelia's house. I've been trying to ignore Dread's pep talk, let him think it's falling on deaf ears, but it's been getting to me, so it's a relief to finally get here.

Amelia answers the door. 'The parents are out,' she announces. 'But they're back at midnight.'

I'll be long gone by then.

'So, your parents still loving our golden boy?' I ask her.

Dread gives me a look. 'What are you on about?'

'Our Dread, the guy who never puts a foot wrong. He's got everything sussed.'

'Jeev, drop it!' Dread says.

Amelia takes me by the hand hurriedly, and leads me into the house. 'It's my birthday, so you know all that bad stuff that's happening to you? You can leave it outside for tonight. OK?'

And that makes me feel bad for trying to pick an argument with Dread over absolutely nothing other than the fact he happens to be standing next to me while I wallow in new depths of self-pity.

There are only nine of us at Amelia's gathering: four guys and five girls. Amelia wanted to keep her birthday low-key, so no one knew about it apart from Dread and Amelia's best friends from school – except no one's told her mum, who's cooked for five thousand.

I get chatting to one of Amelia's friends, Emily. She's cute and funny and she knows nothing about the videos, about Greaves, about anything, which is a relief, but at the same time, I seem to have lost the ability to be normal and make regular conversation. What did I used to talk about before my life went pear-shaped?

And then Ree walks in. She heads straight for me and gives me a hug. I breathe in her peaches and vanilla scent and think that today is the day I'm going to ask her out. She's the only good thing that's happened this year.

'Hey,' she says.

'Hey back,' I say, trying not to grin like an idiot.

'How's it going?' she asks.

I shrug. 'You told me to hang in there, so that's what I'm doing.' When I turn around, Emily's gone back to the rest of the group – probably only too glad to get away from me.

'Did I interrupt something?' Ree asks, eyebrows arched.

'What?' And then I get what she's asking. 'No, course not. We were just talking. Well, Emily was talking. I'm not great company at the moment – there's too much stuff wearing me down. First thing I get from everyone is: are you OK? At least she doesn't know anything.'

Ree purses her lips. 'Fine,' she says, turning away from me.

I'm such an idiot. 'No, I didn't mean that. Yeah, I did, but not like that, Ree. Don't go.'

She turns back. 'Look, you've got loads going for you, your parents and your grandma and friends, everyone backing you up every step of the way. So stop your whining and get a grip. And maybe then people would stop asking you if you were OK!'

She's right. I'm losing the plot. Amelia told me to park my problems at the door, so that's what I'll do.

'Message received,' I say, holding my hands up in surrender. 'So how was that Moroccan film you went to see?'

'It was great – almost made me cry.' That's something I can't imagine happening very often. 'And it reminded me how rusty my French is.'

'It was in French?'

'Yeah, lots of Moroccan films are. France used to sort of rule Morocco, so pretty much everyone there speaks French. Actually, my French isn't so bad, it's my Arabic that's a bit pidgin.' She's laughing at me. 'You should see your face! Have I confused you?'

Confused doesn't go near it. 'All this time I thought you were Spanish or South American.'

'I get that a lot – or Italian, or Greek, or Turkish, or Egyptian. My mum's Moroccan, but to confuse your brain just a bit more,' she says, tapping my head, 'my dad's French, which I do speak fluently as he insisted on speaking only in French to me.'

'And so Ree is short for?'

'Reema.'

'Wow. I had no idea.'

'You could have asked me.'

And that's where she's right, but when you've got all sorts of bad stuff going on in your life, it zaps your brain cells. 'So you're not going to be any help with my Spanish then?' I quip.

She cuffs me on the arm. 'Actually, you're in luck – languages are my thing. My Spanish is almost as good as my French.'

'And people accuse me of having a big head,' I laugh.

'That's probably why we've been getting on so well.'

I'm definitely in love . . .

And then one of the other girls – I think it's Shilpa – gets a bottle of vodka out. After a couple of shots each, everyone pretty much stops drinking – everyone, that is, apart from me, who can't stop, and Ree, who'd never started. I can't find the stop button and I don't want to find it. I'm in the mood to zap a few more brain cells. Life's so much easier after a few vodkas, isn't it?

'Where'sh the bottle gone?' I've searched the table, looked under it, blundered into the kitchen, knocking things over, but it's gone AWOL.

'It's gone,' Dread says.

'Gone where?'

'Come on, Jeev, party's over. Let's go.'

'Party's just started! I'm just getting to know Ree, man – she's great. And it's only,' I peer at my watch, but the hands have blurred time together, 'I dunno, but it's gotta be early.' I vaguely recognize the fact that I'm slurring, that my words are muddled and possibly even incoherent, but who cares? I don't.

'Dread, please, you've got to take him home before my parents come back. He's a mess!' That was Amelia's voice.

'Who's the mesh?' I ask, giggling inanely.

'Sandi, you're going to have to help.' That was Dread's voice.

And that's the last thing I remember before the room spins and I'm falling.

CHAPTER 37

'Thumping' and 'aching' pretty much cover how my head feels when I wake up the next morning. I've got no recollection of coming home, or rather of being taken home, and then taken upstairs, and it's definitely a very good thing that I can't remember my parents' expressions when I was delivered to them. I don't imagine they were very impressed by my state of total intoxication.

The house is dead silent, which means, I fervently hope, that Mum and Dad are at work and Maji has gone out. I don't even attempt to get up until gone midday. Someone, probably Mum, left a tall glass of water and two paracetamol by my bedside table, which I've taken already. They haven't made a difference.

I groan as I get out of bed. Yes, it's my first ever hangover and no, I will never ever touch a drop of alcohol again. But who knows, when the hangover goes . . .

I do remember the first few drinks and how they

made me feel like nothing mattered. The trouble is, things do matter.

I'll still be excluded, expelled, or whatever the hell it is they call it. I'll still be on my own. I won't be in the sixth form with my friends and I won't see them every day, or hang out with them, and I'll end up losing touch with them. So nothing has changed. And I've no idea what I said to Ree last night. Let's face it – she's not going to want to hang around with a loser and a drunk.

My stomach growls. I need food, so I head downstairs, hoping I don't have to face any parental disapproval until tonight. But no such luck – Dad is at home.

'I think we should have a talk, Jeevan,' he says as soon as he sees me. 'But get some food down you first.'

He cooks me a massive fry-up, which I don't think I can stomach until I start eating. He sits down opposite me with a cup of coffee.

I set my fork down. 'I'm really sorry about last night,' I begin.

'We know.'

'No, I really am. I don't know what happened.'

'Jonathan explained.'

Trust Dread to tell them everything.

'Jeevan, your mum and I know that this hasn't been such a great time for you.' *Understatement of the year, Dad*. 'What's happened with that teacher is ridiculous and terrible. We understand that it must be very depressing for you.'

'Yeah, just a bit.' Another understatement.

'We will help you all we can.'

I sigh into my perfectly cooked fried eggs. 'I know, Dad. I just want to go back to school again.'

The doorbell rings just then. 'That will be Raj,' he says. He goes to answer it.

'Jeevan,' my uncle says jovially, slapping me on the back. 'Good party, was it?'

I groan. 'Does *everyone* know?'

'Um . . .' He pretends to think about it for a minute. 'Yes!' he says, laughing. 'Now for the serious stuff, Jeev. I want you to go through everything that happened with that English Literature teacher of yours. Step by step. I want every single detail – even if you think it's unimportant or irrelevant. I want to know everything! Let's see if there is something we can do about all this.'

'There isn't anything anyone can do, Uncle Raj. You're wasting your time. She's got away with it. It's what she was aiming for,' I say. 'It's pointless.'

'No, I'm sure she wasn't aiming for it, Jeev. I think the situation escalated, it grew out of a mutual dislike,' Uncle Raj says.

'No! And it's not dislike, it's hatred! She lied about everything. Even that time when I was supposed to have thrown a chair, broken it and used the leg to threaten her with. It was a complete lie! Total fabrication! The whole class will tell you . . . And anyway, that's not how it started,' I say.

'So how did this little vendetta begin?' my uncle asks me.

How can I tell him? I can't. I'm just going round and round in pointless circles, and I've had enough now. I never want to talk about it again. I never want to see her, or even hear her name ever again. Let them expel me. Let them do what they want.

'I don't know and I don't care!' I storm out of the living room as my dad is telling me off for shouting.

In the kitchen, the sun is glancing in through the window; Maji is sitting at the table with her knitting, warming her back in the sunshine. She sets her knitting down when I walk in and says, 'Come here, *beta*.' She pats the chair next to her.

'I'm just getting my coat,' I tell her, reaching into the utility cupboard.

'Please come and sit with me,' she says.

I sigh, and put my coat back. I can't say no to her, so I slump into the chair next to her. She takes my hand and strokes it. 'You know what your grandfather said when you were born?'

I thought she was going to give me a lecture, or tell me off for being rude to Uncle Raj. 'No.'

'He said, "Shanti may be like you, Asha, but this one takes after me. He's full of fight. See how he makes fists of his hands?" I told him all babies make fists of their hands. "Ah, but not like this. This one has his eyes wide open too. He will know how to fight the world."'

I feel sorry that I've let Granddad down.

'It's not that easy, Maji.'

'No? You will find a way, Jeevan. Now go back and say you are sorry to your uncle.' She picks up her knitting.

I go back to the living room and make my apologies, which my uncle waves away. 'It's OK, Jeevan. I understand. I know you've had enough of the whole thing, but if we brainstorm it again we might find a solution.'

I have the answer. It's sitting in my laptop, where it's been all this time. I think about what Granddad said about me when I was born. It's time to find out how to fight. I take a deep breath.

'Dad, would you mind if I went for a walk with Uncle Raj?'

Dad looks baffled. 'What? A walk? Er, yes, if your uncle doesn't mind. Do you want me to come, too?'

'No, it's OK, but thanks, Dad.'

We head down the road. It's a crisp spring day – the sun's out, the sky is blue, but there's an edge to the air. I take a deep breath. This is terrifying, but I've got to do this. I cut into the path between the houses that leads to the woods. Where it all happened.

'So where are we going?' Uncle Raj asks, puzzled.

'We're here. I need to tell you something – in confidence. Is that OK with you? I need some advice.'

'And this is something you want me to keep from your parents?'

'Yes.'

'That's a tough one,' he says, dubiously. 'But OK.'

So I tell him. I tell him everything.

And, like a good lawyer, he advises me what to do.

'I'm not the only person she's got a major problem with,' I begin.

The four of us, Mum, Dad, Uncle Raj and me, are sitting at the island in the kitchen.

'She's got a major problem with all of us, all the "coloured" kids,' I tell my parents.

'What did you say?' Dad asks. 'And what's that got to do with—'

'If she's racist then it's got *everything* to do with it!' Mum says.

'Wait,' I say. I take another deep breath, a massive lungful. 'I've got something to show you . . .'

At the end of it, Mum and Dad are so lost for words they can't speak, so Uncle Raj takes the opportunity to tell them what to do at the meeting with Rawson.

On Monday morning, we're sitting in Rawson's office again. I'm not even going to mention the déjà vu thing because every other time I've been in here it's ended badly.

I wanted my uncle to come with us, but Mum and Dad decided it was best to keep him as backup.

My parents are in full flow explaining the situation to the Head, who's looking increasingly worried – you can tell by the number of times he strokes his moustache – and this time they are taking no prisoners.

'I hope you finally understand the situation, Mr Rawson,' Dad says. 'There is a great deal of history behind the countless incidents of unfair marking and treatment that Jeevan has received from Mrs Greaves. And in the final analysis, Jeevan is entirely innocent of any wrongdoing. As for the incident yesterday, well, it was a most unfortunate accident, but accident it nevertheless was.'

'Regardless of what Mrs Greaves may or may not have done, and I don't have to remind you that her personal life is very much her *personal* life and therefore not for public scrutiny, there still remains a clear pattern of disrespectful behaviour on Jeevan's part towards her. She has sat here in this office, with us all, and outlined in detail the number of times she has tried to help him, but he has responded in a most belligerent manner. I appreciate that the door hitting her in the face might have been nothing more than an unfortunate accident.'

Lots of parents have rung in about the sex video, apparently, and Rawson has had Greaves's back throughout it all. He still has it, but for how much longer? I wonder.

'I think we may have to speak a little more openly about the whole underlying situation,' Mum says. She gets my laptop out. Mr Rawson is practically blanching. I suddenly realize that he's thinking that I was the one who recorded the sex tape and what I'm about to play for him is the unedited version.

'Jeevan, please step outside for a moment,' he says.

'Jeevan needs to be here,' Mum says, handing me my laptop.

'This is not what you think it is, Mr Rawson,' I begin. 'I caught a conversation between Mrs Greaves and another teacher, Mr Green.' I don't press Play yet. 'I'm going to let you see it, so you can understand what's been going on.'

'All right. Let's see it.'

'The thing is, I don't want it ever to be known that the other teacher in the video is Mr Green.'

'That's not your decision, Jeevan. I'll decide when I've seen the "conversation".'

I shake my head. 'No, sir. It's *my* decision. I think you'll understand when you've watched the video. It's all pretty self-explanatory. But Mr Green's not to know about *any* of this – not about the video, or who recorded it, nothing at all. After you've watched it, I'm going to erase it.'

Rawson is so taken aback that he gets out of his chair and walks around the room, muttering about how irregular this is. Eventually, he sits back down. 'Right, let's see what you have.'

I press Play.

Last night, Mum and Dad asked me if I was sure I

wanted to come back to the school if they could get the exclusion overturned. I thought about it for a while before I said yes. Wouldn't it be better to make a fresh start somewhere else? But then I realized that I didn't want a fresh start – I didn't need one, as long as Greaves wasn't in the school. I haven't changed my mind. I don't know if things can ever go back to normal, but I want them to – that much I know.

'And no one else has seen this?' Rawson asks, when the video comes to an end.

'Only my friends.'

'Which friends?' Rawson asks sharply.

I don't want to tell him, but there's no real reason to keep it secret. 'Jonathan Fellowes, Sandip Singh and Tom Picher,' I tell him.

'And the other video? Was that your work, too? Did you put it on the Internet?'

'Nothing to do with me,' I tell him, looking him straight in the eye. Well, *most* of my answer is true – I didn't work on the video; that was Davy, and I didn't post it; that was Davy too.

Rawson looks wary, but he makes no comment.

'About Mr Green,' I begin.

Mr Rawson nods. 'I fully agree with you. I have to say, Jeevan, I find your loyalty to Mr Green admirable, and I appreciate that this recording does put him in a compromising position.'

Not as much as the first one, I want to say.

'But first things first. Given the circumstances, I have decided to reverse my earlier decision to exclude you. I should point out here that several pupils came forward after the incident last week to say that in their view the whole thing with Mrs Greaves was an accident.'

'Thanks, sir.'

'If you've brought your books with you, I don't see why you can't go and join your next lesson. I'll talk to your parents about the rest.'

I look at Mum and Dad, and they give me reassuring smiles. Mum gives me a thumbs-up, low and well out of Mr Rawson's line of vision. So everything's got to be OK, hasn't it?

But I'm desperate to find out what's going to happen to Greaves and how Rawson's going to deal with her, and how he's going to keep Mr Green out of it. I'm not sure I'll get them, but he sure owes me some answers.

I hover uncertainly. 'Sir?'

'Yes, Jeevan?'

'What about Mrs Greaves? What's going to happen?'

'In all likelihood, she will be suspended pending an investigation. That's all I'll say about the matter and that's all you need to know. Now get to your lesson before you're late.'

Checkmate. Greaves is dead meat!

But it was a close call – I almost lost my king in the process.

It was only when I talked to Uncle Raj that I started seeing everything more clearly.

'Sometimes you just can't see the wood for the trees,' Uncle Raj had said while we were standing at the scene of the recordings. I think he was relieved that I wasn't about to confess to some terrible crime that he would have to keep secret from my parents.

Rawson's got the whole picture now, that's for sure.

It seems, like Mr Green, that he too couldn't see Greaves's true colours until it was almost too late.

I post the update on our WhatsApp group. Ree comes back straight away with a brown thumbs-up and brown girl dancing emojis.

By the end of the day, Greaves will be out. Gone. For good – hopefully.

Is that the end? you ask.

I know what you want to see cos I want to see it too. I want to see her face, her reaction, when Rawson gives her her marching orders. I need to hear that conversation. Will he tell her about the second recording straight off? Or will he ask for her side of the story first?

How will Rawson play it?

I notice Gabbs sitting in the chair in the excluded pupil area tucked to one side outside Rawson's office. That chair's literally got Gabbs's name etched on to it, the number of hours he's idled away there.

He clocks me as I clock him. There's a smile playing on his lips, which I take to mean he's overheard at least some of the conversation in Rawson's office. Which means he knows Greaves will be summoned to the office shortly. I give him a nod as I head out to my lesson and I know he knows exactly what to do. He pulls his phone out of his pocket, smirks and nods back.

I grin. As annoying as it can be, there are times when Gabbs's gabby mouth can come in handy. I have a feeling today might be one of those days.

I'm in the corridor now, on that Walk of Shame, but it's different when you're doing the walk in the opposite direction. This time my head is held so high I'm practically touching the ceiling, my face is split in two by a massive grin, and there's so much bounce in my steps I'm practically jiving. I *am* jiving – until I spot the person at the other end of the corridor.

Her head is down, so she hasn't spotted me. She doesn't even know it but she's doing the Walk of Shame.

She raises her head. Our eyes meet. I flinch instinctively when I see the daggers flying at me, but they shrivel up in the air between us. As she draws closer, I feel the music in my feet, the jive returning. She looks baffled, then scowls her trademark scowl.

And I do what I do best. I give her a cheeky wink before jiving on down to my lesson.

We've got a supply teacher for the rest of the term. She's called Mrs Andrews and she's turning out to be a proper teacher. She's very sharp and she's very fair. She's been briefed about my controlled assessment and let me know that it will be re-marked. Like Mr Green, like all my other teachers, she seems to have no hang-ups about colour at all.

She hasn't bunged me in a pigeonhole and labelled it 'coloured kid'.

I am not 'coloured'.

I am not just that Asian kid.

I am British. I am a human being – I'm seventy per cent water like the rest of you. And like all human beings, I am individual, unique. Yeah, I can hear you shouting – thank God there's only one Jeevan! That's the point, though. We're all unique, we're all individuals. And once you understand that, then you'll understand me.

So if you were to ask me, 'What's your name?' I would respond, 'My name is Jeevan. I'm fifteen, I've got a smart-alec attitude, and somehow I got lucky cos I'm now going out with a scary gorgeous girl with pink highlights. So, shush, don't jinx it!'

That's who I am.

SAVITA KALHAN was born in India, but has lived in the UK most of her life. She graduated from Aberystwyth University with a degree in Politics and Philosophy. She was a Batik artist before getting married in the Philippines and going to live in the Middle East for several years, where she taught English and began to write.

Now living in North London, she spends her time writing, playing tennis, growing veg and super-hot chillies on her allotment, and loves to get the boxing gloves on.

Savita is a member of the Scattered Authors' Society and blogs at An Awfully Big Blog Adventure. She runs a teen reading group at her local library in Finchley.

Her debut novel, *The Long Weekend*, to be republished by Troika, is a tense thriller about two boys who are abducted after school. It was short-listed for the Fabulous Book Award.

You can visit her website to find out more: www.savitakalhan.com.

SAVITA KALHAN

THE GIRL IN THE BROKEN MIRROR

'HARROWING AND TOUCHING'
BALI RAI

Jay's creative writing exercise is to write a fairy tale, to end with 'they lived happily ever after'. But the way her life is panning out, she's not sure it will ever reach that stage. She and her mother are moving in with distant relatives, and they have super-strict rules for girls. Jay is expected to have only Indian friends, if she has any at all. How can she see her school friends, Chloe and Matt?

But this is only the beginning of a nightmare for Jay. When her life implodes, how can she hide the shame – and how will she find a way to keep going?

The Girl in the Broken Mirror is ultimately about hope and understanding, and where help can be found – even in the darkest situation.

'Harrowing and touching. The honesty here was very refreshing, and very hard-hitting, which is much needed' BALI RAI

'This captivating new book from Kalhan explores one young girl's coming of age and negotiation between cultures' BUZZFEED

DISCOVER MORE STORIES

YOU'LL LOVE

AT

TROIKABOOKS.COM

🐦 #TROIKABOOKS